# IN THE OFFENSIVE ZONE

## *with* *My Fake Bride*

## DINEEN MILLER

**VINCI**
**BOOKS**

Vinci Books

vinci-books.com

Published by Vinci Books Ltd in 2025

1

The EU GPSR authorised representative is Logos Europe, 9 rue Nicolas Poussion, 17000 La Rochelle, France
contact@logoseurope.eu

*Not a dedication so much as a thank you to all the hockey players out there.*
*Thank you for making this sport so amazing!*

## By Dineen Miller

Romancing the Sun Kings

*In the Defensive Zone with My Enemy*

*In the Offensive Zone with My Fake Bride*

Messy Love on Mango Lane

*Bloomed to Be Messy*

*Rescued to Be Messy*

*Tamed to Be Messy*

*A Very Messy Christmas*

# Chapter One

I've never been a fan of formal English gardens. Their structured beds, surrounded by short stone or brick walls, filled with topiaries and meticulously shaped shrubs, always felt too controlling to me. Not to mention the rows of flowers lined up like soldiers, as if they were trying to tell you what to do or how to behave in their presence.

Not something I share in mixed company, I assure you. And by mixed company, I mean royals and those who flock to surround them. Much like those stone walls, I never imagined I could wind up hemmed in like one of them.

But today, none of that seems to matter.

Funerals tend to have that effect on a person, I suppose. After the services for my cousin concluded, we returned to his estate for the reception—can you call something dour a reception when everyone would rather be received anywhere else but here?

Upon arrival, I made a mad dash for the gardens to escape the sea of sad faces—both genuine and fake, for the record. Yet, looking out over the perfectly manicured garden and various flowers giving their last hurrah with the imminent arrival of fall, I'm reminded of idyllic days as a child, playing with Sebastian in these very places.

One time, in particular, comes to mind—me chasing after my cousin and taking a turn too fast, which resulted in a nasty tear in my trousers from the aforementioned stone walls. My left knee still sports the scar from that fiasco. Maybe that's why I much prefer pursuing a puck in an open ice rink. The only obstacles are other players, and part of the challenge is to either maneuver around them or body-check them aside. The terrain is always changing, and I prefer it that way.

"Longing to be back on the ice, chasing that puck of yours?" My sister Emalia brushes by me, then perches on the short wall, edging a bed of roses ablaze in reds and yellows that remind me of my team colors.

I hum in the back of my throat in reply—my usual response when she annoyingly reads my mind. Practice starts in a matter of weeks, and I'd much rather be swinging a hockey stick than bracing for whatever curveball—sorry, wrong sport—slapshot life's about to send my way.

She crosses her ankles and folds her hands in her lap, already the picture of royalty. Losing Sebastian left a gap to be filled—an heir to the baronetcy of Tillendale. He never married and was the sole heir to his parents, who died much too young because of various health issues. Perhaps that's why our dear cousin lived life on the edge. He told me once he didn't expect to outlive the age his mother and father reached, and now he's proven himself right, much to my chagrin. And my sister's.

After slipping my hands into my trouser pockets, I

meander closer to where she's sitting. "When will you move onto the estate?"

"Later today."

"That's bloody fast."

She waves her hand in a casual gesture toward the small mansion behind me. "We waited most of the summer, hoping they'd find Sebastian lost at sea somewhere. There's a lot of work to catch up on."

I clear my throat. "I'm sure you'll have things back in order in no time."

She shoots a finely shaped brow in my direction like a bow ready to shoot an arrow, and the gleam in her eye forewarns me of its arrival. "Faster if my baby brother would stay and help his older sister out."

I knew she'd make one last-ditch attempt to sway me. Hearing that my cousin's yacht had gone missing was what brought me back to Tillendale, a relatively small and unknown town in the southern tip of England, of which my deceased cousin is—was—the Baronet.

A title now passed to my sister, making me heir apparent.

The sooner I'm on a plane back to the States, the better. Even as a youth, I never enjoyed the occasional formal functions that required my family's attendance. "The new season is about to start, and I have a contract to honor. The lads are counting on me."

"I know. But I had to try one more time. This won't be fun without you."

I scoff. "What are you talking about? Your favorite game as a child was to play queen. Unlike me, you are well-built for your new role, Em."

"Maybe, but I'd feel better having you close. Especially

since we're not sure Sebastian's accident was really an..."
She mouths the word 'accident' as if doing so would negate
the possible threat.

"Don't buy into those rumors so quickly."

She blinks, pursing her lips for a moment before speaking. "You heard what Mum and Dad said."

"Yes, I was in the room, but again, it could just be the
ponderings and hearsay of their old cronies."

"Those old cronies, as you call them, have ties to MI5."

I lean toward her and lower my voice to a whisper. "So
they say."

With a deep inhale, she turns her head to stare over her
shoulder. "Still makes me nervous. I'd feel better if you were
here."

Hearing the hint of fear in her words softens me. I sit
down next to her and take her hand between mine. "I'm a
hockey player, Em. Not a bodyguard. Your security detail
will do a far superior job than I could with a hockey stick."

My attempt at humor doesn't seem to faze her as she
diverts her stare to our clasped hands. "I don't need your
protection. Just your support."

"That you already have, dear sister. I'm simply a phone
call away."

She sighs in resignation. "Right."

Emalia lifts crystal blue eyes to mine as she squeezes my
hand. Almost two years apart, my sister and I have often
been mistaken for twins because of our shared features and
coloring, although my hair is a shade darker than her sandy
blonde locks.

"When will I meet this mysterious bodyguard you've
hired for me?" I project a tone of humor to my words, more
for my benefit than hers. I'm not yet keen on the idea of

having a bodyguard, but at least we found a workable solution—one I hope will convince my teammates.

"At the airport. She'll meet the car there and make sure your pretty face doesn't get harmed in any way."

"I still don't see the necessity." The words slip out before I can stop them.

Frustration tinges her sigh this time. "Yes, we've been over this again and again, Payton. But it *is* necessary. You're now the heir apparent. You know how the system works."

I nod, clenching my jaw to prevent spewing my own suppressed irritation. When they finally declared our cousin had perished at sea, the wheels went into motion right away to pass the title to the next person in line—my sister, which then put me in the mix.

Initially, I was told I would have to quit hockey and move back to England. I resisted, stating that I had a commitment to fulfill. My contract with the Sun Kings has two more years left. And the powers that be could find nothing that would require my presence in parliament.

So, we made an agreement. I can return to the States as long as I agree to have a bodyguard with me twenty-four-seven. Never imagined she'd take my half-joking suggestion that said bodyguard should be a female who could pose as my girlfriend so seriously. After hours of hashing out ways to make this work, Emalia informed me she'd contacted a firm in London that trained and provided female bodyguards.

Then she had the nerve to outline her brilliant plan—her words, not mine—of me pretending I had a whirlwind romance over the summer and returned with a bride. I told her that seemed unnecessary, as couples live together all the time without involving a marriage contract. She insisted that despite our little deception—okay, major deception—our family values needed to be upheld. However, I know for a fact my sister is a raging romantic because she's read romance novels as far back as I can remember. I'm almost certain she plucked this story of hers from one of her books.

Emalia lifts her face to mine and kisses my cheek. "Make sure you're a dutiful husband, little brother. You wouldn't want to upset your new wifey."

I growl in reaction to her tinkling laughter. "You're enjoying this entirely too much."

She holds her hands out and dons an innocent expression that might fool others but not me. "You always said you wanted to settle down one day."

Now she's playing dirty, repeating something I said after a nasty breakup last year. I rise and take a step back. "Yes, after I'm done living my life and doing the things I want to do."

Her face turns serious as she stands. "Sometimes we have to do what's required."

Em's words twist like a knife in my chest. She had to give up her medical practice to fulfill her newly acquired role of Baronet of Tillendale, which I know wasn't easy.

I take her hands and pull her up to hug her, but she remains stiff. "I'm sorry. I understand this has cost you more than it has me."

She softens and settles against me. "I keep wishing I'll wake up and find out it was a mistake. That Sebastian will walk in with that goofy smile of his and say it was all a joke."

I plant a kiss on top of her head. "I wish that for you, too, dear sister. I truly do."

She lifts her face to look at me. "I know you don't

believe there's a threat, but promise me you'll do whatever your bodyguard tells you?"

Her gaze is relentless in her demand for my agreement, and her tone makes it clear she's left no room for arguments. I only hope my teammates in Florida will be none the wiser as to my true identity. I've done a fair job of avoiding deeper questions about my family. They only know I'm the third male to bear the name Payton Gerard Maxwell. That alone gave them more fodder than they needed in those first months of playing, but with every ribbing, I knew I became one of them, a part of the team. This new title development could change all of that if my ties to the monarchy were to become known.

The true test came last year when a photojournalist followed us for the entire season. I managed to avoid her questions about my familial origins, and thankfully, she didn't do much digging into my family. Not that she would have found much of interest. The Maxwell name was only second in line before now, and most people outside of Tillendale don't know or don't care about what title we might hold. Surely, this ruse won't be any more difficult than that.

"I promise." I strengthen my resolve to not let this become an issue as I hug her tighter for reassurance.

"Thank you." Her stern expression breaks into a gentle smile for the first time today, sending a spike of relief through me. Seeing my sister so troubled these last few weeks weighed heavily on me—probably what finally pushed me to concede to her insistence that I have a bodyguard.

Do I want to play a charade, deceiving my teammates, who have become like a second family to me? No. But I don't appear to have much choice. And I know deep down it's the least I can do for my sister, who's doing her best to accommodate me.

As she said, sometimes one must do what's required. I'm sure the long plane flight will give me plenty of time to get acquainted with my new fake bride and develop a plan to make this believable.

Unless I can figure a way out of this, that is...

# Chapter Two

## LILY

A wad of fabric sails over my arm and lands in a wrinkled puddle of my partially yet precisely packed suitcase.

"You need some shorts." My roommate Delilah dons the expression she normally saves for clients that says, 'Do what I say or die.'

If I were a client, I would comply, but I'm not. I tuck my index finger under the waistband and lift the shorts, studying the large floral pattern that makes my eyes hurt, before dropping them on the bed next to my suitcase. "I have plenty, thanks."

Which is a lie. I don't actually own a pair because, as a professional bodyguard, I'm rarely in a position to dress that casually. Unless a client requests we blend in more or the situation requires it, I opt for some version of my usual business attire. And one can never be over-prepared, something I learned during my very brief stint in the Army.

Once my tour ended, I knew I needed to pivot in a new direction. Intending to take a break and think, I wound up in London, thinking I'd explore Europe. That lasted barely a week before I went stir-crazy and decided I wanted to find some kind of job that would give me the same structure without the constant scrutiny of my gender.

That realization led me to Remington Security, which is owned by one of the best female bodyguards in the industry. And to meeting Delilah, who the firm recruited a year before me. She had a spare room, and I needed a place to land. The rest is history.

Del snatches the shorts off the bed and stuffs them into a gap between my extra pair of black shoes and the stack of pants, which are either black or navy. Another pile of neatly folded button-down blouses in shades of white, pale blue, or cream sits next to it. I add the matching jackets I'll need for this assignment but ignore her contribution because it's easier than fighting with her.

She leans over to study the contents of my carefully planned suitcase, then grimaces at me. "Doll, you're definitely going to need more attractive choices to pull this off. Isn't that part of this whole scenario? You're posing as his wife. Don't you think it will look strange if you always show up," she waves her hand up and down in front of me, "looking like a corporate exec with a stick up her bum."

"Shorts offer little protection in a scuffle, and I certainly can't run in flip-flops." I pluck the items out and toss them at her.

Using her well-honed reflexes, she snatches them out of the air before they make contact. Her grin turns positively evil. "Your principal is rather yummy, don't you think? Perhaps you should throw a negligee or two in there as well."

I roll my shoulders back. "It's a pretense, remember. Not real, in case you don't know what that word means."

"I'm perfectly aware of the meaning, Lil. I'm just

encouraging you to let your hair down a little." She points to my head. "Sometimes, I fear you have that ponytail of yours tied too tightly."

"It's a job, not a vacation, Del," says the woman who doesn't do vacations. Unlike my roommate, who plays as hard as she works, I have one modus operandi—work. I've accepted this about myself, and I'm good at it. But that's the job. When we're on assignment, it's twenty-four-seven. Can't let your guard down even for a moment because that could mean the death of the client. And that's a reputation killer.

She yanks out two pairs of jeans and a few shirts from one of my drawers and hands them to me. "Trust me, you're going to need some more casual attire. I spent a month in Florida for a job, and people there wear shorts everywhere. Even when dining at bougie restaurants." She pats the stack of garments. "These will do."

"Fine." I shove them into the small space left on one side. I could tell her I already packed two pairs of yoga pants and some athletic tops beneath my usual garb. My research revealed this was a popular trend at the moment— to look like you just came from the gym, even if you have no intentions of working out.

Her pout does little to diminish her striking Eurasian features. "And every assignment comes to an end. Why not extend your stay and spend some time on that gorgeous beach? What's it called again? Avocado something…"

"Mango Key Beach."

Del ruffles through two of my dresser drawers. "What about a bathing suit? Do you even own one?"

"I'll buy what I need there."

She darts out of the room, making me believe I can finish packing in peace, only to return, swinging small swatches of red fabric in each hand. "This is my favorite two-piece. Never fails to grab attention."

I grab her wrists before she can toss them in. "I'm supposed to blend in, remember?"

"Yes, during the job." She bounces her eyebrows and singsongs, "But afterward, it's all fair game."

I roll my eyes and snort, releasing her wrists so she can shove the vivid red two-piece—and the shorts—into a gap along the edge. "I'll make sure you get them back."

"No worries, luv. I have a spare."

A spare...like my client, Payton Maxwell, the third. I assume he's adjusting to his new role as a spare heir. The research I did on the Maxwells didn't look much different from what I imagine any average English family would look like. Parents married for almost thirty years. An older sister who worked as a pediatrician until she had to relinquish her partnership in the practice to take her missing, now presumed dead cousin's title of Baronet. Youngest and only son is a hockey player. I will say finding that out surprised me—not a typical profession for a Brit.

I zip up my suitcase and carry it to the door where my backpack is sitting.

"That's it? No books or special items?" She crosses her arms. "They'll never buy a new bride with no possessions?"

"I'll simply explain they're being shipped from the UK. Takes weeks. I'll be on my way back before they can start to question. Besides, no one's going to know the difference."

"What if he invites his teammates over?"

"I'm sure they don't go poking into his bedrooms, but I'll hang some of my clothes in his closet and leave some extra toiletries on his bathroom counter."

"You have that part all figured out, then?"

"As much as possible at this point." I tap my backpack.

"I made some preliminary notes and a list of things to discuss on the flight. That way, we can get to know each other and create a cover story."

"A whirlwind summer romance?"

I nod.

"Fell in love and eloped?"

I shake my head. "They're very traditional. Married at his parents' estate."

"Did they approve?"

Now, she's just being cheeky. "Yet to be determined."

She looks impressed as she shrugs. Then her eyes widen, and her mouth forms a circle all at once. Del dashes back into my room and returns with a white, strapless sundress I bought on a whim last year during a moment of weakness. I'd spent a month on assignment in the Caribbean only to return to the constant drizzle in London. I'd told myself then I needed a pick-me-up.

"Just a pretense." She yanks the tag off, giving me a sly glance. "You would have worn some kind of dress and surely brought it with you. Brides are sentimental that way."

Convinced she has ulterior motives, I lower my eyelids to study her micro-expressions.

"I'm not that easy to get rid of, doll. Remember, I'm part of your team on this assignment."

That's my one comfort in this unusual scenario. I grab the dress and stuff it into the front pocket of my suitcase. "Whatever makes you happy, Del."

She laughs. "And gets me off your back, right?"

"Affirmative."

———

Bodies move around the airport like ants swarming a nest. Delilah flew out the day before to check out the arena and the principal's apartment complex in Sarabella. Since the Maxwells are mostly unknown in the States, and a definitive threat hasn't been confirmed, she and I will operate as a basic team. Meaning, we'll tap into local resources if needed, which she'll establish as well.

I probably know this airport better than most who work here, but the people are always changing. After checking in and dropping off my bag, I scope the general areas from the entrance to security before backtracking to wait outside for my client.

Head constantly on a swivel, I make note of those lingering in the near vicinity. Most move quickly into the airport, carrying bags and suitcases with them as they scurry inside. Those don't concern me. It's the ones hanging around outside that have me watchful.

Like the tall brunette standing to my right, toting only an oversized bag. She crosses her arms and nervously searches the constant flow of vehicles moving through the passenger drop-off zone.

I suspect she's looking for the boyfriend she fears may be a no-show as she checks her cell for the umpteenth time. Mentally, I shake my head, recognizing the impending disappointment as the realization sets in. Indecision will follow next as she tries to decide whether to leave on her own and make the best of the situation. Or, if she's the ballsy type, to find the loser and tell him off.

Of course, there's the slim possibility that she's a hired killer, and this is all an act, but reading people is one of my strengths. My gut tells me she's exactly what she appears, so I move on, scouting the area while watching for the vehicle transporting my assignment.

Maxwell Payton, the third. I hope his insistence on meeting at the airport with the excuse that an escort would create unnecessary fuss isn't his way of being artificially noble. This charade of playing his wife will prove challenging enough as it is.

A black sedan pulls up to the curb, displaying the plate number I memorized from his family's credentials. Before the vehicle comes to a complete stop, the rear door opens, and my principal jumps out, slinging a duffel across his shoulders. For a moment, I'm transfixed by the contours and definition of his forearms as he adjusts the strap across his chest. The picture in his file showed him with short hair. Not the collar-length, tousled style he's sporting now.

I move in closer, prepared to make contact. But then he leans in through the open passenger side window and shakes hands with the driver, whose animated expression reveals pure delight.

"Thanks again, Bruv." The driver holds out a piece of paper and a pen, which Mr. Maxwell takes, then scrawls something across the white surface.

"My pleasure. And if you find yourself in the States, make a stop in Sarabella and say hello." He straightens as the car pulls away.

Not quite what I anticipated, then again, this is my first assignment with any kind of royalty. But I did expect someone softer and with more luggage.

I close the gap but keep a good three feet between us. "Mr. Maxwell."

He spins around. Momentary confusion flits across his face before his grin flashes into place. "Did you want an autograph as well?"

"No."

His smile slips a few notches as his gaze makes a subtle

assessment of me right down to my shoes. "Then you're the bodyguard, I presume."

"That's correct." I hold my hand out. "Lily Evans."

His brows tug together. "You're not British."

"No, I'm originally from the States."

He shakes my hand, then heads toward the terminal doors. I follow him, keeping my focus on every moving part surrounding us until he steps to the side into an enclosed area away from the throng of people.

"Mr. Maxwell—"

He stops and turns around. "Payton, please. I prefer not to feel as if I've stepped into my father's shoes, thank you."

I nod as I knew at some point I would switch to using his first name to fit the whole fake bride persona. Just didn't seem appropriate to start there right away.

"Of course. Payton. We have approximately forty-five minutes to go through security and get to the gate—"

He holds up his hand. "Look, I appreciate what my sister is trying to do here, but it's entirely unnecessary."

"But I've been hired—"

Again, he stops me by lifting his hand, drawing my attention to his forearms and broad hands with long fingers. And for a brief second, I wonder what he looks like in his hockey uniform on the ice.

"Yes, I know. Emalia filled me in, and I informed her I would go along with her little plan to appease her, but I don't need a bodyguard."

"She told me you'd say that." I scan our surroundings, keeping tabs on a few lingerers.

He pulls his head back. "She did?"

"Oh yes. In fact, she said you'd try to convince me to leave."

Finger pressed beneath his full bottom lip, he blinks in

thought. "I suppose I shouldn't be surprised. Emalia knows me better than anyone. But that just simplifies things, don't you think?"

"How so?"

Payton shrugs. "My sister already expects that I'll send you off. So that's settled, then."

"No. It's not." I shake my head as I say this.

This time, he sighs. "All right. Then I have a proposal."

I study his angular features—the pulse in his jawline, the set of his mouth, the pinch of his brows—he's scrambling for a way out of this. The least I can do is humor him until he finally realizes I'm not going anywhere. "I'm listening."

Hope flashes in his crystal blues, almost making me feel guilty that I'm about to kibosh his plan. "You can escort me through security to my gate. You can even wait until I get on the plane if you'd like. Then you'll have completed the most important part of your assignment."

"How do you figure?"

"Any threat," his brows lift, "if there *is* any threat, is here in the UK. Not in the States. So once I board the plane, you're free to go."

I shake my head for the second time, and I suspect it won't be the last. "Then we'd best get you to your gate."

# Chapter Three

I should probably feel guiltier than I do, leaving my sister to deal with her new title and responsibilities. However, I know she'll be a whiz at it. She's built for it, whereas I am not.

Dealing with this bodyguard is proof enough of how out of my element I am in this scenario. At least she's agreeable to my proposal. Once I'm on the plane, I won't have to give it another thought.

Give my bodyguard another thought...

I lift my phone a little higher so I can study her without her noticing. She's sitting across from me, constantly watching either me or what's going on around us. I feel like I'm an ant in an ant farm, constantly under observation. The analogy even makes my skin crawl.

Though I will say Lily is madfit—our British term for 'hot'—for a bodyguard. I don't know exactly what I expected, but not this. With her light honey-brown hair pulled back into a ponytail, she appears younger. But that could be the light dusting of freckles covering her high cheekbones, which tells me she spends time outside. I could easily mistake her for a college student except for her attire, which seems more in line with a business executive.

She may be sitting, but my experience as a hockey player has taught me to be sensitive to a body about to change position or direction. As a forward, that's part of my job, so I can predict the best avenue to score a goal. And Lily is poised to move at a moment's notice, so that tells me she's athletic as well—another feature I find very attractive. Most of the very few women I've dated wanted nothing to do with the outdoors or any physical activity at all in some cases.

The flight attendant announces boarding is to begin, and since I'm flying first class, I rise and head toward the door. Lily follows close behind, still doing her job. Once I'm on the plane, I can relax for the duration of my flight without those hazel-green eyes watching me and everything around me. I'm still convinced my cousin's tendency for recklessness was his demise and therefore there's no credible threat to me. However, if I needed a bodyguard, I'm not sure I'd want one so breathtaking.

"Welcome aboard." The attendant smiles at me as I hold my phone out for her to scan my ticket.

As I look over my shoulder to nod my thanks to Lily, the attendant scans her phone.

I step to the side and face her. "What are you—"

Lily wraps her hand around my arm just above my elbow and, in one swift and impressive move, turns and propels me forward. "Let's not draw attention."

Once we get about twenty feet down the walkway to the plane, I stop and pull her aside, careful to keep my voice at a whisper. "What are you doing?"

Her gaze unwavering, she leans in and whispers, "My job."

"But you agreed to my proposal."

She waits for several people to pass by. "Actually, I didn't. I shook my head."

"But you said, 'We'd best get you to *your* gate.' Meaning my gate."

"Yes, your gate. And that's where *we* are."

I don't miss her implication or how she's handling me. A steady stream of travelers are now heading our way, inspiring a Hail Mary plan I'm begging the universe to let work. "Just go back and tell them you're sick or have a sudden family emergency."

Since timing *is* my strong suit, I launch myself in front of the latest pack of boarders, creating a barrier between Lily and me. Once on the plane, I stow my duffel and sit, watching the front to see if my bodyguard has decided I'm not worth the trouble or if she's as tenacious as I'm beginning to suspect.

After several people board and pass by, I pull out my phone and begin reading the book I started last night, doing my best to pretend that the movement next to me isn't Lily settling into her seat.

The small privacy door between the seats slides open. "Did you really think that would work?"

I exhale in resignation before lifting my head in her direction. Sunlight streaming through the tiny windows to my left highlights her hazel green eyes, making her irises appear almost backlit. The effect is captivating. "I'd hoped."

If that were true, then why do I feel somewhat pleased she didn't bail on me?

She leans forward, ruffling in her backpack, then sits back with a notebook and pen in her hands, which she promptly opens. "I made a list of things to cover so we can get our nuptials story down. The closer we keep to the truth, the better."

"Is this really necessary?" I probably sound like one of the petulant toddlers my sister used to treat, but I can't help it. I'm scrambling for some way to get out of this before I return to my *normal* life in Sarabella. When I threw the idea out about a female bodyguard, I honestly didn't expect Emalia to take me seriously.

She blinks at me. "Which part? Creating a believable story to keep your friends and teammates from knowing who you really are while I protect you? Or your continuous objections that are wasting valuable time and energy? Mostly mine."

"Well, when you put it that way..." This woman clearly doesn't like to be trifled with. I file that away, enjoying her forthrightness.

"Then let me rephrase. Let me do my job, Payton. That way, you can continue to do yours. That's the crux of this, isn't it?"

As much as I don't want to admit, she's right. I want to get back to the life I've worked hard to create outside of my family ties and responsibilities in England. Never mind that my sister outplayed me, which she's always excelled at.

"Fine. Let's get on with it. What's our story?"

An almost smug expression tilts her lips, which I find myself looking at more than I should. She's the enigma I never expected, that's for sure.

Lily folds back the cover of her notebook. "We met the first week you flew home for your cousin's funeral." She glances up as if to gauge my reaction. "Sorry for your loss, by the way."

The flash of compassion in her eyes twists something in my chest. I react with a curt nod. "Thank you."

She returns my nod and then refocuses on her notes. "What did you do that first week?"

I tilt my head back in thought to six weeks ago. "Let's see. I attended a polo match, had drinks at the pub with some friends, and…" I snap my fingers, "I helped my sister with her annual fundraiser event."

Lily taps her pen against her lips, drawing my attention there yet again. "Hmm, polo might work. Drinks with friends…perhaps I tagged along with one of them as a last-minute invite. That could work. What was the fundraiser for?"

"Underprivileged children. She started it not long after she went into private practice."

Something flashes behind Lily's eyes, then disappears with a smile that's decidedly forced. "Drinks with friends, it is. We wound up talking all evening and spending almost every day together after that."

She falls silent as she writes in her notebook. Does she not enjoy children or fundraisers? That seems highly unlikely.

I find myself wanting to learn more about her. Where did she come from, and how did she wind up being a close protection officer? What was her family like? Did she have any siblings?

"What about you?"

Her gaze jumps to mine. "What about me?"

"I should know details about you as well, correct?" I add a whimsical tone to my voice. "Seems odd that we talked for hours, yet I know nothing about you."

She checks her watch. "We met barely an hour ago."

"At the pub, the night we met. I'm practicing my part." I wink at her, just for effect.

A flight attendant stops next to my chair. "Would you like something to drink or something off our menu?"

I grin up at her. "Just some water, please."

"Are you sure I can't get you something more...enjoyable?" One side of her mouth lifts in a sly smile.

She's flirting with me. Normally, I'd engage and enjoy this rare occasion. In the States, one of the other guys on the team, such as Luke or Wade, would get the attention while I hung about like their wingman.

I swing my gaze to Lily. "I'm sure my wife would enjoy something."

The attendant's momentary flash of shock settles into a contrite expression. "So sorry. Of course! What can I get you?"

Lily's lips twitch up just so on the sides. "Some water, thank you."

The attendant nods, then turns around to walk back to the galley.

"Well done...husband." Lily's voice drops to a husky whisper.

If I weren't in on the ruse, I'd believe it myself. Suddenly uncomfortable, I shift in my seat. "Might as well start practicing now."

The flight attendant returns and hands us each a cup of water. I guzzle mine down, then hold my cup out to her. "I think I need a refill."

———

"Did you always want to be a hockey player?" Lily waits for my answer, pen poised over what I guesstimate to be her fourth page of notes.

In the last two hours, we've covered everything from

food and entertainment preferences to quirky details like my complete intolerance for anything sweet that's been salted— why eat it then? The entire purpose of eating a chocolate or a caramel is to enjoy its creamy sweetness. Why ruin it?

Yet, I still think I'm lacking enough details about Lily.

"I started playing as a child in a junior league and never looked back."

She tilts her head. "How did your parents feel about you wanting to make a profession of it?"

Not sure how this is pertinent to our convincing people we're married, but I don't mind answering it. "They've always been supportive of my choices, even if they don't entirely understand them."

Her mouth tenses for a moment. "That's nice."

"What about your parents? Do they approve of their daughter being in such a dangerous line of work?"

She clears her throat and studies her notebook. "They passed away when I was very young."

The twist I felt earlier in my chest returns twice as hard. "So sorry. That must have been difficult."

Her shrug doesn't hide the wariness I see on her face. "I don't remember much about them."

"Did your grandparents raise you, then? Mine like to play second parents to my sister and me, always nosing into our business." I finish with a chuckle.

She shakes her head. "My parents didn't have any family, so I grew up in the foster system."

I don't recall ever meeting someone who spent their childhood as an orphan. At the moment, I dearly wish I had some of my sister's diplomatic abilities.

"Sorry again." I let out a self-deprecating laugh. "I'm honestly not sure what to say."

"You don't need to say anything. It's simply the facts.

On the bright side, we won't have to make up any stories about meeting my parents. Makes things easier."

As much as I wish at times that my parents—and grandparents—would show less interest in my life, I can't imagine not having them in my life. And my sister, of course, whose penchant for bossing me around is either her way of showing she loves me or her superpower. Maybe both...

I run my hands down the front of my trousers. "Right. So, what's your story then? Do I tell my teammates you're a...you know, a..."

"Bodyguard?" A gleam of mischief sparkles in her eyes. "After high school, I did a short tour in the Army, then moved into the private sector, doing security in London. It's vague but detailed enough."

"You mentioned keeping things as close to the truth as possible, so is that true?"

"Pretty much."

"Why did you leave the military?"

She studies me. "That's complicated. Let's just say I realized I wanted something different."

Color me intrigued and completely fascinated. I want to ask her to expound, but I get the sense she holds this close. If I planned to spend more time with Lily, I'd wait for her to trust me before asking her for details about her past. But somehow, I have to find a way to cut this arrangement short before I'm back with the team.

"Hmmm. I can relate to that. That's how I wound up playing ice hockey in another country. I wanted something different."

"But for different reasons, I'm sure." She says this with a finality that tells me the subject is closed.

The lights dim in the cabin, drawing our gazes upward. A yawn bubbles up before I can squelch it.

Lily closes her notebook. "Get some rest, Payton. We've covered enough for now."

I nod as I reach to close the small door between our seats, but she stops me.

"Sorry, but I need to keep eyes on you at all times."

"But we're on a plane."

"Whatever threat's out there—"

"If there even is one," I interrupt.

"A single moment of vulnerability is all it takes, Payton. Trust me on that." Her gaze never wavers as if to bring her point home.

Aside from the jitters now coursing through me, I confess I find the thought of her watching me as I rest somewhat unsettling yet comforting at the same time. On the ice, I can count on Luke or Ethan to have my back, but in life, I'm largely on my own in the States. Returning for Sebastian's funeral reminded me how much I'd missed our family gatherings.

And as my eyes close, shutting out a last glimpse of Lily's ever-watchful presence, I'm struck with the thought that she must feel the same.

All the time.

# Chapter Four

## LILY

Most of the time, my assignments are willing participants, but I've never had one try to run away. So not only do I have to keep an eye out for anything unusual or threatening as we move through the small airport in Sarabella, but I also have to maintain a careful watch on Payton's movements in case he tries to bolt again.

Like now, I have to course-correct him because he's heading toward the exit. "Baggage claim first, big guy."

"Big guy? If that's your wifey nickname for me, I ask that you please try again."

I squelch a laugh bubbling up. Payton's sense of humor can be quite disarming. And distracting, which is a full-on negative in my book.

"You are taller than me," I sing-song. When I was a kid, I hated being the tallest kid in the crowd, but then, as I got older, I learned to use it to my advantage, like staring down a bully who was a good six inches shorter than me. Worked every time.

He leans his head toward me. "Not by much."

The look he gives me as he says this isn't what I expected, as if he likes that I'm tall, finds it attractive, even. Most guys I've encountered seem to only want cute little petite women. And that's never been me.

As we reach the luggage carousel, I guide Payton to the far end, away from the gathering crowd and closer to the side exit in case we have to leave fast, then send Del an update as to our location.

Just for the record, I don't mind him pointing out my height. I'm used to it, mostly. I shot up in eighth grade, earning me the nickname 'mosquito legs.' And I'm often asked by shorter women to reach items on upper shelves at shops. So I'm tall. Big deal.

"We'd be eye level if you wore heels. Do you ever wear heels, Lily?"

Is he trying to flirt with me? "Not if I can help it. Can't run well in them."

"That implies you've had experience."

"You could say that." I spot my bag and move us both closer to the circling belt.

"I revealed all kinds of details about my life. Surely, you can spare a few more about yours." A surly undertone accompanies his statement.

"I've told you all there is to know about me. Anything else," I shrug, "NDAs have my lips sealed."

"So, that's your full story?" He uses his fingers to tick off each one. "You grew up an orphan, did a brief stint in the military after high school, and went into private security in London."

"Good job, Payton. I'd give you a sticker if I had any."

He turns to face me. "There has to be more than meets the eye."

As his eyes move down my form to emphasize his point,

heat rides up my neck to my cheeks. Why am I reacting this way to him? I've done protection details for celebrities who make most women's toes curl, yet mine remained completely straight.

"Nope. That's it." I go to reach for my bag, but Payton gets there first, lifts it to the floor, and extends the handle. And he does all this without breaking eye contact. Does the man have eyes in the back of his head like some kind of secret antennae?

"What do you do in your spare time?"

I grab my suitcase and glide my bag toward the exit with Payton in tow. "Sleep."

"What about books? Do you read? Do you have a hobby?"

"Not much time to read in my line of work. And I'm never home long enough to engage in hobbies. Unless you count working out."

"That's something." His interest seems piqued. I always look for a way to connect with my principals for the sole purpose of building trust, which reduces resistance.

*Observation #1: If my principal's talking, he's distracted and much easier to manage.*

I snap my gaze to his. Maybe a little test of the waters. "From what I understand, you have a fairly regimented workout schedule. That's challenging in my line of work. Can't always keep a routine."

"Yes, but sometimes regiments can feel too controlling, so I prefer to shake things up." He runs his forefinger and thumb around his mouth as if drawing an imaginary goatee, which isn't hard to imagine with the hefty five o'clock shadow already there. His eyes dart back and forth like a wild animal searching for an escape.

The glass doors whoosh open. A wall of humidity

envelopes us as we step outside. Payton slips his phone out of his jeans pocket. "Shoot. I meant to arrange an Uber when we deplaned, but a certain someone distracted me."

Now I'm a distraction? Somehow, I have to figure out how to get him to take this seriously. Otherwise, it will be a constant battle to keep him safe.

Recognizing Del behind the wheel, I point to the dark gray SUV pulling up to the curb. "Already taken care of."

Making sure to reach the vehicle before him, I open the rear door for Payton. "You first."

His gaze drifts from me to my suitcase, and I can almost hear his thoughts.

"I can handle my bag, Payton. Please get in."

He turns to face me after getting in to say something, but I shut the door. Once my bag is stowed, I climb into the back seat on the other side. Del adjusts the rearview mirror so we can make eye contact.

I give the subtlest lift of my brow to let her know this assignment is far from the norm, then glance at Payton to make our communication less obvious. He's staring at me again and hasn't bothered with his seat belt.

"Buckle your seat belt."

*Observation #2: When flustered, the principal loses track of details.*

And judging by how his knee is bouncing up and down, he's nervous, too. He must have really thought he'd convince me to stay behind in London. Now I understand why his sister dangled a carrot for this assignment to make sure her brother didn't finagle his way out of their agreement.

I never expected such an offer, but when Payton's sister interviewed me, we clicked. She said if I could manage her brother, she'd put me on her permanent security detail. It's an ideal position that would secure my future. As much as I love my work, I'm not a fan of the constant change of assignments and locations. I'd rather have a long-term position…something stable and familiar.

The closer we get to Payton's apartment, the faster his knee is bouncing. Once I catch Del's eye in the rearview mirror, I touch my left brow to signal the principal is in meltdown mode. When we stop at a traffic light, Del taps her nose to let me know to check my phone, then leans forward slightly.

Seconds later, I hear the ping of a text.

Del: He has a roommate.

"What?!" Ignoring Del's warning glare, I swivel my head to look at Payton. "You have a roommate?"

His eyes widen slightly. "Yes, I do."

"That wasn't in the brief. And your sister didn't mention it."

He lets out a noisy breath, sounding almost relieved. "It's temporary. Luke's getting married in a couple of months."

Which means I'll have to stay in Payton's room. "This could be a problem."

His brows furrow. "How did you find out?"

Del glances at him over her shoulder with a cheeky grin. "That's our job, luv. We make it a point to know everything."

Payton wags his finger between us. "Wait. You two work together?"

I shove his hand down on the seat, registering the callouses on his fingers. "Yes. Why didn't you say something earlier?"

He lifts his shoulders. "I didn't think it would matter."

"You were that sure you could get rid of me?"

One side of his mouth tilts up with his sheepish expression. "Yes."

I realize I'm still holding his hand at the same time he glances down at the tangled knot between us. With a grunt, I yank my hand back. "This complicates everything."

Payton's smile stays in place, matching the mischievous gleam in his eyes. "I suppose we'll get to test our acting skills sooner than planned."

———

Acting skills? He still thinks this is a game. Mentally, I'm shaking my head. This assignment is going to take more patience than I expected. But I tuck that thought away for another time to explore. Right now, we have a roommate to fool into believing we're a married couple.

Once Del parks the sedan in front of the apartment building, Payton jumps out before me and takes his chivalrous self to the trunk to extract my suitcase. I can't help but wonder if he's playing nice to make up for his 'oversight,' which I suspect was more out of his conviction that he'd fully expected us to part ways in London.

While I keep an eye on him, Del puts her window down. "Sorry, luv. I only discovered it last night, and by then, you were already on the plane. Figured it would wait until you landed."

I step closer to the vehicle so he won't hear me. "He tried to lose me at the airport."

At the thud of the rear trunk closing, she glances backward. "You might want to do some damage control just in case there's anything else he didn't tell his sister."

"Copy that."

With a parting wave, Del backs out as I follow Payton and my suitcase, which he insisted on taking, toward his apartment. I assess our surroundings while analyzing the trepidation sitting in my stomach like a lead pipe. Am I just nervous about convincing this roommate that I'm Payton's wife, or am I picking up on something else?

Right away, I spot the temporary cameras Del installed as we step onto the sidewalk leading to his door. A staircase spanning to the second level sits to the left. The open design of the stairs gives me a clear view of what's beyond them, but the lighting's somewhat dim, creating shadows that could conceal a threat.

Payton stops in front of the door but doesn't unlock it.

I glance over my shoulder to make sure no one's coming from behind. "What are you waiting for?"

His gaze slides from the door to me. A fine sheen of moisture covers his forehead, which could simply be the stifling humidity or nerves. Or both. "Listening to hear if Luke's inside."

"This would have been easier if you told me sooner."

He holds his hand up. "I didn't think it would be necessary."

"Because you were convinced you'd come home alone." My half statement, half question, makes him cringe.

"Well, yes."

I point to the doorknob. "The faster you rip the Band-Aid off, the better."

He nods, but before he can use his key, the door flies open. A large hulk of a man fills the doorway. Casually dressed, dark hair, brutish features. Instinct compels me to take a step forward, preparing to insert myself in between the brute and Payton, just in case this unidentified man isn't the roommate.

"Payton! You're back!" The two men lock hands and pull toward each other as they slap each other on the back. "Great to see you, man. How was your trip?"

"Good as can be expected, considering."

Hulk man frowns at me. "Is this your sister?"

Payton barks out a laugh, then scrubs his hand over his mouth. "No, um, this is Lily. She and I met my first week back." He turns to me. "Lily, this is my roommate, Luke Jameson. He's also captain of the Sun Kings."

Donning my best smile, I extend my hand. "Pleasure to meet you, Luke."

"Likewise." He bounces his eyes between us before settling on me. "And you came with him?"

My priority at the moment is not to explain why I'm here to Luke, but to get Payton out of view or harm. "It's really warm out here. Why don't we go inside?"

"Of course! Sorry." Luke opens the door wider, clearing a path for us. He takes my suitcase from Payton and rolls it inside.

Cool air wafts around me. Air conditioning. A luxury Del and I don't have in the UK. I let out a soft breath once I see the door's closed. "Much better."

With a combination of humor and confusion in his expression, Luke crosses his arms and stares at us as if he's waiting for an explanation.

And Payton's standing there as if he's at a loss as to what to do or say next. I sidestep to Payton and twine my hand with his, which seems to startle him back to the present. He glances at me before focusing on Luke.

"Lily and I...we're..."

Luke raises a brow. "Together? That's great, man. Fast, but great."

I can tell Luke's being polite. His words are supportive, but his stance is uncomfortable.

Time to uncover the elephant in the room. "Payton and I just got married."

"Seriously?" Luke lowers his arms.

In an attempt to appear happy about it, Payton nods, but there's a tinge of green peeking out of his tanned face.

"Wow. You work fast, Pay." Luke frowns as he studies us. "Does anybody else know?"

Payton shakes his head. "Not yet. And I'd appreciate it if you'd let me be the one to tell everyone."

"Of course." Luke glances between us, still appearing unsure about the situation.

And Payton acting like a cornered dog in an alley isn't helping. I squeeze his arm, encouraging him to say something. We both need to play our parts if we intend to pull this off. Right now, this is feeling more like a one woman show.

He covers my hand with his while gazing into my eyes like a love-sick puppy. "What can I say? When you know, you know. The closer my return date came, the more we knew we didn't want to be apart."

I've read studies done with couples that involved extended times of just staring into each other's eyes to truly see one another, the goal being to build connection and affection. I didn't put much thought to it, but considering the way my heart just tripped up, I think I'll reassess my opinion on that.

And make a point to limit eye contact with Payton. Although, he does have quite attractive eyes. He's the classic stereotypical light brown to blondish-haired male with blue eyes. Not a pretty boy by no means. More on the rugged side, especially considering the faint scar on his cheek, which I assume came from a recent scuffle in the rink, which gives me an idea.

Payton said Luke is the team's captain. If we can convince him our fake marriage is the real deal, we'll have a leg-up on convincing the rest of the team.

I drag my eyes to Luke and smile. "I know we could have lived together and given it more time, but Payton's family isn't big on that kind of thing. And his nan is having some health issues. Since everyone was there, it just seemed ideal."

With a nervous laugh, Payton jumps in. "More like fate. Just meant to be."

Luke's frown deepens, reminding me of an infant trying to mess their diaper. Not that I have any experience with babies, but I did have to be around one on an assignment last year. Every time I saw that tiny human, he was eating, sleeping, or pooping.

Suddenly, Luke breaks into a massive smile and holds his hands out. "Congratulations, you two." He steps back with a sheepish expression on his face. "I'm sorry I blew your entrance."

Payton frowns. "What are you talking about?"

Luke takes on a puzzled look and shakes his head. "Tradition, man. She's your new wife, and you brought her home. You're supposed to carry her over the threshold."

I shake my head...vigorously. "That's not necessary."

"Of course it is." Luke reaches for the door. "You want to start things right, don't you?"

"I'm too tall. Payton might hurt himself." Might as well use my height as an advantage here. I long ago accepted I wouldn't be one of those petite women who gets swept up into the arms of a man who towers over her and weighs twice what she does.

Little did I expect Payton to rise to the challenge. And that mischievous gleam of his is back. Next thing I know, he grabs my hand, drags me outside, then sweeps me up into his arms without even a grunt.

I stiffen at first, but then our eyes lock, and my body relaxes.

"Right." Surprise lurks in his eyes.

Concerned I might be too much, I tighten my grip around his shoulders to make this easier for him as he swings my legs through the doorway and sets me back on my feet.

He straightens and gives me a cheeky grin, displaying deep lines that bracket his lips like parentheses and adding to the ruggedness of his face. "There. It's official now."

Our gazes meet again and hold. I think I must be in partial shock because I can't stop staring at Payton and reliving how he so easily carried me inside. And I can't seem to shake the feeling of his arms holding me like vises against the warmth of his chest.

Luke clears his throat, then grabs a set of keys off the table by the door. "I just remembered I have some errands to run. You two enjoy getting settled in."

# Chapter Five

## PAYTON

I've never been a fan of innuendos. And Luke's was fairly clear. I'm sure it comes with the newlywed territory, which would be fine if that's what Lily and I actually were. I reach for her suitcase, fully planning to take her bag to the spare room, then stop as the full ramification of our situation slams me like an opponent gone rogue, flying down the ice in a breakaway.

I turn back around to face Lily. "I...did not think this through."

Her lips purse together. "No, you didn't. Which room is yours?"

"Mine?"

She rolls her eyes and lets out an exasperated sigh. "Yes, Payton, yours. I certainly can't sleep on the couch."

"Of course not. I will."

Brows pinched, she studies me. "Don't you think that would raise questions with Luke?"

I blink and shake my head. "Right. Of course. I guess I'm struggling with the lies more than I originally thought."

Her expression softens as she takes a step closer to me. "You could just tell everyone the truth. Would certainly make things easier."

For a moment, I consider her suggestion. Besides simply loving the game, I pursued a career in hockey to build my own life. Not something defined—or dictated—by my familial connections to royalty. I simply wanted to be a regular bloke.

Now, in light of this new title of heir apparent, I feel like I'm fighting to hold onto my dream. If I tell Luke and the rest of the team the truth, that will change the whole dynamics of what I've worked so hard to put in place—my anonymity and autonomy.

I shake my head. "No, let's stick to the plan."

"You mean the original plan you never intended to keep?"

Just enough sarcasm to soften the harsh reality. "Right, again. Sorry about that." I gesture to the first door. "That's my room there."

She darts off with her suitcase in tow.

I follow her into the room, then divert to the dresser. She'll need places to put her clothing, so I start opening drawers on one side and sweeping items out by the armful.

"Payton, what are you doing?"

A pair of balled socks falls from my arms to the floor, as if to punctuate the moment. "Making room for your things."

"That's unnecessary. I'm used to living out of a suitcase. I'll stow it in your closet or under the bed to keep it out of sight."

I glance at the empty drawer. "I'll just dump these over here for now and show you the wardrobe." I drop the pile of clothes onto the bed and stride to the generous walk-in. "There's plenty of room in there."

Lily stops next to me. Shelves cover a small section to the left, then two levels of hanging bars extend to the back. On the opposite side, the same thing but instead of shelves, shoe cubbies fill the space.

"That's quite a closet." She seems surprised.

My clothes only take up half the space. "One of the highlighted features of the place. Probably intended for couples. Real couples, that is." I try to inject some humor into my tone. My wardrobe feels small with her musky vanilla scent wreaking havoc with my senses.

When she swivels her head to look around, I find myself fascinated with the swish of her ponytail and the delicate curve of her neck, reminiscent of one of the porcelain ballerina figurines my sister likes to collect.

That is not something I should be noticing right now. This is a business arrangement and nothing more. However, Lily is unlike any woman I've ever met. She's edgy yet reserved. Assertive when necessary, yet inquisitive without being intrusive. And she has a mind that'd put a top-tier coach's playbook to shame. Having her in my bedroom may prove to be more of a challenge than I expected.

She unzips the top of her suitcase and tugs out a small zipper case. "Bathroom?"

I probably look like a skittish pup the way I jerk myself back to reality, dart toward the loo, and push open the door. "Plenty of vanity space, so feel free to spread out. And towels are in the linen cupboard, amongst other things. Make yourself at home."

A slight blush creeps up her cheeks. Does she react to all men like that? Or just me? And why am I hoping it's the latter?

Brilliant. Could I sound any more like a prize idiot? I can't recall being this rattled before. Last season, an enforcer on our opponent's team decided to target me for the entire second period because I skated into their goalie during a shot on goal. The lot of us fell like dominos as one of their blokes tried to block me, and we wound up a tangled mess in the crease. After that, I had to constantly watch my back to avoid getting battered into the boards. But even that didn't unsettle me as much as Lily does.

She rests her hand on my upper arm. "Relax, Payton. We'll figure this out. I'm fine. You're fine." Her brows dance together as she studies me. "Why don't you rest while I unpack? I think you need it."

I inhale deeply, realizing at the same time that I'd been holding my breath, then exhale. "Right. I'll go and read a book. Or something."

Naturally, I shut the bedroom door when I leave to give Lily privacy, but as soon as I hear the click of the latch, the tension in my shoulders releases, and weariness from the long flight hits me harder than a crosscheck.

The last thing I remember is sitting down in my favorite reading chair and opening the Kindle app on my phone.

---

Soft voices filter in, rousing me into a foggy state of awareness. The clink of a dish followed by the sound of running water lures me back to reality.

And my current predicament.

I'm tempted to keep my eyes shut and pretend I'm still asleep—pretend that none of this is real, that there isn't a gorgeous bodyguard standing in my kitchen, ripping apart a head of lettuce with startling gusto. I make a mental note to never let those hands near my head, as I'm quite attached to it.

Perhaps losing my head isn't what I should worry about, though. I'm beginning to think there's more to Lily—and I mean a lot more—than just the abbreviated story she gave me. She's stronger than she appears, too, which I can tell she uses to her advantage. Best way to surprise your opponent is by deception, of course.

We are neck-deep in subterfuge here, and Lily's carefully guarded depths draw me in like a cat with a few lives to spare. And I'm almost certain I'd lose a few.

Resolved to table this examination until a later time, I stretch my stiff limbs as I yawn.

"He's awake." Luke's voice rumbles through the room.

Lily glances at me but says nothing. However, her smirk tells me one of two things. Either she realizes what a pathetic bloke I am, or she's satisfied with her work destroying a head of lettuce.

Not entirely sure which I prefer, to be honest. "Please tell me I didn't drool. How long was I out?"

Smirking, she dries her hands with a towel that says 'I only puck around in the kitchen.' I dearly hope she didn't read it. "Almost two hours."

Without looking up, Luke shakes his head. "Didn't think you'd opt for sleeping, Pay."

If this is what it's going to be like when I tell the rest of the team, I may have to reconsider this strategy. I scan Lily's face for her reaction but see none. Not even a slight blush or an awkward gesture. So, unlike me, innuendos don't seem to bother her, yet she blushed when we were in the bedroom.

I stand and wander over to the kitchen area of my open-plan apartment. "What are we making?"

Lily raises her brows, seemingly surprised. "We?"

Luke slides a package of steaks across the island toward me. "Payton's the master cook of this residence, which I'm going to miss, by the way. Sophie's great in the kitchen, but not like Payton."

"Oh, really?" Lily leans against the counter with a gleeful expression.

"Don't tell her I said that." Luke shoots a warning gaze with his words, then gives Lily a look of disbelief. "He hasn't cooked for you yet?"

I clear my throat. "No, never had a chance. I was staying with my parents, so we always went out."

A slight twist of the truth. I went out some while I was back. Just not with Lily. I dart my gaze to her, making sure we're on the same page.

She dips her chin as her brows lift, as if to say 'well done' while Luke stoops to grab a pot out of the drawer.

"Then tonight, you get to show off your cooking skills to your new wife. We'll take care of the salad. You do the rest."

My new wife...

I mentally shake myself to brush off the weight of those words, reminding myself that all of this is temporary. I'm confident the investigation into my cousin's death will be resolved quickly, and then Lily can be on her way back to England. Or wherever she calls home. I make a mental note to ask her more about that.

After doing my best to impress my fake bride with my cooking skills, the rest of the evening glides along with good food and easy banter. However, I noticed Lily grew very intent when Luke mentioned his father and that they were recently reunited. Again, she displayed her curiosity without being intrusive, but I personally found her questions quite telling as they seemed to focus on the familial aspect, especially regarding Luke's sister.

I suppose that makes sense. Lily said she grew up in foster homes. I can't imagine what that was like. My family's always been close—sometimes *too* close, if you ask me. But to go through life without that kind of support system... I make a mental note to call my sister tomorrow and speak to my mother, as well.

Once we finish clearing the remnants of our meal and load the dishwasher, Luke excuses himself, pleading weariness and an early morning ahead of him. I *do not* miss the wink he sends me as he passes on the way to his room. And the click of his door punctuates yet another awkward moment about to ensue.

Lily busies herself wiping the counter and hanging the dish towel over the oven handle. After which, she finally lifts her gaze to mine. She glances toward the spare room and whispers, "I need to do a perimeter sweep and check the cameras."

"Cameras?" I whisper back.

She nods. "Del set a few up yesterday. Just precautionary."

This feels way more serious than it ought. "I'll come with you, then."

"No. It's dark out. Too risky." She picks up her phone and swipes the screen. "I won't be gone long."

I close the distance between us so I can keep my voice down. "What about *your* safety? A woman walking around at night alone? Sounds even riskier if you ask me."

"I can take care of myself, Payton. That's what I'm trained for, remember?"

The image of her ripping apart the head of lettuce

comes to mind. I fear if I got in her way, she'd fold me like a pretzel.

"How could I forget?" I clear my throat. "What if Luke walks out?"

"He won't."

"How can you be so sure?"

"Because I drugged him."

"You what?!"

"Shhh!" She snorts and bends over, shaking with silent laughter, then finishes with a long sigh as she straightens. "I'm just kidding. He made it pretty clear he was giving us our privacy."

"Fine. But if you're not back in ten minutes, I'm coming after you."

She takes a long breath that matches her slow blink. "If that makes you feel better."

Feel better? If there's one thing we Brits do to extreme, it's proper etiquette. However, letting her go outside alone at night goes against every fiber of who I am as a man.

She shuts the door quietly behind her, and I can't rip my eyes from it. Tomorrow, we have our first practice for the upcoming season. Will she insist on hanging about the arena to keep her eyes on me like she did on the plane?

If so, what do I tell the blokes? That my new wife is clingy? That we can't stand any kind of separation? That I want her there to boost my morale? I mentally groan because, no matter what I say, I'll look like a right muppet who panicked and ran straight to the altar. Might as well ask her to wear one of my jerseys so she can truly fit the part.

Wouldn't that be a sight? Lily wearing my jersey as she cheers me on...

And that's the image that captures my imagination as I stare at the door, waiting for my fake bride to return.

# Chapter Six

## LILY

"So, how's the honeymoon going?" Del's snarky tone makes me grin.

"Awkward as hell." I didn't want to tell Payton that my true intention for leaving was to touch base with Del. She's already done a perimeter sweep for tonight and made sure the cameras are sending signals to her phone and mine. I just needed a few minutes to clear my head and get some perspective.

"What did you expect? He's royalty adjacent and British." She says 'British' in an uppity nasal tone.

I crack a laugh. "But you Brits are always cracking sex jokes and innuendos all the time."

"To deflect, luv. We either refuse to talk about it or poke fun at it. And I prefer the latter."

"Duly noted." Never a dull moment with Del. I've learned not take her too seriously, but I know in a life and death situation, she's the most serious and effective person I've ever known.

"So, what's on the agenda for the rest of the night?"

"Hashing out a plan for tomorrow." Just the thought makes me sweat even more than the muggy nighttime air.

Del sighs. "Boring. You're spoiling my fun. You know that, right?"

I choose to ignore her poke. "We almost blew it with his roommate. If Payton acts as nervous as he did tonight, I'm not sure we'll pull off this cover."

"Then do something to defuse the tension, luv."

"Like what?"

She hums over the connection. "You could kiss him."

Even though she can't see me, I roll my eyes. "That's completely unprofessional and would only complicate things."

"Interesting that you didn't flat-out refuse." Her voice trails off with implication.

"Don't start reading into things, Del. And I don't want to fluster him any more than he already is." Anticipating the end of this conversation, I turn around to head back to the apartment. So much for gaining some perspective.

"I meant in a strictly professional capacity, of course. You're posing as a married couple. Couple's kiss, in case you didn't know."

"I know that." I bark out.

A soft chuckle accompanies her words. "Just checking, luv. I know you didn't grow up around that kind of thing. Maybe you should do it now and get the awkwardness out of the way."

She's right, as always. I never knew my father, and cancer took my mother away before I even started school. "We'll navigate that when, *and if*, it becomes necessary. I don't want to rattle him more than he already is."

"Hmmm. You sure he's the only one rattled in this scenario?"

"Okay, we're done for tonight. I will check in tomorrow around the same time."

"Deflecting now. This is getting very interesting."

"Good night, Del." I end the connection before she can worm another unwelcome thought to take residence in my brain. The last thing I need in my head are images of kissing Payton. Although, Del made a valid point. There may come a time when we're in a situation that warrants a show of affection.

The problem is that I'm unsure whether discussing this with Payton would do more harm than good. Sometimes, you have to keep a principal in the dark about certain aspects, but that usually has more to do with potential danger and kissing doesn't fall into that category.

Cool air makes the dampness on my face tingle when I walk back in. Payton's still poised in the same spot as when I left, a mix of concern and confusion on his face. I close and lock the door quietly so Luke won't hear and wonder.

When Payton opens his mouth to speak, I put my finger over my lips and then point toward the bedroom. Once inside, I kick off my shoes in the closet and tug out a set of pajamas off a shelf to change into after I shower.

He shoves his hands into his jeans pockets, causing his shoulders to hunch near his ears. "Do you have to be with me at the arena the entire time?"

"No. Most of the time, I'll do surveillance from outside. Del's already scouted the facilities for weak points. Do you carpool with Luke?"

"Not really. He often has plans with his fiancée."

"Good. We'll use the single car as an excuse for me to drive you back and forth each day."

He nods. "Should I make a proper introduction to the blokes so they can meet you?"

"That's up to you." I walk toward the bathroom. "We can be flexible with things like that. You could say I'm shy and not ready to meet your friends yet."

He quirks a lopsided grin, bringing back those creases bracketing his mouth. They're like giant dimples. "Not sure they'd believe that once they actually get to know you."

"Why, Mr. Maxwell, are you implying I'm not genteel enough?" I slide in a mock British accent I know sounds horrible, because Del as much as told me so when I tried it on her one day as a joke.

A guttural laugh rumbles from his chest, which oddly spikes my pulse. "Now you sound like my mother."

I grin. "Yes, but I made you laugh. The easier we keep our rapport, the more believable this will be."

He seems relieved at first. "You're good at this."

"That's my job." I pat my pajamas. "Let's talk more after I shower."

Payton drops his gaze to his feet, appearing awkward again. At this rate, I predict this facade will last barely a day, which would make this assignment much easier if he would just come clean about his situation. But I get it. I've worked with enough clients to understand the intrusion personal security creates when the principal isn't accustomed to it.

I toss my PJs onto the counter and start the water, still mulling over ways to solve this predicament. Unfortunately, Del's voice about kissing Payton won't go away. Maybe I should have had her switch places with me. Then again, I'm not sure Payton could handle Del.

Washing off a day of travel and humidity never felt so good. I wrap a very plush towel around me and step out of the shower. The large closet and oversized bathroom confirm my assessment that Payton prefers creature comforts, which I'm sure he has the money for but doesn't like to make it obvious. Most likely, part of his desire to keep his family connections unknown here in the U.S.

A loud thud comes from the bedroom. I pause to listen, then raise my voice. "Payton?"

When I don't get a reply, my adrenaline kicks in. With one hand holding the fold of my towel, I bolt out of the bathroom, yet I don't see Payton or anyone else, for that matter. The bedroom door is closed, and no sounds are coming from the living room.

"Payton?"

He pops up from the other side of the bed, rubbing his head. "Yes?"

"What are you doing? Are you all right?"

He glances down. "I was making a pallet on the floor and hit my head on the nightstand."

I rush over to make sure he's not bleeding and push his hand aside. "No blood, but you'll have a nice little bump there. Are you dizzy or nauseated?"

He doesn't answer, so I search his face for signs of incapacitation. He seems fine except for the way his blue eyes make a slow drift from the top of my towel, up my neck, and then to my face.

Our gazes lock, making me acutely aware of the tension building between us. And that I'm dressed in only a towel. Those blasted images induced by Del's comment about kissing him flood in like a raging storm.

Feeling exposed, I grab the bottom of the towel to keep the overlap closed and spin around. "I'll be right back."

After dressing and combing out my wet hair, I return to the bedroom to find Payton lying on the pallet, reading a book.

"Payton, sleep in your bed. I'm fine on the floor."

He lowers his book. "That wouldn't be very gentlemanly of me, now would it?"

"That's unnecessary. This is a professional arrangement. And I've probably slept on the ground or a floor more often than I have in a bed, to be honest."

He's quick to hide his surprise but not fast enough in hiding the flash of concern lingering in his eyes. "All the more reason you should take the bed."

"I'm your bodyguard, Payton. Nothing more. Perhaps this would be easier if you didn't think of me as a woman."

He sits up, draping his arm over his leg. In doing so, the blanket he'd casually draped over himself falls away, revealing the rest of his torso. And an impressive six-pack, I doubt comes just from playing hockey.

Warmth spreads in my belly. Since when do I react to a bare chest like a blushing schoolgirl? And I saw plenty during my military days. This should be no different. I want to turn away to hide the heat rising in my face.

But the look he gives me is borderline smoldering. "That's impossible, Lily."

Is that why he's acting so awkward around me? Because he's attracted to me?

I'd be a fool and bad at my job if I didn't admit—if only to myself—that I'm drawn to him as well. And that is something I will have to work double time to shut down, especially since we'll have to share a room indefinitely.

This assignment just turned way more complicated than I ever expected.

———

Before he heads to the arena for practice, Payton likes to take a morning jog on the beach.

I'm not complaining, mind you. Here, I thought I'd have to squeeze in a workout here and there when time and circumstance permitted—and when Del was on watch. But I may wind up in even better shape once this assignment is done.

I will say I found Payton's efforts not to wake me this morning rather endearing. Although, the way he jumped when I said good morning still makes me laugh. He didn't appreciate my humor at his expense, though, but his expression bordered on sheer delight when I walked out of the closet dressed in workout clothes and sneakers.

Just shy of sunrise when we arrived, the beach was nearly deserted, but now shell hunters and fellow joggers dot the sandy shoreline in growing numbers. The sound of waves crashing on the shore settles something in me, and for the first time in a while, I feel like I can breathe. How did I miss how wound up I was?

"How much further do you want to jog?" I keep my pace matched to his, which turns out to be almost the same as my norm.

"Getting tired?"

"Nope. Just noticing the beach is getting more crowded. I would suggest we head back soon. For your safety."

"All right." He slows down and comes to a stop, barely winded. "Then how about we pick up the pace?"

"Sure. No problem." I do a quick scan of the area, assessing any threat or choke points. Cottages line the upper part of the beach. Further down, I notice the Sandpiper Inn, where Del is staying, and the neighboring restaurant, the Turtle Tide.

All very picturesque and inviting. Something about it

makes me want to linger, to soak in the tranquility of it all. I snap my attention back to my principal. Right now, that's all I can allow to take up my headspace.

Payton tilts his head as he studies me, then swings his gaze to a seawall in the distance. "We're about a hundred yards from that wall. Think you can manage a sprint?"

I shrug. "Sure. No problem."

The growing sunlight adds to the twinkle already sitting in his eyes. "Care to make a race of it?"

Curiosity piqued, I lift my hands to my hips. "Why?"

"Just a little fun. Unless you think you can't handle it. I can slow my pace to make it fair."

I know I shouldn't take the bait, but his smug expression is making that really difficult. "No need. I'm up for the challenge."

He moves closer, invading my space just enough to kick my pulse up a notch. "Then let's make it interesting, shall we? If I win, you tell me what made you join the military."

I snort. "Nothing made me."

"Okay, then why you *decided* to join the military."

Why am I even considering this? It's a distraction, more than anything. "And if I win?"

He traces the sides of his mouth as he thinks. "I will promise not to try to lose you again."

Hands on my hips, I blast him with a glare. "Did you have plans to do that?"

The look he gives me says he'll never confess. "Do we have a deal?"

I sigh. "Fine. Deal."

He takes a spot next to me, facing the seawall in the distance. "Ready, set...go!"

We launch in unison, racing down the moist sand just above the shoreline. Halfway there, the burn in my thighs starts, but I push harder to keep pace with him. However, I suspect he's pacing himself to make me believe I have a chance. I'm tall, but his stride is longer.

About thirty feet from the wall, I give it all I have, testing my theory. Payton does the same and shoots ahead of me easily, reaching the wall a good three yards ahead of me. Just as I suspected he would.

Am I irritated that he beat me? Mildly. I think I'm more annoyed that he held himself back.

He rests his hands on his hips as he catches his breath.

*Observation #3: Payton is more athletic than he looks. And very competitive.*

I lean my rear against the wall while resting my hands above my knees, keenly aware of our surroundings as I catch my breath. A drawing of a mermaid on the cinder blocks to my left stares back at me with a slight smile and a red bikini top that reminds me of the one Del insisted I bring.

He dons a smug grin. "Happy to give you a rematch anytime."

"I bet you are, big guy."

"Whenever you're ready." He raises his brows, letting me know he's waiting for me to divulge my life secrets.

I straighten. "Now?"

"No time like the present."

We walk side by side, heading back the way we came.

I take a moment to decide how much I intend to share with him. The problem is, I want to tell him the entire story, which isn't normal for me. I haven't even told Del everything.

So I'll just tell him what's specific to his question. "When I graduated from high school and aged out of the system, I really didn't have a place to go. I couldn't afford college, but I liked the idea of being part of something structured." I shrug. "The military made sense."

"Was that because you were used to being in the system?"

His question hits close to home, surprising me that he would make that connection. "In a way, yes. I was usually the one looking out for the younger kids, so it felt familiar."

"To protect those in need."

I dart my gaze to his, locked in a moment of unexpected understanding. How is he able to read me so well when he hardly knows me?

"You sound like you have some experience."

He nods. "British royalty is very service-oriented. It's ingrained from an early age. Even though my family doesn't hold a major title, we've always taken our position quite seriously."

"Why did you pursue hockey, then? Did you want something less serious?" I end with a laugh.

His jaw pulses. "No. I feel the same about hockey and train hard. My decision was more about living my life on my own terms."

Now I feel bad that I laughed. "I can relate to that."

He studies me. "Can you?"

I feel like a bug under a microscope as if my answer will determine what he does next. "I left the military for much the same reason."

"And became a bodyguard." He glances away for a moment.

"Yes. Like you, I wanted control of my future."

"We have a lot in common, Lily." His blue eyes mirror the encompassing sky as he stares at me with that infernal dimpled smile that makes my stomach flutter.

I use checking the time on my watch to change the subject. "We better hurry, or you'll be late for practice."

He doesn't say anything else on our walk back, and neither do I. The silence is a relief, actually. Most of my assignments have required minimal communication. I'm more of a background fixture than a centerpiece.

But with Payton, I find myself wanting very much to be the center of his attention.

# Chapter Seven

## PAYTON

I drop down on the bench and yank at the laces on my skates to get out of my gear. Except my mind isn't here. It's still on the beach, thinking about what Lily shared. But it's more what she didn't say that lingers with me and what was implied.

She had no family or anyone close to help her once she became an adult, so she had to find her own way in the world. The thought of her alone like that puts an ache in my chest, akin to getting hit with a puck.

Yet her tenacity inspires me. She didn't frame her past in a negative light—simply as facts and a logical choice. As much as I'd like to disassociate myself from my family title, I've always appreciated their support and encouragement, even if they didn't totally agree with my life decisions. No matter what happens, I know they're there for me. I know they're there for me if all else fails.

Maybe that's why launching out on my own to a new country didn't seem that scary to me. I knew I'd have a place to land if things didn't work out. But they did, and I'm loathe to let the life I've built for myself go.

Luke sits next to me on the bench and gives me a gentle shove. "Mind on something else today?"

I rub my hands down my face. As uncomfortable as it makes me, it's easier to let him think what he wants. "Guess you could say that."

He lets out a deep chuckle. "That's understandable. You're newlyweds."

Keeping my face down, I continue to unlace my skates. I've never been great at hiding my facial expressions—I felt my cringe when he said 'newlyweds.' I should be more careful and think before I react.

"When are you planning to tell the team?"

I convinced Lily to drop me off and leave before any of my teammates caught sight of her to avoid questions and finish practice without saying a word about it. But he's right. If I don't say something, he'll think there's trouble in paradise.

The rest of the guys wander in to shed their gear and shower. I might as well get this over with. I attempt a wide grin that I hope is believable.

"No time like the present." Once I slip off my other skate, I stand up.

Luke lets out a loud whistle. "Listen up. Pay has something to share."

All eyes are suddenly on me. The words lodge in my throat when I open my mouth. I think my sweat is sweating at this point. "A curious thing happened while I was back home. I…well, I…"

Luke stands and pats me on the back. "Payton got married."

A mix of disbelieving 'whats' and 'no ways' break out

before several of the blokes walk over and congratulate me. I can see the questions resting in their eyes as they study me, but I keep a smile in place. Coach Markelson shakes my hand and congratulates me. All of it I accept with no explanation. Lily suggested I only divulge details when asked. That most of the time, people won't ask out of respect for my privacy. Turns out she's right.

But Wade has never been one to let etiquette deter him. "What on earth possessed you to do that, my English friend?"

I sputter at first, but once again, Luke jumps in. "Love, you idiot. What other reason could there be?"

What reason, indeed? If they only knew.

Luke gives me an affirming nod, then starts conversing with Coach.

I grin. "What he said."

Wade studies me, doubt clouding his eyes. "Sounds like a whirlwind romance. Did you two elope?"

"No, we had a small private ceremony at my parents' home just before we flew back." Movement in my peripheral vision catches my attention. Luke gestures at me while talking to Coach Markelson and Derek, our assistant coach, who nods. I assumed Luke's sharing his introduction to Lily, since he's the only one who's met her so far.

Wade rests his hands on my shoulders. "I guess congrats are in order then, Pay-man. I hope you two are very happy."

I catch a glimpse of something sad flit by in his gaze, and file it away for another time. Wade's never mentioned any current or past girlfriends, so now I'm wondering if he might have had a bad experience. That would explain his hesitancy to congratulate me at first.

Why am I even concerned about this? If he knew the truth, he'd probably be relieved. Or angry as hell.

I rush through my shower and then send a text to Lily that I'm almost ready as I get dressed. But before I can leave, Coach stops me.

"Payton, Olivia and I would love it if you and your new wife…?"

Takes me a second to realize he's waiting for me to fill in her name. "Lily."

He grins. "If you and Lily would come over for dinner, Friday. Do you think she'd be up for that? I can only imagine what a big adjustment this is for her. For both of you."

I've always known Coach to run on the diplomatic side —part of what makes him a great coach, but when it comes to his team, he's usually very forthright. But there's a hesitancy to his words, as if he's picking them carefully.

I can't think of a reason to decline. Not one good enough to make sense that won't fuel whatever's concerning him. Just what I need—an evening spent not only convincing him and his wife that I'm married but also assuaging their concerns that I made the biggest mistake of my life because I have a feeling that's what this is about.

"I'll check with Lily, but I'm almost certain she'll agree."

"Good man. You're already thinking like a 'we.' Took me months to get the hang of that."

I think I just got marital advice when this is more about making sure my bodyguard approves. "Right."

Coach squeezes my shoulders. "Great. We're looking forward to meeting Lily."

*Looking forward to meeting Lily.*

The words have spun in my head like fans chanting for the last two days. It's bad enough that Lily insisted on driving to Coach's place, stating that was also part of her job. When I probed further, she simply said that being in control of as many factors as possible was key to my safety.

The notion had me checking the passenger side mirror the entire trip over. Thankfully, I noticed nothing unusual except for the lady walking her bright pink poodle on the sidewalk. Her owner had matching hair. I may have to tell Luke's fiancée, Sophie, about that one since she likes that color so much.

I switch the bag holding a bottle of wine to my other hand for at least the fourth time as we walk up the path to Coach's front door.

Lily glances at me. "Relax, Payton."

"Easier said than done."

Before I can push the doorbell, she nudges my shoulder, forcing me to face her. "Then reframe the situation."

I'm instantly intrigued. "How so?"

She tilts her head. "Pretend this is a game you want to win."

I think my eyebrows just merged with my hairline. "A game? You're bloody kidding, right?"

The corners of her mouth tip up in a mysterious smile that captures my full attention. "We'll make it a competition to see who does the best job of convincing everyone we're madly in love."

The nervous energy pulsing through my body coalesces into pinpoint focus like a shot on goal during the last minute of a period. She's challenging me, and I relish it.

My gaze skims her lovely face, settling briefly on her lips. "You're on."

Lily leans in until she's pressed against me and lifts her head to the side of my head farthest from the door. Her lips brush my ear as she speaks. "Someone's at the door, about to open it. Act as if I'm telling you what I want to do when we get home later."

The corners of my mouth slide up of their own accord, and heat instantly rises up the back of my neck. I close my eyes, turning my head slightly toward her as if to lean into her words, which I totally am. No acting needed.

The sound of the door opening, followed by a throat clearing, pulls us apart.

Coach divides his grin between us. "Glad you two could make it."

I hand him the bottle of wine I brought. "A little something for tonight."

Ever the dutiful fake wife, Lily beams at him. "Thank you for having us."

"Come on in. Olivia has some appetizers set out to hold us over until dinner."

As we step inside, a group chorus chimes out. "Surprise!"

Good thing I handed that wine bag to Coach because it would have hit the floor, making a mess. Even Lily jumped and grabbed my arm. Not to cling to me but to yank me behind her.

I grab her hips in a subtle tug to shift her next to me. "Wow, everyone's here."

Smiling, Lily plays along by slipping one arm around my waist and resting the other on my chest. Doesn't take long for the heat from her hand to feel more like a branding iron through the fabric of my shirt.

I cover her hand with mine, feeling almost prideful that

I get to present Lily to everyone. And I mean everyone. Even Derek's wife, who I'd begun to think didn't exist, is here, hanging on his arm.

"Ladies and gentlemen—"

A snicker comes from someone—I suspect one of the young rookies just promoted up—from the back of the room, to which Luke gives his signature grunt to shut it down.

"I'd like to introduce you to my Lily." I shake my head. "I mean my wife, Lily."

Chuckles fill the room as Sophie rushes up. "Hi, I'm Sophie. Luke's fiancée. It's so great to meet you!"

Smile ever in place, Lily shakes her hand, then lets out a soft yelp when Sophie hugs her. "Nice to meet you, too."

Lily shoots a questioning look my way. I shrug and grin. Like a royal couple in a greeting line, Lily and I are greeted and congratulated by almost everyone.

Olivia walks in with a tray of fluted glasses filled with champagne. "Everyone, grab a glass so we can toast the new couple."

After Lily and I take one, Coach stands next to me. "Since we didn't get to see you two get married, we thought we'd surprise you with our own little celly."

Forcing a grin, I lift my glass up. "Quite the surprise, indeed."

"And so thoughtful." Lily's hand on my waist tightens as if to remind me why we're here.

Coach rushes over to help Olivia pass out the rest of the glasses.

Wade lets out a soft whistle. "Toast time."

To which Coach waves him on.

You never know what you'll get when it comes to Wade.

He's as unpredictable off the ice as he is on it—a great trait in hockey, but I'm not sure it works in his favor otherwise. But one thing is certain—his actions always come straight from the heart.

He lifts his glass as the room quiets. "To Payton and Lily. May their love always burn bright for each other, and may they always know their way to the bedroom."

A banter of laughter and snickers fills the room. I don't bother to stifle the groan that erupts from my chest. Nor do I miss the blush seeping into Lily's cheeks as she glances shyly at me. We stare at each other for a moment, and something delicate shifts between us like a shared moment of intimacy, so I wink at her.

Her eyes widen just so...my reward. Put a point on the scoreboard for me.

Elias smacks Wade on the bicep. "Not the time, bro."

Luke grunts under his breath. "There's never a time for that, man."

Wade's expression turns downright repentant. "Sorry. I was just trying to keep the mood light."

Mathéo chuckles openly. "You definitely made me laugh."

With perfect timing, Coach's wife, Olivia, lifts her glass. "To the happy couple!"

Soft cheers and whistles fill the room. Lily takes a sip of her champagne, then presses a kiss on my cheek near the corner of my mouth. At the touch of her soft lips, my eyes close of their own accord as I instinctively lean into her.

As she pulls away, I catch her smug expression, followed by a subtle wink of her own.

I suppose part of me thought she was joking about making this a contest of sorts, but now that I know she's serious, I will take great pleasure in waiting for my chance to even the score.

Most of the guests wander toward a large table covered with all kinds of finger foods and a large sheet cake decorated with wedding bells. Silver balloons and blue streamers swag the nearby windows, acting like a backdrop.

Once there's some distance between us and the rest of the crew, I turn to face Lily. "You are a sneaky minx."

She flashes a smile. "Just trying to do my part to keep it believable."

I hum. "Well played, wife."

She makes a show of mock innocence as her gaze swings toward the gathering of people eating and drinking as they converse. "You think so, husband?"

I ease into a grin. "If this bodyguard gig doesn't pan out, you should consider going into acting."

She tilts her head. "No, thanks. I prefer my life on the real side."

Am I crazy to wish this thing between us could be 'on the real side'? I don't see how I can date my fake wife when she's technically on the job as my bodyguard. But I do wonder...

Before I can say anything, Luke heads toward me, excitement gleaming in his eyes. Coach follows close behind, along with Wade, Elias, Mathéo, and Ethan. These guys are not only on my line but also have become my best friends. And I feel like a proper git lying to them like this.

Luke stops about two feet away and holds out a folded jersey. Some kind of gag gift that probably stays 'tied down' or 'whipped.' I can hear the sound effects now.

"Hope you don't mind if we make this a double celebration." Holding the shoulder seams, Luke lets the jersey unfold like a flag, revealing the back. My last name blazes across the top.

Okay, maybe the joke's on the front. Perhaps an image of a bride dragging a groom up a wedding aisle. He turns the jersey around. No joke here. Just our team logo.

And a letter 'A' sitting above it to the right.

I grab the sides, scanning the fabric again to make sure I'm interpreting this correctly before bouncing my gaze between Luke and Coach. "Are you serious?"

Luke lets go, giving me full possession. "You've earned it, Pay. We all agreed that you'll make a great alternate captain."

The slick fabric of a jersey never felt so good in my hands. "Thanks. I won't let you down."

But in a way, I feel as if I already have by not telling them who I really am. Any and all lingering thoughts of confessing the truth about Lily and my family get shoved into the deep, dark recesses of my mind. Telling them would be like a slap in the face of the trust they're investing in me.

The rest of the evening passed in a blur of chatter and food. And cake. Let's not forget the cake they insisted we feed each other. I fully expected Lily to take the opportunity to score another point on the 'faking it' board, but she kept looking to me for clues. Or concern.

For the most part, I not only faked being a married man, but also one in a good mood. Because all I could think about was that letter on my jersey and how unworthy of it I'm feeling in light of my deception.

I almost sighed in relief when we left. And the only thing breaking the silence in the car as we drive—correction —Lily drives us home, is a slew of texts erupting on my phone.

She glances at me. "Everything okay? It's getting noisy over there."

"Probably just one of the blokes." I unlock my phone, careful to keep the screen turned away so as not to blind Lily while she's driving.

> Luke: Congrats again, Pay. On both fronts.

> Wade: Yeah, man. And sorry about the bedroom comment.

> Mathéo: I'm still trying to forget that one. And I'm French!

> Wade: French Canadian, sir. Get your facts straight.

> Ethan: Why is this suddenly about Wade?

> Luke: Because he's Wade?

> Mathéo: Then make it about Lily. She's definitely hot.

> Luke: Rein it in, Barbie Man, or you'll sound like Wade.

> Mathéo: Hey! No insults.

> Wade: Ha ha! Join the club of inappropriateness, my friend. Glad to have you.

> Ethan: All kidding aside, Pay. Lily is great. You two are a perfect match.

I run a hand over my mouth and type a quick message I hope will shut them down.

> Payton: It's all good, mates. Thanks for tonight. Really appreciate it.

I shove my phone back into my pocket, feeling far from good. Somehow, I have to find a way to make this work.

# Chapter Eight

## LILY

Payton's silence on the way home was telling. My guess is he's struggling with the whole fake wife scenario in light of the honor he received tonight, which is understandable.

During my brief time in the military, I learned the importance of working with a team and trusting we had each other's backs. That required transparency and authenticity. I imagine hockey is similar, and Payton's secret must be weighing heavily on him, which makes me totally regret kissing him.

I was playing my part, and perhaps I fell prey to Payton's competitive streak. How could I not counter his sexy wink? And how was I to know the surprise celebration was also about honoring him with the title of alternate captain?

A perfect storm of bad timing.

We arrive at his apartment before Luke since he stayed behind to help clean-up. I guess one of the perks of being a guest of honor is no KP duty. Always nice to have some bonuses on the job.

After we walk inside, I drop the car keys into the bowl sitting on the table by the door and send Del a text to confirm we're secure. As I follow Payton into his bedroom, he tosses his new jersey on the bed and drops onto the end with a bounce, holding his head in his hands.

In case Luke walks in, I close the door. "Want to talk about it?"

He sits up and shoots a steely glance at me. "Is playing therapist part of your job, too?"

His attempt at humor falls flat, sounding more like sarcasm. But I'm not offended. I understand where he's coming from. Well, kind of. These guys are his friends. Some closer than others. They care about Payton, and he obviously cares about them. They're much closer knit than I expected.

Relationships have always felt messy to me. Not sure why, other than I learned quickly not to get too attached at an early age. Thus, I keep most people I meet at arm's length. Del's probably the first person I've let in to some degree, but that took several years of her basically wearing me down with her constant presence and ridiculous jokes.

"No, but I'm happy to listen. You'd be amazed how often a principal spills their guts to their bodyguard." I take a spot on the opposite end of the bed.

He shifts to face me. "Is that what I am? A principal?"

I shrug. "Or client, if you prefer."

Nodding, he returns to his previous position. "I'd prefer not to be in this situation at all."

"You could still tell them the truth before this goes any further. They seem like a supportive bunch. I'm sure they'd understand."

He drops his hands, letting them hang between his knees, and sighs. "It's not just this fake marriage thing. I've never told them anything about the title my family holds because I consider it inconsequential to who I am here. And that was the point. But now, it seems..."

"Deceptive?"

Payton groans. "Yes, I suppose. For lack of a better word."

"Would you prefer dishonest?"

He glares at me. "I think you're better at being a fake wife than a therapist."

I try to stifle a giggle and fail. "Just trying to help. No judgment here. That's definitely *not* part of my job."

As I rise with the intention of getting ready for bed, he catches my wrist. The feel of his calloused fingers on my skin is rough yet stimulating in an unexpected way. The memory of kissing his cheek flashes front and center in my mind and sticks there. The rough stubble of his five o'clock shadow, his spicy clean scent, the warmth of his skin against mine...

"What would you do?" His eyes plead with me for a genuine answer.

I drag my focus from the sparks running up my arm to his question. "I can't answer that, Payton. This is your life, and you know it better than anyone."

That's the one area I think I can relate to most about him. Clearly, he wants to live his life on his own terms. After growing up in multiple foster and group homes, being told what, how, and when to do anything and everything, I jumped into the military because it made sense. And felt familiar. While enlisted, I learned a skill set and gained independence, but ultimately, I realized I wanted to live life on my own terms.

He lets go of me. "You're right. I need to figure this out on my own."

Still feeling his touch, I brush my wrist with my other hand. "Sleep will help. Let your unconscious mind chew on it overnight. Things always look clearer in the light of day."

He nods, yet says nothing.

In the week since we arrived in Sarabella, Payton and I have established a nightly routine, taking turns in the bathroom and getting settled for the night. Again, I take my place on the left side of the bed while Payton sleeps on a pallet on the floor on the opposite side. I can't imagine he's sleeping very well, and though I'm sure his tossing and turning is due to what happened earlier, I can't help but feel a twinge of guilt.

I keep my voice to a whisper in case he's fallen asleep. "Payton, are you still awake?"

"Yes, why?" He sounds husky but not sleepy.

"Why don't you take the bed tonight? You'll need a good night's rest for your game tomorrow." It's their first pregame, which Payton explained didn't count toward their standings but did help their coaches evaluate the team and the rookies and helped get the fans excited about the new season, especially in Sarabella.

"I'm fine." He roughs out.

I grab my pillow and walk around the bed to his side. Payton's sprawled on his back with one muscular arm swung over his forehead, revealing part of his bare chest.

And there's enough moonlight seeping into the room for me to notice. "Swap with me."

He sighs. "Lily, I already feel like a proper git as it is. That would just make it worse."

Damn his chivalrous nature. Time to switch tactics.

"Then let's share the bed." I gesture toward the king-sized bed that's remained undisturbed on one side. "There's plenty of room. Unless you don't think you can handle it, that is."

I know I'm probably playing a little dirty here, but challenging him seems to be the best way to stop his bullheadedness so he can consider an alternate solution.

He flings his arm down. "I'm exhausted enough to throw a bit of caution to the wind." He sits up, making the muscles on his abdomen tighten in a very appealing way, then gathers his pillow and blanket as he stands. "But I'll sleep on top of the bedcovers."

I return to my side of the bed. "Whatever works for you, big guy."

"We're back to that nickname again?" He sighs through his words.

"Still waiting for you to pick out mine, husband." I find a little humor always helps diffuse a potentially awkward situation.

Payton positions himself on the bed—on top of the navy comforter—then spreads out his blanket to settle over his feet and lies back with a sigh that shifts into a groan of relief. "Guess I'll sleep on that too, wife."

Within seconds, my smile widens at the sound of his soft snore.

---

After driving Payton to the arena this morning and running surveillance for a few hours until Del took over, I took a quick jog before returning to the apartment to clean up for the game tonight. While getting dressed, I found one of his jerseys—notably without the 'A'—hanging in front of my clothes with a note pinned to it that pushed an odd flutter through my stomach.

*For tonight. To keep things believable.*

My phone buzzes with a text. I pick it up, fully expecting an update from Del to find Payton is now texting me.

Payton: Left you something in the closet.

Lily: I just noticed.

Payton: Figured you'd need it for the game.

I may not be a sports fanatic, but I'm fully aware of what wearing the jersey means under normal conditions. Ours is far from normal.

Lily: It's missing a letter.

Payton: Uh oh. Is that grounds for a divorce?

Lily: Only if I get sent to the penalty box.

Payton: Hmm, that could be interesting.

I think he's flirting with me. And with a little innuendo, I might add.

As much as I'm looking forward to seeing Payton play, I'm not excited about posing as the doting wife, who's eager about watching her husband skate around an ice rink and whack a puck into the net for the next three hours. But duty calls.

A strong sense of anticipation accompanies me to the game tonight. I've been to plenty of stadiums, but never a hockey arena. I shift my shoulders in the oversized jersey as I make my way to the area on the seating diagram Payton texted me, explaining this was where the WAGs—wives and girlfriends—sat during the games.

As I get closer, I spot Sophie's bright pink hair band first. A swatch of pink peeks out above the collar of her jersey, which has "Jameson" across the back. She wore a pink and white polka dot dress to the party with matching pink shoes, so I'll assume she's a pink freak. I kind of like that—the way she wears her passion boldly. And the blonde woman sitting next to her has Ethan's last name, so that must be Mia.

Phone in hand, I shoot off a text to Del.

Lily: Entering the lion's den

Del: Play nice

Lily: Grrrrrrr...no promises

I pocket my phone as I reach the aisle they're sitting on. Both women smile at me simultaneously. That's a good sign.

Sophie jumps up and rushes in for a hug. "You made it!"

At least I'm prepared this time to return her embrace. "Of course. I can't wait to see Payton play."

Which is true, actually. I'm curious to watch how he moves on the ice as compared to our morning runs. Payton's one of those joggers who makes running appear effortless as he floats along. He's a natural athlete. And at this rate, I'll be able to manage a marathon with ease. Not that I'd want to, though.

Mia smiles and wags her hand her way. "Come sit."

Sophie waves me in ahead of her, so I guess they want me to sit between them. I shift into high alert because that can only mean one thing—they want to get to know me. Hopefully, the game will be the bigger attraction tonight.

"How are you settling in? Have you had a chance to explore Sarabella?" Sophie blinks her big eyes at me with her ever-present smile. This girl is like cotton candy—sweet and pink.

"Just the beach. Payton and I jog on it every morning."

Mia's eyes widen. "Every morning? Oof. That's dedication."

I leave out the part that I have to go where he goes, of course. "Helps to have a running buddy."

Sophie rests her hand on my arm, so I swing my attention back to her. "If you need help finding anything, just text me." She digs into a large brown bag at her feet and hands me a business card sporting the Sarabella Herald Tribune logo and 'photojournalist' next to her name. "I know Sarabella inside and out."

"She does." Mia nods with a wide grin. "If it weren't for her, my wedding would have been a disaster."

Sophie giggles. "She's exaggerating."

Mia snorts. "Not really."

I can't help but smile at these women. Kind of reminds me of a foster home I stayed in briefly when I was about ten years old. The family had two girls around my age. I felt like I had sisters for the first time in my life, but then their father got a promotion that required them to move out of state. Back to the group home I went and the next time I was placed with a family, I knew better than to get too attached.

Pregame announcements blast through the speakers. Cheers and shouts fill the arena in epic volume as the first line of the Sun Kings is introduced. When Payton's name is called, my heart does a little flip-flop, then shifts into overdrive when I see him skate out fully geared. Despite the helmet hiding a lot of his face, I can still see those oversized dimple grooves on each side of his mouth. And I don't miss how he taps the 'A' on his shirt as he takes his place on the ice.

The national anthem is sung by a local talent, and I'm fascinated with how the fans pass a huge American flag across the seats on the other side of the arena. Once the announcer introduces the players, they take their positions in the center of the ice. Payton takes his place for the puck drop.

For most of the first period, I study him, impressed with his skill and how he skates on the ice. He's graceful yet powerful. I'm drawn to his every move and search for his return after he leaves during rotations. The more I watch, the more I'm convinced he's more comfortable on skates than walking on his own two feet, except when he gets shoved into the wall, which Sophie said were called boards. But I'm more concerned with the opposing team player who slammed Payton for the third time in the first period.

I lean toward Sophie. "Is it me, or does that guy keep going after Payton?"

"Oh, it's not you. That's Houston Jennings. He's had it in for Pay since the end of last season."

"Why?"

She shrugs. "Not sure exactly, but I suspect it's because the Sun Kings knocked them out of the Kelly Cup playoffs last season. Pay stole the puck from him and shot the winning goal."

I need to find out more about this guy. While Sophie and Mia go to the concessions for sodas and soft pretzels, I use the restroom as an excuse to send a text to Del so she can do a quick check.

Del's reply hits my phone just as I'm about to head down the steps to my seat.

> Del: Nothing comes up immediately. Let me dig a little more.

Hmmm. Something must have caught her attention if she wants to do further research on this dude. In the meantime, I'm concerned for Payton, but not enough to alarm him. I'll wait for an update from Del in the meantime.

"Everything okay?" Sophie's voice breaks my concentration.

Somehow, I missed her and Mia walking up to me.

I pocket my phone and take the offered soda and pretzel. "Thanks. What do I owe you?"

"Our treat." She frowns at me. "Are you sure you're okay? You looked super serious when you were looking at your phone."

"Just concerned about Payton." Before they can ask any more questions, I head down the steps to our row. This time, I wait for them to take their seats first. That way Sophie can sit by her best friend, and I can manage one of them at a time.

Not that I mind their company, but I'd rather not be the center of further scrutiny. And until I hear from Del, I'm on high alert for anything else suspicious.

Second period starts in a few minutes, but Payton won't be the only player I'm keeping my eye on.

# Chapter Nine

## PAYTON

Who would have thought a text conversation could be so stimulating? I reread the messages from Lily, still amused and somewhat surprised at my comment about the penalty box. Seems I'm a new fan of innuendos, however, I suspect that's because of Lily. She's occupying more and more of my head space lately, and I'm not entirely sure how I feel about that yet.

I reposition the ice pack on my shoulder, stretching my neck to the side to subvert the ache radiating up from my shoulder. That last slam? Absolute corker. Might need to check if all my bones are still where they should be.

Our staff physical therapist checked me out, then gave me an ice pack and the all clear. I'm certain I'll have a nice colorful bruise there by morning. Just a perk of the job.

Luke strolls over and stops in front of me. "How's it feeling, Pay?"

I shift the ice pack down a little. "All good. Cleared for second period."

"Good. Ethan and I will make sure Jennings doesn't take another shot at you."

Most of the time, hockey players shake it off. We know what this game takes and that the fans love a few skirmishes. No big deal. It all stays on the ice. But Jennings is definitely holding a grudge. "Cheers. Guess he's still pissed."

Luke grins and smacks my other shoulder. "Yeah, man. That steal last season was epic. Just part of the game. He'll get over it."

"Hope you're right. At this rate, I'll require a complete bodysuit made of ice packs."

Using his fingers, Wade peels out a whistle, which I'm sure would make those cows he talks about on his family farm come running. "Listen up. Score's zero zero. You boys need to light the lamp."

Luke mutters. "Here we go again."

Mathéo smacks Wade on the chest. "You say that almost every game, cowboy."

Hands out at his sides, Wade grins. "I know. It's a tradition, Barbie Man. Can't break the pattern now. That would be bad luck. And I'm itching for a shutout."

When we head out to the ice, I glance toward the seats where the WAGs usually sit. Lily waves, smiling. And she's wearing my jersey. I figured she would, as she's quite dedicated to playing her role, but part of me wondered if she actually would.

My mouth goes dry, and I'm pretty sure my pulse took a detour. I lift my stick in acknowledgment but have to drag my eyes away. Seeing her wearing my number is a distraction I don't need right now. Not with an overgrown toddler coming after me with a stick. I'm determined to get through second period without any more crosschecks or slams from Jennings.

Plus, we need to score some points so we can take this game home. So what if it doesn't count in the standings? Starting the pregame season with a loss isn't great for morale.

Halfway into the second period, Jennings is back to his tactics of chasing me down or staying in my face. He's already taken a penalty for hooking Ethan when he played interference during the last play. I have no intention of letting the bloke take me down again.

Ethan and Luke swap places with Elias and one of the rookies, joining me on the ice. The tension in my shoulders settles a margin, knowing they've got my back because I'm open and waiting for the puck so I can make a shot on goal.

Elias shoots it my way, and I'm after it. Problem is, Jennings is heading my direction like a bull on a stampede, as Wade would say. He'll block my shot easily if I don't change direction.

I skate behind the net with the plan to make a wrist shot into the corner of the net. Next thing I know, I'm flying up against the boards only to fall to the ice in a heap, trying to catch my breath from the impact and wondering what the hell hit me.

A quick upward glance confirms it was Jennings again. I'm guessing he anticipated my move and changed direction, surprising Luke and Ethan as well. The whistle blows as I struggle to get up. Luke helps me up, and Wade, of all our players, gives Jennings a strong crosscheck—something he rarely does as a goaltender—and zings some choice words at him.

Jennings makes the mistake of shoving back. Ethan drops his gloves. The two wind up hanging on to each other, throwing random punches into each other's necks and faces, which knocks their helmets off.

The fans are going nuts in the stands with shouts, stomping feet, and pounding the glass nearby. Finally, the refs move in and separate them.

Luke dips his head to see my face. "You okay?"

Still bent over, I nod, but in truth, the pain radiating in my side isn't easing up. "Just need to catch my breath."

The crowd boos when a penalty is called for both Ethan and Jennings. I can't help but feel some satisfaction when the ref calls a major penalty and gives Jennings five minutes in the sin bin.

"Go get checked out, man. We got this."

Luke helps me skate over to the exit, and I head down the tunnel with one of the trainers to the locker room. Every move keeps the pain waves coming. I'm sitting on the medic table, getting examined, when I hear Lily's voice from the hallway.

"I'm his wife. I want to make sure he's okay." Her words are confident with just the right amount of concern. Even I'm inclined to believe her.

"It's all right. Let her in." I raise my voice as loud as I can without making my side scream. Our medic already helped me out of my jersey and upper gear and seems to be on a mission as he prods my midsection. He hits a tender spot that makes me jump and hiss through my teeth. The last thing I need is a broken rib. That will keep me out of the game for two to three weeks, at least—not to mention practice.

"Is it broken?" Lily asks matter-of-factly, staring down the medic as if she's in charge.

"Could just be a fracture. We'll check to be sure." The medic helps me lie down on the table. "You'll need to step out while I do the X-ray."

"Here?" Lily's eyes widen.

I nod. "We have a portable machine."

"Color me impressed." She ducks out of the room.

After the medic does his thing, he lets Lily know she can come back in while he studies the images. I'm still sprawled on the table when she rests a hand on my shoulder, her warmth pressing into my skin, setting off a slow burn beneath it. Instead of the pain radiating out of my side, all I can focus on is what her touch is doing to me. An image of tugging her against me while she's wearing my jersey and kissing her plays out in my mind.

Best. Painkiller. Ever. Someone should bottle this.

She pulls over a wheeled stool and sits next to the exam table, keeping her voice to a whisper. "Del's checking out that guy."

I snap my eyes open and lift my head to look at her, but regret it immediately and groan. "Why?"

She raises a finger to her lips to hush me, which I find oddly stimulating. "Isn't it obvious? The guy has it in for you."

Shaking my head, I whisper back, "There's no way he had anything to do with what happened to my cousin."

She glances toward the medic. "Best to be sure."

"He's harmless." I sling my arm over my eyes.

"Tell that to your ribs." She snickers.

A grin is all I can manage at her humor. "I'll be fine. He's just holding a grudge."

"Yeah, that's what Mia and Sophie told me."

I turn my head and take in those gorgeous hazel-green eyes staring at me with concern. She has her hair pulled back like usual. "How's that going? Making some new friends?"

She rolls her eyes. "Pretending to." She shrugs. "They do seem nice, though."

"They're great. I'm glad you don't have to sit by yourself."

"They're a bit distracting, and I don't need distractions."

If she only knew how big a distraction she is to me right now, sitting there wearing my jersey. "Would you mind standing up a minute?"

She frowns at me. "Why?"

"You'll laugh at me."

"I already am." A mix of humor and challenge flash in her eyes.

I'm seriously loving how she does that. "No, you're not."

Her expression turns smug. "Inside I am."

"Why?"

She grins. "That was my question."

I let out a chuckle, then regret it. A groan slips out before I can stop it. I clutch my side. "Take a little pity on me, please."

"Fine." She sighs, then stands.

I make a spinning motion with my hand, asking her to turn around.

She rolls her eyes again, then turns her back to me as she tugs her ponytail out of the way.

And there it is. My last name riding across the top of her shoulders like a declaration of possession. Maybe I should thank Jennings for busting my ribs because I don't think I'd do a very good job keeping myself in check around Lily right now.

She glances over her shoulder at me. "Happy now?"

If only she knew the chaos she's causing. We're not technically a couple, but being together all the time is making it harder and harder to remember that. The line of separation is definitely blurring.

"Yes. Now I can survive the rest of the game." I keep my humor and sarcasm at an even balance.

She spins back around. "You're not honestly thinking of going back out there, are you?"

"As soon as the medic clears me."

Speaking of whom, he walks over, carrying a tablet with X-ray images filling the screen. "Not happening, Pay. Can't just tape you up for this one. You need to lie low for at least a few days, maybe longer. Then we'll decide when you can resume playing."

I groan again, but not out of pain.

Lily holds her hands out. "See? Worked out for the best."

"How so?" She's right, in a way. At least it's an exhibition game. I should be fine in a couple of weeks when the season officially starts.

"You don't have to deal with that brute anymore tonight."

No. But I still have to navigate the tall beauty wearing my jersey as if she owned it.

---

Lily maneuvers me in and out of the car like a pro. Once inside my apartment, she helps me sit on the bed and then removes my shoes. Getting my shirt off doesn't hurt nearly as much as I expected. Probably a combo of the rib strap the medic gave me and the painkillers working.

Letting Lily undress me like this feels…intimate. She's caring and slow in her movements to cause me as little pain as possible. Thankfully, I had a pair of joggers in my locker that I could sleep in. Otherwise, that would be downright awkward.

After arranging several pillows, she helps me lie back on the bed. "Thanks."

"No problem. I'll go get you a glass of water in case you need to take another pill during the night."

I close my eyes and listen to her movements in the kitchen. Luke won't return for a while, so I'll have to check the score on my phone or wait until morning. Between the exertion from the game and the painkiller, I'm floating in a very pleasant state of happy sleepiness.

She walks back in and sets a glass of water on the nightstand. "Let me know if you need anything else, okay? Doesn't matter what time it is. I know how hard it is to navigate up and down with one of those." She gestures to my midsection.

"You've experienced the joy of broken ribs?" I shift on the bed, trying to get my pillow in the right place, but wind up grunting like an angry pig.

"A few times." She leans over to help me get more settled, engulfing me in her subtle scent of vanilla and musk. It's maddening, honestly. She's as fierce as they come, yet graceful and gorgeous enough to knock me completely off my game.

"Do tell."

She perches gingerly on the edge of the bed. "Not that interesting."

"Says you." I grin, feeling more playful than usual. Must be the painkiller.

She laughs softly. "You should go to sleep, Payton. Your body needs rest to heal."

When she gets up, I reach for her hand, flinching in the process. She leans in, relieving the tug on my side. Her ponytail falls forward with her motion, cascading across my arm like silk.

Our gazes sync. "Thank you."

The lamp light reflects in her eyes, making them appear more green than hazel. "It's no problem."

"Is this normal?"

"Is what normal?"

"Do you wind up taking care of your injured *principals*?"

She smiles at my use of her word for me. "Sometimes."

"Is that how you broke your ribs?" I know I'm babbling, but I'm not ready to stop talking to her. Or to let her go.

She sits back down as she holds my hand. "Maybe."

"NDA?"

"Yes." She dips her head with her reply.

"Hmm." I close my eyes, giving in to the drift. "Wish you could tell me more."

She doesn't say anything at first, but then her voice floats in, soft and with a tinge of regret. "I do, too."

Did I imagine that? Does she feel the connection growing between us, or is that just a side-effect of the job? I want to open my eyes so I can read her expression, and see her gorgeous face, but I can't seem to lift my eyelids anymore.

"You're lovely." I tighten my hold on her hand to emphasize my slurred words.

"Thank you," she whispers and squeezes back.

I want to say more...so much more, but I'm falling fast into a deep sleep.

And into some serious feelings for my bodyguard.

# Chapter Ten

## LILY

Since Payton's in no condition to go for a jog, I make a quick loop around the apartments to get some exercise in and to clear my head, but all I can think about is what he said to me as he fell asleep last night.

*You're lovely...*

His words keep repeating in my head and echoing in my heart. I know I pump my legs harder as if to punish myself. Falling for a principal is a no-no. And if I want that shot at a permanent position on Dame Maxwell's security detail, there's no way I can entertain the idea of getting involved with Payton, even after this assignment ends.

*You're lovely...*

His smooth voice echoes through my thoughts again, sending warm prickles through me.

No one's ever told me I was beautiful. Not that I can recall, anyway. In the military, it was "frowned upon." Same thing with being a bodyguard. No mixing of business and pleasure. I've seen what happens when lines get crossed, and edges turn fuzzy. In my line of work, that's a formula for disaster. And when lives are involved, there's no room for mistakes.

My phone vibrates, forcing me to stop my jog and pluck it from the holder strapped around my arm.

Del: Didn't find anything worth noting. He's just a hockey player with a bad temper, it seems.

Lily: Good. Thanks for the confirmation. Any updates on his case?

Del: Checked yesterday. They're still investigating.

Lily: Hmm, interesting. Keep me posted. We'll be at home base today.

Del: Roger that.

I slide my phone back into place and jog back.

Luke walks out as I reach the sidewalk in front of the apartment, and he's carrying a box. "Payton's up and on the couch. I think he's itching for a shower."

Oh my...I hadn't given that part much thought. Reflecting back on my own run-ins that ended with cracked or broken ribs, I remember the challenge of showering and especially washing my hair. At least Payton's is shorter than mine.

I nod, then gesture at the box. "What's that about?"

His gaze drops to the folded brown flaps. "The apartment Sophie and I found is ready early. And you two don't need a third wheel around."

Not having to continue the charade twenty-four-seven

would certainly make aspects of this arrangement easier. "I assume Payton knows?"

"Yeah. He seemed pretty happy about it."

Probably because he'll get his privacy back—not to mention his bed—since I'll take over the guest room. "I bet he is."

Luke shakes his head and chuckles. "You two are really great together."

My mind does a whirlwind inventory of the last week. Guess we're pulling things off better than I thought. "Um, thanks."

He continues to his SUV in the parking lot.

"Luke, wait." I walk toward him and step off the sidewalk as he stops and turns around. "If you don't mind me asking, what makes you say that?"

He shrugs, causing the box he's carrying to slide up and down his torso. "Nothing specific. You two just seem to be a good fit. And I've never seen the Pay-man distracted like this. Tell him he better watch it, or one of the rookies will take his place."

His chuckle tells me he's joking, but still, I can't let that piece of knowledge pass without some serious consideration, probably for the best that I'm moving out of his bedroom. That should help minimize distractions for both of us. I'm still bothered by how I didn't see Mia and Sophie walking up to me at the game ahead of time.

I grin appropriately. "I'll make sure he knows."

But my smile fades quickly as I enter the apartment and find the couch empty. "Payton?"

Only silence. I stride into the bedroom, but the bed and the corner chair are vacant. The sound of the shower turning on draws me to the bathroom door. I knock loud enough to be heard over the noise because I really don't want to walk in and surprise him. Or me, for that matter.

The door opens. Payton has his arm cradled against a very large, dark bruise on his injured side. Besides being shirtless, he's only wearing a pair of blue boxers with yellow hockey sticks all over them. I snap my gaze back to his face and keep it there.

His expression turns downright uncomfortable. "I didn't get a shower after the game last night, and if I don't wash this funk off soon, I might crawl out of my skin. Any chance you could help a bloke out?"

My brows shoot up of their own accord. "You want me to...*bathe* you?"

"Just my hair. And well, maybe my legs as bending over hurts like the dickens. And perhaps my back?" He says as an afterthought.

"In other words, you mean yes." I let out a breathy sigh, resigned to my fate.

He gives me a slow nod. At least he has the wherewithal to look embarrassed. Most guys would look at this as an opportunity.

"Fine. But the boxers stay on. You can take care of those areas yourself." I think the heat riding up my face matches the red tinge climbing his neck.

"Of course." He growls out.

Thankfully, I'm already wearing the bare minimum—yoga shorts and a tank over my sports bra. I kick off my running shoes and pull off my socks. "Let's get this over with."

"Way to make a bloke feel wanted." He jests as he moves like a snail into the shower, which, to my relief, is oversized.

"Face the shower head and be quiet." I note the bar of soap but see nothing else—no puff or even a washcloth.

I dart over to the linen closet and almost sigh with relief when I see a stack of washcloths. Now to soap up this large hockey player as fast as possible.

Steam fills the bathroom as I open the shower door and step in behind him. Payton has his head under the nozzle with his chin tucked. A bruise covers one shoulder and down part of his bicep. I get to work, lathering his back and legs. My work has put me in some very interesting and sometimes precarious positions, but this takes top spot on the list.

*The time I soaped up a principal in the shower.* There's one for my future memoirs.

"Back's done. Spin around." I keep my tone professional. This is simply a business transaction. That's all.

He turns around, brushing his wet hair back, and stares at me with those crystal blue eyes. "Dare I ask if this has ever happened before?"

He better not be flirting with me.

"Nope." I pop my 'p.'

Next, I wash his arms, taking great care not to move the one on his injured side too much, but the bruise that covers most of his ribs is next level. I suppress a cringe as I soap his torso, skirting around the discoloration. When I run the washcloth down his other side, he makes a snickering noise.

*Observation #4: Payton is ticklish.*

Not that it's important or relevant. Just…interesting.

By the time I finished the front of his legs and feet, the steam and water have saturated my tank top and the tendrils of hair surrounding my face are dripping. I plop the washcloth on the soap holder and grab the shampoo bottle.

"Dip your head."

I have to say, the man follows orders like a soldier. And I think I'm slightly impressed by that. When I start massaging the shampoo through his hair, he lets out a guttural sigh that stills my hands.

He lifts his chin and opens his eyes. Our gazes lock for a moment that feels more like minutes. I could get lost in those blue depths…and drown if I'm not careful.

"Lily?"

"Yeah?"

"The soap is burning my eyes."

"Oh! Sorry." I grab the washcloth and wipe his eyes.

He scrunches his face. "I think that's making it worse."

"Tip your head back." I swipe the spraying water gently over his eyes and work my fingers through his hair to rinse the soap out. "Okay, you're done. I'll leave so you can do the rest."

"Thank you, Lily." His words catch me as I'm one leg out of the shower, and his expression is so earnest you'd have thought I'd saved his life.

I can only nod because my voice can't get past my fickle heart that's pounding in my throat. I grab a towel, drying off as I rush out of the bathroom. Just in time to get a text from Del.

Del: How's the invalid?

Lily: Fine. No problems.

No way am I going to tell my partner that I just bathed our principal. I'd never hear the end of it.

Del: Good. Just heard from Dame Maxwell.
Apparently, the police are looking into a
suspect.

Lily: Seriously? What did they find?

Del: No details yet. I'll keep you posted as
usual. In light of this, Dame Maxwell would
also like more regular reports.

Lily: How regular?

Del: Daily.

My head says this is about an overly worried sister who's concerned about her brother. However, my gut says this could also be her way of assessing how I work. Suddenly, this feels more like a performance evaluation when I was being considered for a promotion in the military. Except this is even more important to me because I want this more than I've ever wanted anything in my life.

I lower my hand holding the phone as Payton walks out wrapped in a towel. Water droplets fall from his hair, making a path down one side of his chest. I'd love to make a similar trail down his pecs with my fingers to see if they're as muscular as they look.

But if I want a shot at that position on Dame Maxwell's security detail, I have to shut that kind of thinking down. That's just immediate gratification rearing its ugly head and will only mean failure in the long run. I can't let Payton Maxwell get under my skin.

Or my heart.

"Shower's all yours. And thank you again for your help." His sheepish expression turns borderline rakish, which seems to wake up every cell in my body. "Happy to return the favor if you ever need it."

I snicker. "Not gonna happen, big guy."

Is this his way of getting even for my impromptu kiss last night? I grab random pieces of clothing to make my escape to the bathroom because that bruise down his side does nothing to diminish his sexiness, but then stop. "Can you dress yourself?"

His expression appears guarded. "I'll figure it out."

Did I offend him with my refusal of his offer to return the favor? Surely he was joking because there's no way anything can ever happen between us.

---

When I walk out of the bathroom, Payton isn't on the bed as I'd expected he would be. And when I leave the bedroom, I find him on the couch, dressed in a T-shirt and jersey shorts, reading his book again.

I stop in front of him and point at his clothing. "How did you manage to get a T-shirt on, let alone pull up a pair of shorts?"

He glances down at his attire, then shoots a rather mischievous look up at me. "I googled how to get dressed with broken ribs, which recommended sitting down."

I glance over at his metal bar stools and gesture at them. "Too bad you didn't think of that for the shower."

The dimples on one side of his mouth deepen with his lopsided smile. "I don't believe that would have worked quite as well as having your help, which I confess, I found quite enjoyable."

I resist the temptation to grab his book and smack him on the back of his head. "Tomorrow you're on your own."

He raises a single brow. "Yes, ma'am."

While Payton reads that infernal book of his, I get the guest room ready for me now that Luke has vacated the premises. I'm sure Payton will enjoy having his space to himself again. I'm not even going to consider the slight pang I feel at the thought of sleeping in separate rooms tonight.

With Del's go-ahead, I run to the store to restock his fridge. How domestic of me? Washing sheets, cleaning the bathroom after a very hairy hockey player, and now grocery shopping? This role of pretend wife is feeling a little more real than I'd like at the moment, yet strangely appealing on a level I'm not sure I understand.

If anyone's watching his movements, they'll most likely think I'm Payton's flavor of the week...or the month, although I don't get the sense he dates a lot. And so far, neither Del nor I have picked up on any irregularities or anything suspicious. The longer I'm here, the more I suspect his cousin's disappearance was truly due to an accident. Nevertheless, Del did say they have a potential lead.

When I return to the apartment, Payton's sitting on the couch, still reading. For some reason, I find that aspect of him as sexy as his physicality. The more I get to know him, the more I see a man who's diverse and well-rounded. I wonder if that's due to his semi-royal British upbringing.

I hand him a bottle of water. "Stay hydrated. That will help."

He closes his book. "Thank you."

"I'll make us some lunch."

His expression turns playful. "I didn't expect your role as my fake wife to include actually taking care of me."

My turn to lift a brow. "Neither did I."

The ding of my phone saves him from having to reply.

I'm expecting an update from Del right about now, but the text isn't from her.

> Sophie: Hey Lil! Mia and I were wondering if you'd like to be part of the planning committee for the team's next fundraiser. Might be a great way for you to make some connections, too. We're meeting at the Turtle Tide tomorrow for lunch. Hope you can come.

Somehow, Sophie got my phone number. And she's calling me Lil, as if we've been friends for ages. An odd warmth fills my chest. Probably because I'm about to get mad at Payton for giving her my contact information before checking with me first, he's the only one who could have. I stare at her text, trying to figure out one, how she got my number, and two, how to get out of this.

"Sophie just texted me." I lower my phone and stare at him.

"Did she?" His attempt to appear innocent is almost laughable.

"Why did you give my phone number to her?"

He gives me a thoughtful look, but that competitive gleam is back in his eyes. "I figured that would be the normal thing to do. You know, for believability."

"For believability..." For lack of a better comeback, I repeat his words. That warmth I felt a moment ago is definitely shifting to something more hot. And angry.

"You might enjoy it." He opens his book and starts reading again as if there's nothing abnormal about this.

I take a step closer to him, like a cat ready to pounce. "Did you forget we're not really married? That my focus is supposed to be protecting you, not playing house?"

He lowers his book again. "I'm perfectly safe inside my

apartment. And your partner seems to have outside surveillance well under hand. Do you want to sit around here and watch me read?"

I don't miss the soft chuckle he counters my growl with as I head into the kitchen. Not only do I have to figure out a way to get out of Sophie's invitation, but how to out maneuver Payton, who's proving to be quite proficient at more than just hockey.

# Chapter Eleven

## LILY

"You let him outsmart you." Del's laugh screeches in my ears.

I filled Del in with the details of the morning when I checked in to ask her for some ideas to navigate my way out of helping Sophie and Mia. Even though the door is shut to my room, I keep my voice down so Payton won't hear.

"I did not! And why are you on his side?"

"I'm always on your side, luv. But I'll always be honest with you, too. He got you on this one. Might want to change tactics."

With a harrumph, I drop to my bed. "I only made it a competition because he was struggling with deceiving his friends."

"And it worked bloody well. Better than you expected, I'd say."

I fall back on the bed with a grunt. "Helping to plan a fundraiser wasn't part of the job."

"Well, it seems it is now, so I say roll with it. Who knows, you may wind up making some new friends." Her carefree tone is seriously grating on my somewhat frayed nerves over this situation.

"You sound like Payton."

She laughs again. "My, my. Has the happy couple hit their first bump on the proverbial road?"

I snap back to a sitting position. "Will you stop enjoying this so much?"

Del lets out a long sigh. "You really don't have a choice. Just go and make the best of it. If you come up with excuses, they'll think you're being evasive or snobby, which will only complicate future interactions. You don't want that, do you?"

"No, I don't. I don't want this either, but I'll go just to make you happy," I quip.

"And Payton?"

"Don't be ridiculous."

"I'm merely saying—"

I end the connection so I don't have to hear the rest of that sentence because she might be right. What if I am doing some of these things out of concern for Payton? I mean, of course, I'm concerned for him as his bodyguard, but am I overly worried? Or unnecessarily so?

One thing I learned early in life was not to become too invested in a person or a situation because, ultimately, I'd wind up hurt or disappointed. That belief served me well during my time in the military and made even more sense as a bodyguard. Care for your principal, but don't get emotionally involved.

Unfortunately, I may have crossed that line already, which will only damage my chances of landing that position with Dame Maxwell.

Maybe getting out of the apartment is a good idea. A little time away from Payton might help reset my perspective. Del's covering surveillance and has constant eyes on the situation, so I really don't have a valid excuse not to go.

I send a quick text to Sophie, telling her I'll be there, to which she replies with one of those celebratory emojis.

Now to figure out what to wear, so I look the part. My professional attire might bring up questions I'd rather not have to answer with more lies. So jeans and a cute top it is.

And just for the record, and contrary to what Payton thinks, I'm not going to enjoy this.

Tantalizing aromas fill my nose as I walk into the Turtle Tide. Payton said to be sure to try the hush puppies because that's one of their specialties. Along with the house-made remoulade dipping sauce. Something his former roommate turned him on to.

Sophie waves from a booth near the back, and as I approach, I see the top of Mia's blonde head. But nobody else. Unless you want to count the basket of hushpuppies already sitting in the center of the table.

To be polite, I sit on Sophie's side since she's patting the spot next to her. "Where are the rest?"

Mia gives me a confused look. "Rest of what?"

"The other wives and girlfriends?"

"We're it so far." Sophie lets out a giggle as Mia snorts.

She dons a conspiratorial expression. "We're the ones who count."

Their silliness makes me grin. "You're joking, right?"

"Not really. But we're just getting started, so I'm sure more will join in once we have things figured out." Sophie taps her pen on her notebook.

I bounce my gaze between them. "Okaaaay, then what's the fundraiser for?"

"Underprivileged children. The team wants to do something really special this year, so we're trying to come up with ideas." Sophie pulls a notebook out of her tote. Pink, of course.

After a pause, Mia sighs. "I was thinking we could do some kind of amusement park."

A fundraiser for kids in need? An amusement park? I think my heart just clenched, and not in a good way. When I was twelve, a state fair arrived in town, close to the foster home where I lived. I'd never been to one and asked if we could go. My foster father looked at me as if I'd sprouted horns, then cracked open his next can of beer. Yet another moment that taught me to keep expectations low.

"Um, I'm not sure I'd be much help with this kind of thing." I glance at the door, trying to figure out an escape. Maybe Payton needs me to babysit him after all.

Sophie blinks her large eyes at me. "When Payton texted me your number, he said you had some experience with stuff like this."

"Like what?" I ask with a hefty dose of caution. Did he share details about my life? Because I don't normally tell anyone about my past. Payton only knows because it seemed necessary for our cover story. Not that I have anything to hide. I'm just not a fan of sharing my life history.

"Organizing people and events." Sophie blinks at me as if what she's saying is obvious. "What kind of work did you do in London?"

"Security." That's generic enough and should satisfy their curiosity.

Sophie looks thoughtful. "Like with large groups?"

I give her a quick nod. "Sometimes."

"That's great! You can help us avoid complications."

Mia tilts her head at me. "We had so much fun together at the game, we figured we'd make a great team."

A great team? Anything I might have wanted to say is lodged in my throat. My heart's melting at the thought of Payton thinking about me and these two women believing I'm worth their time and effort. But my head wants to knock him a solid in the skull with one of those pucks he plays with for the same reasons.

This is a job, not my life. I can't get invested. Or attached. My time here is limited, but they don't know that. They can't know that. And then there's that annoying tug on my heart that appears to be winning. Wait until Del hears about this. I can hear her laughing now.

My stomach feels like a swarm of bees took up residence, but I settle back into the seat, resigned to spending the next two hours planning an event for children who might never get the chance to do something like this. Like I never did.

"Okay, count me in. Where do we start?"

Sophie opens her notebook. "Today's all about brainstorming." She jots down Mia's idea with a fancy number one beside it in blue ink.

I lean a tad closer to study the page. "I fully expected pink."

Mia rolls her eyes. "If you only knew."

Sophie giggles. "She's still a little salty about that. I used pink ink when I was planning her wedding."

"And I about went blind trying to read it until I begged her to switch to a darker color."

"But my notes were pretty. You have to admit that."

Sophie implores her best friend with a humorous expression.

"No, I don't." She dips a hushpuppy into the sauce and pops it into her mouth.

I nab one and do the same just so I can tell Payton I at least tried them. An explosion of flavors hits my tongue, almost making me groan. He's right. These things are doughy balls of heaven. "Wow. Payton said these were good."

Sophie sets her pen down. "Be careful. They can be addictive."

Mia finishes chewing and sips her water. "How did you two meet exactly? I don't think I've heard that story yet."

I grab the glass of water they so thoughtfully had waiting for me and take a long drink, mentally composing my first words. "At a pub. Turns out we had a few friends in common."

Sophie nods. "Ah, that makes sense. Payton's kind of shy."

Shy? Maybe awkward at times like that first night trying to figure out our sleeping arrangements, but there was nothing bashful about Payton when I helped him take a shower, especially that last comment of his.

I nab another hushpuppy and break it in to pieces on my napkin. "I've never thought of him as shy."

Mia and Sophie glance at each other.

Now my interest is completely engaged. "What am I missing here?"

Sophie smiles. "I'm guessing Payton never mentioned he tried to ask me out once."

I snap my gaze to hers, feeling a sudden rush of heat and discomfort in my chest. Am I jealous? Is that jealousy?

No, it can't be. There's no reason to feel that way. This is just a job.

"No, he didn't." My words sound clipped even to me.

Sophie rests her hand on my arm. "It was nothing. Seriously. Just an awkward moment when I did his interview for the paper."

"Did you turn him down?" Why am I asking this? It's not like I care...

She giggles again. "Didn't have a chance to. Luke walked in and basically staked his claim on me."

Mia snorts, then laughs. "Hockey players."

Sophie beams a smile at me that's pretty much irresistible. "If Payton wasn't shy with you, that just proves you two are meant to be together. I'm so glad Payton found his person."

I nod, then nibble on a piece of hushpuppy as I sift through this odd mix of emotions running through me. "Me, too."

That seems the right thing to say in this situation, for believability. But I can't help wondering what that would feel like. To be someone's person...to be claimed by someone...to be wanted.

Payton's quirky smile and humor, his agility and speed on the ice, and his concern for me...he's the total package. I've never encountered anyone like him before, and I may never again. But none of this is real. That's what I need to keep telling myself, or else I could easily fall for a guy like him. And not just him. His group of friends, too.

Hopefully, my heart will start believing what my head is screaming at it.

# Chapter Twelve

PAYTON

When Lily walks in, it's like the atmosphere shifts. I know I'm treading dangerous ground here, but she's all I've thought about since she left. And as engaging as this book is —the history of hockey, so, of course, INTERESTING— I've lost count of how many times I stopped reading to glance toward the door whenever I heard a noise outside.

But then the sound of the lock turning hits my ears, and every fiber of my body comes to life in anticipation of seeing her face. And I'm not disappointed when she walks in, giving me another chance to appreciate how her jeans and floral T-shirt perfectly accent her fit curves.

"So, was it a smashing time or just mildly tolerable?" I grin, expecting either a confirmation that her lunch with Sophie and Mia turned out fun, or more grumbling about how it's not part of her job. Spoiler alert—I'm hoping it's the former.

Her expression tells me nothing as she walks over and hands me a small takeout container. "Thought you'd like some hushpuppies."

I close my book and hold my hand out. "How thoughtful."

Our eyes catch as our fingers brush. And I don't miss how she lingers for a moment.

She frowns, then pulls her hand away. "You didn't tell me you asked Sophie out once."

Interesting...she sounds almost jealous. Or is she just annoyed I left out a detail like I did about having a room-mate? Yeah, I properly mucked that one up. But in my defense, I genuinely thought I could give my bodyguard the slip. Now I'm rather glad I didn't...

"I didn't think about it, to be honest. Is it important?"

She turns around to head toward the kitchen area. "Not in the grand scheme of things, but it might have helped avoid an awkward moment during lunch."

As much as I want to pop a hushpuppy into my mouth, I set the container down on the coffee table because this discussion just turned more intriguing than fried dough. "How did that wind up part of the conversation?"

She gives me an exasperated look. "You went back to England, and six weeks later, you returned with a wife. They're curious about our relationship." She pulls out two mugs and fills the kettle. "Sophie described you as shy, by the way."

"Did she now?" I remember that day well, and I was somewhat unsure at the moment, come to think of it. Then Luke walked in and made it clear Sophie was off limits, and the rest is history.

"Yes, she assumed I asked you out first." Lily takes a bottle of water out of the fridge.

"Dare I ask what you told her?"

She's avoiding my gaze, so I can't help wondering if this bothered her. I'd be an idiot to deny the chemistry between us, but is it to the point that Lily could feel threatened by my past interest in Sophie?

"That you asked me. I said you flirted with me all evening and wouldn't take no for an answer." She unscrews the bottle cap and takes a sip.

"Oh, really now?" I set my book on the coffee table as well.

"No. Of course not." She smirks at me as if she's won a game I had no notion of. "I let her make her own assumptions."

I grunt as I work my way up from the couch. "Like what?"

"Isn't it obvious?" Her exacerbated expression returns in full force, which only makes me think she really was jealous.

"Maybe to you, but I wasn't there, so enlighten me." I grin, waiting for her to continue.

She swings her hand through the air in a grand gesture to punctuate her words. "That because you weren't shy with me, we're meant to be together."

I chuckle and pad my way toward the kitchen when the kettle whistles. Might as well tug this delightful thread she's exposed while I can. "You almost sound jealous, Lily."

She raises her brows at me and deadpans, "That's ridiculous."

The air buzzes between us as I lean on the counter with my good arm a few feet away from her. The downside of cracked ribs is the pain. The upside is that if it didn't hurt so much, I'd probably make a move on Lily right now because I want nothing more than to pull her against me and explore those lush lips. Then I'd tug her hair loose so I could run my fingers through the silky strands as I kissed her again.

"Payton?"

I shake myself back to reality. "What?"

She squints her eyes at me. "Where did you just go?"

"Sorry. Must be the ribs. They're aching quite a bit at the moment." Which is true—I'm overdue for some ibuprofen.

Her suspicious expression shifts to concern. "Sit down. I'll bring you your tea and some pain medicine."

That was a close one. "Thank you, wife. You always take such good care of me."

"Don't mention it," she replies sarcastically.

A few minutes later, Lily brings me a cup of tea, a bottle of water, and two ibuprofen.

"Cheers."

"You're welcome." She walks back to the kitchen, grabs her own mug, and heads toward her room.

"Where are you going?" I sound like a petulant child. What kind of sop am I turning into here? I know it breaks all the rules, but I want nothing more than to take whatever's forming between her and me to the next level. If she'll even let me.

A smug grin splits her face. "I have a date with some very important reports and people. You're not jealous, are you?"

"Of course not. That's ridiculous." I sling her words back at her with a cheeky grin.

And while I'm momentarily proud of my success in seeing her smile slip ever so slightly, I'm borderline bereft when she closes the door, leaving me alone with only my book and a hot cup of tea to keep me company.

And a box of hushpuppies.

It's time to switch tactics. That's what I told myself an hour ago when I got the bright idea to make Lily dinner. Not an easy feat with my ribs, but I was determined. I managed to figure out something to cook with minimal movements that didn't require bending over or lifting heavy items.

That brought me to spaghetti and meatballs, a specialty of mine. Turns out I can roll a ball of raw meat with one hand and fill a pasta pot with water, one measuring cup at a time. Before long, the aromas of tomatoes, garlic, basil, and savory Italian meatballs permeate the kitchen.

As the sauce simmers, I set the table, which looks decidedly bare. Then I remembered the hibiscus bush outside of my apartment building. I grab a pair of shears and head out the door with the intention of clipping a few blooms I'm sure won't be missed. I'd rather they be lilies for obvious reasons, but these will do in a pinch.

Just as I'm about to clip a third bloom, I see Lily racing toward me, and she doesn't look happy at all.

"Payton!" She comes to an abrupt stop in front of me, then starts pushing me toward the apartment. "What are you doing?"

I quirk a grin and hold up the flowers. "Isn't that obvious?"

"Get inside. Now." She hustles me through the door—or rather I let her—and then turns the lock once we're back in the apartment. "What were you thinking?"

She's standing there with her hands on her hips, looking at me as if I just broke some cardinal rule. Perhaps I did. "I didn't see the harm in stepping outside for a moment. Your partner has eyes outside, so I figured it was safe enough."

She drops her hands to her sides and takes a step closer to me. "Safe enough won't keep a bullet from piercing that humongous head of yours, and with those broken ribs, a child could take you down in a heartbeat."

I search the cabinet for a container to serve as a vase and find a tall glass. "I'm sorry. I was only trying to make a special dinner for you. My way of saying thank you for taking care of me."

Her stern expression falters a smidge and, as she parts her lips to say something, a knock sounds on the front door. "Are you expecting someone?"

I shake my head.

She checks the peephole, then opens the door, still looking rather peevish.

Wade swaggers in, followed by Ethan, Mathéo, Elias, and finally, Luke.

"We thought we'd pay our Pay a visit." Wade chuckles. "Get it? Pay our Pay…"

Ethan pops him on the arm. "Give the Dad jokes a rest, man."

Luke grunts. "Sorry. When I told them I needed to stop by and get a few things I forgot, they insisted on coming with me."

I dart my gaze from Luke to Lily, who's shooting me a warning look, then another until I finally get what she's worried about. If Luke goes poking around in his old room, the jig will be up, and they'll know something isn't right here.

"A text might have been nice. I was making dinner."

Wade lifts the lid to my sauce and inhales. "Are these your famous meatballs, Pay-man?" He roams his gaze to the other guys. "Looks like we came just in time, boys. Let's help Pay wrap this up so he can rest."

Mathéo takes the flowers and glass from me. "I'll finish setting the table."

He proceeds to grab additional silverware and napkins, which tells me they intend to stay. Normally, when this happens, I just go along with the flow. They're my friends, and I do enjoy cooking for them.

But I had an evening planned that I hoped might warm Lily to the idea of something happening between us. Although, after the stunt I pulled with the flowers, I may as well declare tonight a lost cause.

Elias gets to work, slathering the French bread with the garlic butter I prepared, while Ethan pours in the box of pasta and stirs.

Luke bounces his gaze from Lily to me. "I left my jackets in the coat closet."

"I'll help you." Lily darts over the closet to the left of the front door and helps Luke sift through the hanging articles.

A short while later, another knock sounds. Lily shoots a questioning look my way, to which I shrug. I can't imagine who else would be stopping by at this point.

She opens the door, revealing Sophie and Mia.

"Surprise!" Sophie gives Lily a hug, then heads toward me, holding a pie. "We brought dessert. Luke texted we were doing dinner here, so Mia and I stopped to pick up a few things for you."

Mia holds up a grocery sack. "I have the ice cream and whipped cream."

Suddenly, my intimate dinner for two has turned into a party of nine. Good thing I made a large pot of sauce.

I sigh and head to where Ethan's stirring and grab another box of pasta from the cabinet. "We're going to need more."

## Chapter Thirteen

### LILY

So many people in one small apartment...

Sophie and Mia chat with Mathéo, asking him questions about his unexpected table-setting skills. They appear quite impressed with his explanation about his *mémé*, his grandmother, who taught him many things 'French.'

Wade and Ethan delegated Payton to the couch, and they're picking apart a replay of an NHL game that featured an unusual play by the goalie that helped the team score the winning goal in overtime.

They're all so comfortable and easy around each other, as if they've done this dozens of times, which I suspect they have. Something tugs in my chest, a longing of some kind that I'm unsure what to do about.

My phone vibrates in my back pocket, so I excuse myself to go to the bathroom. Must be Del, as she's pretty much the only person who texts me. Except for Sophie and Mia, now that we're in a group chat for the fundraiser, but they're here. And these days, most of my conversations with Del seem to happen in restrooms.

Del: Having fun?

> Lily: I honestly don't know how to answer that.

Del: Everyone checked out as expected.
Nothing to worry about.

> Lily: That's what you think.

Del: Trouble in paradise?

> Lily: Remember that assignment in India?

Del: Oof! So many people!

> Lily: Exactly.

Del: Think of it as a fact finding mission on
that yummy client of yours.

> Lily: Already found out he tried to ask Sophie
> out. That was before Luke staked his claim
> on her. Her words.

Del: I'm liking hockey players more and
more.

> Lily: Of course you would.

Del: Judge much?

> Lily: Eye roll emoji

Time to return to the fray before someone knocks on
the door to see if I'm okay, which is a great question,
considering. If I'd known this assignment would require
pretending to be friends with other WAGs as well as
Payton's fake wife, I may have reconsidered taking it.

But that permanent position is what I've been shooting

for, figuratively speaking. I just hope, in the end, I can say it was worth it.

When I return to the living room, everyone is lined up in the kitchen, filling their plates with food. Someone threw a salad together while I was gone, which I find impressive, even if I suspect it's one of those kits. I'm starting to appreciate how these people do life together.

Definitely brings back a lot of memories of the group home I spent time in as a teenager. By the time I was thirteen, I was labeled as "difficult." Most likely because I was tall for my age and took it upon myself to protect the smaller kids.

After a few complaints from parents who had no business parenting, in my opinion, the label stuck, and I wound up a permanent resident in the group home, which was fine. I was tired of getting bounced around so much by that point. At least I knew what to expect on a daily basis.

But Payton and his friends are different. They're a community by choice, not because of circumstances. I've never experienced that nuance before, and frankly, I find it unsettling. I'm better at identifying the best exit route or avoiding choke points. Of making sure my principal gets from point A to point B safely. Not socializing and building relationships.

Somehow, we all crowd around Payton's dining room table. He's the consummate host, ensuring each person has what they need without lifting a finger because everyone is quick to jump up and take care of whatever he suggests, so he doesn't exert himself any more than necessary.

I find it all very amusing. And even...heartening. I get that these guys spend hours together every day on the ice, doing a job they love. But they're friends, too. Payton asks about Mathéo's *mémé*, who lives in Canada still and just had hip surgery. He's bummed he couldn't fly out to be there with her, but everyone reassured him she understood and had plenty of other family members to help, details they already knew about him.

And then there's Elias, who's decided to quit dating since his last girlfriend cheated on him. I wanted to tell him that most of the time, life isn't fair, but then Sophie jumped in and said he couldn't give up on love. He just hadn't met the right person yet, and that she and Luke were proof of that, which only made me more curious about those two. I mean, she's the very definition of sunshine, and Luke's as grumpy as they come.

All of this swirls to a screeching stop when Sophie pins me with a question. "What do you think, Lily? Should Elias give up on love?"

My hand pauses mid-air, holding my next bite of garlic bread. I lower my hand. "I think…" I clear my throat. "I think anyone who can make garlic bread this good is a great catch."

An unexpected rumble of laughter erupts around the table. I smile, genuinely glad I dodged that bullet.

Payton leans over. "I made the spread. He just finished what I started."

I turn my head so only he can hear. "Are you feeling a little jealous?"

He says nothing, but I don't miss the slight pulse in his jaw muscle. Is he trying to impress me?

"Aww! Look at the lovebirds." Mia beams at us. "Aren't they cute?"

Heat flushes up my cheeks despite my attempt to appear unaffected as I continue eating.

Payton gets to his feet and raises his glass of wine. "I would like to make a toast to my lovely bride to thank her for taking such good care of me." He turns to face me, capturing my gaze with his.

There he goes again, using 'lovely' to describe me. But this is for show, right? Maybe the word just rolls easily off his lips.

I try to communicate a cease-and-desist message with a few blinks, but he continues.

"I know we rushed things, and the last thing we expected was for me to be laid up while we're still technically in our honeymoon phase…"

Whistles and catcalls fill his pause, which was clearly his intention, and succeeds in making me squirm in my seat. The man moves as smooth off the ice as on, I have to admit. But I'm not ready to give up this fight.

He flags his hand to quiet the snickering. "She is truly the woman of my dreams. To Lily!"

Everyone raises their glasses, be it wine, water, or, in Wade's case, a beer, and cheer, repeating Payton's last two words. I stand up, intending to add my own lethal toast, but before I can say anything, Wade drawls, "Lily, the only way to top that one is to kiss the guy. I think he earned it."

An awkward laugh slips out before I can stop it. I think my stomach just made friends with my toes. "That's sweet but—"

Payton's grin turns downright evil. "Isn't she adorable? And here you thought I was the shy one."

The last thing I see is Sophie's brows shoot up before Payton's head, which I'm convinced grew four times bigger in the last hour, closes in, and his lips brush mine.

I have two choices. Lean away, making it obvious we're not the happy couple they think we are, or let him kiss me and make him answer for it later.

His kiss is tentative at first. Almost cautious. Then his

hand slides behind my head as he continues, not giving me a way out. But I can't think of an escape because all I want right now is to explore his lips that taste like garlic and tomato and wine, and give in to all these exhilarating sensations rolling over me that leave me feeling wanted and... safe. Like I could let down my guard around him.

But I can't—not and do my job well. However, I can even the score a little. After all, I'm the one who suggested we make this a competition. I lean closer and deepen the kiss. His spicy scent nearly intoxicates me, making me almost forget why I'm doing this, but I resist the pull and run my hand over his injured side. Not enough to seriously hurt him, but enough to make him jump ever so slightly and end the kiss.

I cover my mouth with my fingers with a gasp. "I'm so sorry, honey. Guess I got caught up in the moment and forgot about your ribs." I mimic a contrite grin at the rest of the table. "Must be that honeymoon phase he mentioned."

Sophie giggles while Mia fans herself with an expression of approval on her face.

Payton holds his side as he lowers himself into his chair. "No worries, *dear*. I'll be fine."

"I should get him an ice pack. Can I get anyone anything?" Before anyone can answer, I make a beeline for the kitchen on shaky legs.

Between the military and working as a bodyguard, I've been around a lot of men. Some are attractive, some are not. Some kind, others not so much. A few I admired, a lot I considered nuisances to be ignored.

I've always kept my guard up with little trouble. But Payton just blew all my pretenses out of the water and proved my walls aren't as impenetrable as I thought.

*Observation #5: Payton is mischievous, and his kisses are dangerous.*

Maybe it's time to set some boundaries before our competition turns my heart on end.

---

The thing about a dinner party—and that's the only way to describe what this turned into—is there's always the cleanup to look forward to. And I mean that in the most sarcastic way. Thankfully, Payton's friends are as quick to help as they were to helping put this dinner on the table. All things considered—excluding the kiss—it was a nice evening.

Payton and Elias sit on the couch, chatting, while I'm loading the dishwasher with Mia's help.

"Ethan and I have this agreement that whoever cooks doesn't have to do the dishes." She hands me the next rinsed plate to add to the rest.

"So you take turns?"

"No, I cook, and he cleans." She giggles.

I laugh. "Then why have an agreement?"

She shrugs. "I figure if he decides he hates cleaning up, he'll have to cook more."

I stare at her. "You're a sneaky one, aren't you?"

"And proud of it." She snorts, then laughs again.

As I'm about to add another plate to the dishwasher, I catch Luke and Sophie leaving the second bedroom. My breath catches as I search out Payton, but he's in a deep discussion between Ethan, Mathéo, and Elias.

"I'll be right back, Mia."

"I'll be right here." She singsongs as I walk over to Luke and Sophie.

"Couldn't wait until the honeymoon, huh?" I force a

laugh, half hoping my joke is actually the truth and not something else.

Blushing like a banshee—do banshees blush?—Sophie glances at Luke, who nods and walks away. "Sorry. He was just trying to find the hockey stick he saved from the game when he proposed to me."

He proposed at a hockey game? Was he playing? How would that even work? And there's my point of deflection. "How did he propose?"

"It was the most romantic, yet somewhat terrifying, moment of my life to date." She hesitates, leaving me to think I'd succeeded because she was about to launch into the entire story, but then she asks, "Are you and Payton okay?"

I school my expression, careful not to clench my fists at my sides. Body language is a dead giveaway, and I don't want to ignite any unnecessary fires. "We're fine. Why?"

She glances over her shoulder. "We didn't mean to snoop. It's just that all your stuff is in this closet."

With a snort, I wave my hand at the bedroom door. "Oh, that. Payton hasn't had a chance to make room yet. His closet is twice as big as mine."

"But you have stuff on the nightstand." She clasps her hands, appearing nervous. "I have big ears and a mouth that stays shut, if you know what I mean."

In another life, I think I could actually trust this woman and let her in. But this isn't that time or place. I scramble for an excuse as close to the truth to maintain our believability.

There's that word again. "I am a very restless sleeper and didn't want to risk bumping him during the night, so I slept in here."

With a slight press of her lips, she stares at me before glancing toward Payton.

I rest my hand on her arm, much like she has with me. "I promise. We're fine."

Her concern softens into a warm smile. "I'm so glad. I mean, that kiss." She fans herself. "Passion like that doesn't happen all the time. Take it from someone who knows."

Again, I take advantage of the spotlight shift from me to her. "Oh, do tell." I scan the room in search of Luke and find him at the coat closet, holding up the lost hockey stick like a trophy.

"I'd pretty much given up on love when he showed up." The expression on her face as she stares at him almost makes *me* fall in love with the guy.

I swallow down the lump in my throat. "Was it instant?"

She turns wide eyes my way. "Not at all. We hated each other in the beginning."

That's unexpected. "Seriously?"

"Oh, yeah. Mostly because of assumptions. He assumed I was trying to dig dirt up on him for my articles about the team, and I thought he was an overbearing grump who didn't deserve the time of day." Her eyes tilt as she laughs. "But then we got to know each other better."

"And fell in love..." I add a wistful tone to my statement.

"Hook, line, and sinker. But then he blew it a couple of times."

I blink. "Excuse me?"

"Yeah, he had some stuff to work out with his father, but now they're great. And so are we. His sister Kinsley is adorable. You'll meet her at the wedding. She's one of my bridesmaids, too. You'll love her. You'll come with Payton to the wedding, right? I already added you as his plus one. But if I'd known, I totally would have addressed the invitation to Mr. and Mrs. Payton Maxwell. Oh, but I think I sent the invitations before you two met. But it all worked out in the end, right?" She grabs one of my hands. "Please say you'll come?"

Takes me a few seconds to catch up on her verbal diatribe before I realize she's waiting for my confirmation. My heart constricts as I realize I'm holding her hand as tightly as she's clutching mine.

The closest thing I have to a friend in my life at present is Del. We were kind of thrown together through assignments and I needed a place to live. Thankfully, we liked each other well enough to make it work, although our definitions of having fun are vastly different. She's more of a party animal, while I'm the quintessential loner, content to do things on my own.

A longing I thought I'd let go of a long time ago rushes back like the waves I've watched surge onto the shore. I've never had a circle of friends who hung out just because they wanted to. Not because they happened to be thrown together in the same house or unit. For the most part, I've shied away from building friendships, figuring it didn't make sense, considering my life is constantly in flux.

But none of this is real, and I won't be here for long. Soon, this assignment will end, and I'll be on a plane, returning to England, then off to wherever I'm assigned to next. Still, for right now, how can I resist making this woman happy by simply going to her wedding?

I nod and smile. "I wouldn't miss it for the world."

Sophie squeals, hugging me, and I hug her back.

The funny thing is…I think I actually mean it.

# Chapter Fourteen

## PAYTON

Everyone has left, leaving Lily and me alone. She's collecting the remaining glasses and dessert plates from the coffee table, appearing rather domestic at the moment. Not that I care about details like that. My family may be more traditional, but I wouldn't describe my mother as a homemaker.

But watching Lily isn't so much about what she's doing as how she does things. She's gorgeous, athletic in her movements, yet graceful and complex. The more time I spend with her, the more I want to explore those complicated depths she keeps so carefully protected. I'm curious to know everything about her—the good, the bad, and even the ugly. And I suspect she's seen more of the last two than the first.

And that makes my chest ache. I want to show her there's beauty and goodness in this life. But if I'm really being honest? I want to be that for her. I want to be the one who takes care of her instead of always being the one she protects.

I understand she has a job to do, which could end at any

time. Especially once the authorities realize they're chasing after nothing. However, I'm convinced Lily and I could have something amazing together, but the ticking clock in this scenario is getting louder and louder. And I feel like I'm in the third period of a tied game with less than five minutes to shoot the winning goal.

She continues to wipe down the counter while I stand on the other side of the island. Despite the late hour and the ache in my side demanding that I lie down, I'm not ready to go to bed. She probably thinks I haven't noticed how she's avoided me since we kissed. With a house full of guests, it's easy to stay busy, but I noticed.

And I don't like it because that kiss was epic. I didn't expect it to turn into a massive PDA show. She did that, and I'd be an idiot—let alone flat-out lying—to say I didn't enjoy it. More than enjoy it.

I read once that fireflies adapt their flashing patterns to attract a mate. Consider me sucked into the glow that is Lily because she figured me out on day one. For the first time in my life, I can picture myself in that kind of relationship—something serious that could lead to, well, more. Maybe even a lifetime.

Perhaps it's because she has to be here twenty-four-seven as part of her job or because she wound up taking care of me and my cracked ribs. I probably could have showered on my own and survived subpar cleanliness for a few more days. If I were alone, I'm positive the rest of the blokes would have stopped by to help with what I needed. Outside of the shower, of course. But Lily's been a champ through it all.

Somehow, I have to get her to engage with me. "You play dirty."

She stops mid-sweep across the counter and blinks at me. "Black."

Why is she naming a color? "What?"

"Just calling the pot what it is." A sly grin tilts her pouty lips while she resumes her cleaning.

Now that I know what those lips feel like, I want them even more. "Touché, Kettle." I hold up a finger with my thought. "You know, I've been trying to think of a good nickname for you. You have one for me, so it only seems fair."

She continues to move around the kitchen, appearing half-distracted. "And?"

"I thought that was obvious."

With a definitive yet controlled breath, she brings her full attention to me. "Enlighten me."

How the tables turn. And it's my turn, indeed. "Kettle. That will be my endearment for you from now on."

She tosses the dishrag into the sink. "Think again, big guy."

You'd expect the snark in her voice would deter me, but it has quite the opposite effect. "I will if you will."

"Will what?" She strides to the front door and checks the lock, then does the same with all the windows as she's done every evening.

"Think of a different nickname?" I do love sparring with her like this.

"I never meant it as a nickname." She's sounding more and more irritated. Or is she flustered?

"Then what is it?"

She gestures her hand at me, waving it up and down. "A fact. You're a big guy."

That adorable blush seeps up her neck and into her

cheeks as if she hadn't intended to vocalize that thought. "How nice of you to notice."

She lets out something between a growl and a grunt and storms toward her bedroom.

"Where are you going?" I let out a soft hiss through my teeth as my side reminds me I can't twist like that right now.

"To bed." She tosses over her shoulder, then stops in front of her door. Her shoulders slump just before she spins around. "Do you need any help before I go to my room?"

She says this like a robot as if it's a required duty. That's the last thing I want her to think of me as—a requirement.

"I'm fine, but thank you for asking."

"No more going outside unattended." She glares at me.

"I wouldn't dream of it," I reassure her.

"Good. Glad we have that clarified."

"Sleep well, Lily." My gentle tone seems to disarm her for a moment, which was my intention.

She nods and then retreats to her room, closing me out yet again. I stare at her door for a long while, waiting—hoping—willing—it to open. That she'll walk back out because she forgot something, giving me another chance to engage her in conversation because I'm not looking forward to sleeping alone.

While the minutes and hours pass and sleep evades me, I hatch a plan. I may have tried to lose Lily at the airport, but now I'm determined to get past those walls of hers and see what really makes her tick.

---

"Are you sure you're ready for this?" Lily tries to grab my suitcase, but I beat her to the punch. I toss hers into the trunk as well, just to prove to her I'm fine.

"I can play without pain, so I'm cleared." I won't mention to Lily that I still feel some tenderness in my ribs. She'd worry more, which I'm finding quite adorable. And I'm convinced her concerns fall beyond her being my bodyguard. Over the last two weeks, she's constantly reminded me of my 'compromised condition,' making me more vulnerable.

Honestly, my ribs aren't the vulnerable spot I'm concerned about.

As much as I'd love to start something with Lily, I can't seem to find a way of making something work between us. Not unless she moved to the States, but I don't see that happening. If the tables were turned, I wouldn't want to give up playing hockey. And I'd never ask her to sacrifice her career for me. Sarabella's a small town, so I'm fairly certain there's minimal demand for a bodyguard.

That brought me to the idea of a long-distance relationship, but even that didn't make sense. Not when we'd have an entire ocean separating us. Sure, it might work in the beginning, but with my schedule, there's little room for transatlantic flights. We're allowed time off when necessary, but more than that would mean letting my team down, and that I can't do.

She shields the sun with her hand, throwing a shadow over her face. "But what if you get hit again?"

I can feel her eyes on me these days without seeing them. It's as if every cell in my body is in tune to her now, which makes the dealing with my growing feelings for her an even bigger challenge than I anticipated.

"I'll be fine." I hop into the driver's seat, but she blocks the door before I can shut it.

Her gaze drills into me like an opponent on the ice. "What are you doing?"

I rest my hands on the steering wheel. "Isn't that obvious?"

One side of her mouth ticks up before she suppresses it. "That's my job."

"Then consider this a break."

"I'm the bodyguard, Payton. Remember?"

"It's just to the arena. Hop in." I nod my head toward the passenger seat, unrelenting in my stare.

"That won't mean squat if we get into a situation."

"What kind of situation?"

She tosses her hands out to her sides. "I don't know, and that's the whole point."

I shut the door before she can grab it again, and I can honestly say I don't think I've seen Lily turn that shade of red before. When she reaches for the handle, I lock the doors and start the engine.

Her eyes are rounder than the globe light perched above the walkway to my apartment. "You wouldn't dare."

I can't hear her, but I can read those full lips of hers well enough. I'm almost afraid to see how she'll react when we get to the arena and she finds out I may have tampered a bit with her plan to indiscreetly follow our team bus to Savannah. We're playing the Ghost Pirates tomorrow and the Gladiators in Atlanta two days later. When I found out she'd never seen the amazing architecture in Savannah, I hatched a plan of my own. Just because we can't be together—although I'm still trying to find a solution—it doesn't mean I can't do special things for her.

After shifting into reverse, I back up a foot, then rev the engine and grin, which seems to aggravate her even more. And judging by the way her hands are fisted at her sides as she marches around the vehicle to the passenger side, she's as fired up as my car engine at the moment. The excitement pulsing through me reminds me of that first skate onto the ice during a game, filled with anticipation over what the next few hours could hold.

I unlock the doors.

She slides in and slams hers.

"Take it easy there. My car has done nothing to you." I shouldn't enjoy this as much as I am, but getting under her skin is fast becoming my favorite pastime.

"No, but its owner is a pain in the butt." She jams her seatbelt into place.

I chuckle and pull out as her phone pings. "Del?"

She knifes me with a glance. "Probably. She's already heading up to assess the situation in Savannah… thankfully."

Her hesitation and then additional comment sends a pang of doubt through me. "Will my driving get you in trouble?"

After glancing at her phone, her expression turns curious. "What would you do if I said yes?"

I blurt out a laugh before I can stop it. "Absolutely nothing."

Her mouth drops open just enough to satisfy my ego and draw my attention to her full lips. "Then I guess it's a good thing Del doesn't have eyes on us at the moment."

"Would she really take issue with me driving? Surely, you've had other principals who insisted on driving themselves."

Her expression tightens into a frown. She taps out a message.

"Am I right?"

No answer.

"I'll take that as a yes."

She flips her phone face down on her lap and stares out

the passenger window. "You can take it however you want, but if I get even a hint of trouble, I'm taking over. Understand?"

I glance her way to see if she's serious, which she is. Dead serious. "As in, pull over and swap places? Seems like that would make us more vulnerable."

"It would. There are other ways to do that."

"You don't mean…?"

Her frown turns into a smug smile. "I've done it before."

"You're kidding, right? I thought they only did that in the movies."

The slight arch of one brow answers me.

I rip my focus back to the road. Just when I didn't think this woman could impress me anymore, she surprises me again. Not by the implication of her doing something dangerous, like taking control of a moving vehicle, but by the sheer fact that it's one of many skills in her secret bodyguard tool belt, which I'm finding more and more attractive on a daily basis.

Lily Evans is definitely unlike any woman I have ever met in my life.

# Chapter Fifteen

"A girls' weekend?" I stare at Sophie as if she just sprouted horns. Although, we're talking about sweet and sunshiny Sophie here. She's more likely to sprout sunflowers.

"Surprise!?" Mia draws her exclamation out to a question as her voice trails off. I'm beginning to appreciate Mia's unabated sarcasm.

I'm guessing that has to do with the fact that Payton pulled one over on me...again. I expected to follow the bus at a discreet distance, alone. Now I'll have two chatterboxes in tow to distract me. Del is going to love this.

Although the upside is I won't have to stay out of sight. Seems WAGs aren't allowed to travel on the team bus, but there's nothing that says they can't go to away games on their own. How quaint.

"Isn't it great?" Sophie stares at me with saucer eyes. Something she's really good at.

I've decided that's her superpower. "Sure."

Next to her, Mia snorts. "Such excitement. Don't overdo yourself."

Like I said, unabated sarcasm. Guess I didn't sound excited enough. "Sorry. I'm not always great with surprises."

Which is true. As a bodyguard, my job is to prevent surprises as much as possible. But I also have to be adaptable.

"It's okay. I get it." Sophie gives me a quick hug. "We're going to have a blast on the ride up." She pats her big brown bag, "I brought my research for the fundraiser so we can get a jump on planning."

Mia grins. "Great idea! I've got plenty of snacks so we can stay fueled up, too."

"Perfect." I force a smile, all the while searching out Payton's location by the bus, and notice the guys are starting to board. I hand Sophie my keys. "Load up your stuff. I'll be right there."

As I walk toward Payton, Mia's giggle catches my ear. "She probably wants to kiss him goodbye."

I let this slide because Payton's the true object of my ire at the moment. He gives me a questioning look, to which I reply with a gesture indicating I need him to step aside from the group and meet me where I'm heading a few feet away and out of hearing.

He reaches me as I stop near the arena entrance. "Do you like my surprise?"

As I lift my arms to cross them, I think better of it and drop them to my sides. Too many eyes watching, especially Sophie. She'd read something into it for sure if I did that.

"What were you thinking?"

Payton shrugs. "I figured you needed a reason to be at the games, so I created one. Sophie and Mia jumped on the idea when I told them you'd never seen Savannah."

"And how am I going to do my job if I have to gallivant around with these women to keep up *your* ruse?"

A flash of guilt passes over his face. "You said Del would be on location. Surely, she can monitor things and give you a little time off."

"It doesn't work that way, Payton. Del and I are a team of two. There is no back up to give us a break."

"Why not? Am I not important enough?" He says this jokingly, but his curiosity is genuine.

I sigh, knowing where this is headed. "The risk factor isn't that high—"

"I knew it!" His words pounce on me as if I'm a puck.

And now I'm thinking in hockey metaphors? Good grief...

"Since there is no visible threat—"

"No known threat," I interject.

He gives a curt nod. "My point is, there's no reason you can't take a few hours to explore a fabulous city with two friends."

Friends? I have friends now? "Says you."

"Yes, I say so. Savannah is known for its beautiful architecture and historic landmarks. You'll love it."

A surge of emotion I'm not familiar pulses through me. Payton did this for no other reason than to make sure I didn't miss out on seeing something beautiful. Makes me want to grab his face and kiss him to express how much his thoughtfulness touches me.

I shove that desire down and relent. "All right. I still have to clear it with Del, though."

"Of course." He looks toward the bus. "Seems we have an audience."

I glance over my shoulder to find several concerned

faces watching us, including Sophie. "They probably think we're arguing. Especially Sophie."

His gaze slides to me. "Why?"

"She saw my stuff in the second bedroom the night everyone crashed our—your dinner, so I told her I was trying not to disturb you while you slept."

He chuckles at my corrections. "Did she buy it?"

"I thought so, but now I'm not so sure."

Payton brushes my hair back from my face and tucks it behind my ear, sending a shock through my body. His hand is so warm and right there near my cheek. The urge to press my cheek against his palm almost overwhelms me as the memory of that kiss crashes in. Anytime I think about it, it's like I'm there all over again.

"What are you doing?" My voice comes out husker than I'd like.

"Keeping things believable." His smile may be saying that, but the heat in his eyes tells me something entirely different. "I enjoy seeing you with your hair down."

"I don't like driving long distances with a ponytail. It gets annoying."

"You should wear it down more often. It suits you." He cups my face.

My eyes flutter shut before I realize what's happening. I force them open. "I think that's sufficient to convince them."

He tilts his head and leans in. From behind, it must look like we're kissing, but Payton keeps just enough distance between our faces so that our lips don't touch, and his eyes are hooded as to appear closed. "Just making sure."

His breath fans my lips with his warmth, causing me to long for him to actually kiss me. But then the scent of his spicy soap floods my nose and slaps my senses awake. I could easily lift up on my feet, bringing my mouth to his. For believability, of course, not to mention that my body is begging me to do it.

But this is just for show, so that would be unnecessary. Unless this is his competitive nature peeking out, and it's always about the game for him. Any game.

*Observation #6: Payton is a bit of a thrill seeker.*

After encountering plenty of them during my time in the military, I know the type. Although, Payton is nowhere as extreme.

I slide my hand up his chest and over his shoulder, pressing against him in a hug, which puts my mouth conveniently near his ear. "This should help, too."

He hums his agreement, and as I'm about to pull away, the scoundrel wraps his arms around me and crushes me against him. His hold is so tight I can't even wiggle enough to put a little air between us. He's a wall of muscle that's driving my heartbeat so hard and fast I'm convinced you could see it pulsing under my skin.

"Now, who's playing dirty?" I whisper, making sure my lips brush against his ear.

His breath hitches, making his grip loosen enough that I can break free. But his blazing stare stops me from fully leaving his embrace.

"Call it even?" His voice sounds rough, almost strained.

And that, my friends, is how it's done. I tilt my smile to the side. "Not on your life."

A soft, deep laugh rumbles through his chest. "Game on."

Mia leans between the front seats. "That was some kiss, Lily. You're going to make the rest of the WAGs envious if you two keep that up. I didn't think Payton had it in him."

I dart my eyes up to my rearview mirror and take in her borderline awed expression. "Just because Payton tends to be shy doesn't mean he's not passionate."

Why do I feel the need to defend Payton? I could use the excuse that I'm maintaining believability, but the truth is, I know in my gut that it's true. Payton is the kind of guy who gives himself completely to what he loves. I see that in him when he talks—and reads—about hockey, in his friendships with his teammates, and in the way he talked to his sister when I happened to overhear the tail end of his conversations with her this morning.

Plus, he's sexy as hell. I've been in some very precarious situations with my job, but I'm beginning to think this one is by far the most dangerous because my heart's getting too involved.

There. I acknowledged it. Now I have to figure out what to do about it. I still haven't had a chance to text Del about this girls' weekend development, but I can hear her cackle already.

I'm almost positive she won't like it either because that will require her to be more hands-on while I'm indisposed, pretending to run around with THE GIRLS.

Mia giggles. "I guess I just never thought of Payton that way."

Sophie bends over and tugs her pink planner out of her bag. "Oh, I had a rush of ideas last night about our fundraiser."

Bless that woman for changing the subject because whatever this is rising in me needs to settle back down.

"Let's hear it." I check my mirror again to see Mia's completely focused on Sophie now.

Another bullet dodged, I suppose. Sure hope there aren't more like them.

Sophie folds back the cover of her notebook. "I know we talked about doing a carnival, but we'd have to charge too much to recoup the cost and meet our donation goal. But then I realized we could do something similar in the arena. Kids love to ice skate. We could have the guys do drills with them and even set up a mini hockey rink at one end of the ice."

Mia bounces up and down. "And we could give the kids rides on the Zamboni!"

Sophie grins at her. 'Exactly! I wrote that down, too." She points to an item on her list. "And we can use the lounge as a concessions area since it has a kitchen and popcorn machine. I already called Rebecca Piedmont, the team owner, and she said she'd cover the cost."

"Girl, you are on fire!" Mia gestures to Sophie's notebook. "What else do you have on that list?"

"That's it so far. We need more activities. Do you have any ideas, Lil?"

My childhood isn't exactly a pool of resources to draw from, but I do remember loving to color and make things on rare occasions. "What about multiple tables set up with different crafts? Kids love being creative and don't always get the opportunity. When they finish one, they could move on to another table to do something different."

"Oh, I love that idea!" Sophie jots it down, then studies me. "Sounds like you had some experience with this. Did you have younger siblings you helped take care of?"

I tilt my head. "Something like that."

Mia groans. "I had to babysit my little brother all the

137

time. And the only thing he liked to play with was Legos. I knew I was in trouble when I began looking at everything in terms of how I could build it with Legos."

Even that one makes me laugh, which seems to please Mia. I'm beginning to see her sarcasm for what it is—a shield to hide some kind of insecurity. And I'm more than familiar with shields and cover-ups. I became a pro at it growing up as I did, turning it into a skill that's served me well as a bodyguard, but I also recognize it in others.

By the time we reach the hotel, Sophie has organized our ideas into an action plan. The woman is an organizational force to be reckoned with, that's for sure. As we walk into the lobby, I do a scan to locate Payton and assess any potential threats or situations. He's waiting with the rest of the team and winks when he spots me.

Next, I search for Del. By the elevators, a blonde woman turns around and tugs on her earlobe, which is our signal for 'we need to talk.' She looks pensive as well when she swings her handbag in the direction of the restrooms.

"I need to run to the bathroom. Can you guys watch my bag for a sec?"

"Sure." Sophie rolls my suitcase closer to hers.

Mia swivels her head toward me. "Probably a good idea. It takes a while to get the team checked in so we'll have a few minutes. I need to go, too."

Blast. There goes my plan to talk to Del. Unless I can make up some excuse to take longer. I make sure Mia enters the restroom first so Del won't jump the gun before she knows I'm not alone.

She's sitting at the vanity mirror in the lounge area, fussing with her hair, a.k.a. wig, with the contents of a make-up case strewn about the counter. I give her barely a glance as I follow Mia through the archway leading to the bathroom stalls. Mia darts into the first one, and I take the next. Hopefully, she's not one of those women who waits around for her friend.

A few minutes later, I hear her leave the stall, then the sounds of water running. "Lily, do you want me to wait for you?"

"No, I'll be right behind you."

The faucet squeaks when she shuts it off, followed by the tug of paper towels from the dispenser. "See you out there, then."

When I hear the bathroom door tap shut, I dart out and wash my hands.

Del rounds the corner as I'm drying them. "That was a close one. I didn't know the Olsen twins were coming."

"Neither did I. Payton turned this into a girls' weekend." I use air quotes on the last two words.

She crosses her arms and leans against the wall. "You need to tell him no more surprises."

"No kidding." I toss my paper towel wad into the receptacle. "Obviously, I'm going to have to be more specific with him. He's very good at finding his way around the rules."

"I suspect he's also good at finding his way around you."

I frown at her. "What does that mean?"

The corners of her mouth tip up just so. "Do I really have to spell it out? The man is smitten with you. I'm the one watching, remember?"

Good thing she's at the arena. Everyone saw that one but her. "We're just playing our parts."

Del rolls her eyes. "Oh, doll, if you think that, you're more gone than I thought."

I give her a pointed look. "I'm not gone. I'm right here. One hundred percent."

She sighs and taps a finely manicured nail on the

counter. "Sweetheart, this vanity is more solid than you are right now. I've never seen you give in to a principal like you have this one. Makes me wonder what's going on behind closed doors. Incidentally, that includes shower doors."

Her laugh dances over the tile walls, echoing in an almost maniacal way. I never should have broken my resolve and told her about that. "We need a new plan."

"Come down with a bad case of the flu?"

"No, those two will just play nursemaid." I prop one hand on my hip and run the other through my hair.

"Love the new look." She eyes me suspiciously.

"You know I don't drive with a ponytail."

"Uh-huh. Whatever you say." Her teasing tone tells me she's not letting this go.

"You'll have to cover for me when I'm with them."

She pushes off the wall. "No worries. I brought my bag of tricks."

I point to her blonde wig. "Might want to go with something less obvious. Hockey players have a type."

She dons an innocent expression and shrugs. "Maybe that's part of my plan."

"Sounds like trouble to me."

Del shoots me a toothy grin. "When have I been anything but?"

# Chapter Sixteen

## PAYTON

A large crowd fills the arena tonight, but there's only one face that interests me at the moment. Following Luke, I leave the ice while the next line jumps over the boards to take their turn. As soon as I sit down, I'm searching for her. Even before I grab a water bottle to slake my thirst, my gaze makes a hungry sweep to find her.

And there she is, sitting by Sophie, smiling as she talks while her head moves back and forth, assessing everything that's happening around me. Our gazes lock, and, even though ice separates us, there's no mistaking the fire zinging between us.

A winded Ethan drops onto the player bench to my right and swats me on the arm. "If you stare at her any harder, your eyes are going to pop out and freeze into little round balls."

I grin while the others laugh. He's right, but I can't look away. She's wearing my jersey again, and after her teasing yesterday—all for the sake of believability, of course—she's occupied my head space nonstop. I want this to be real more than anything I've wanted before—except for hockey. But it's a close match.

She has to feel something for me. No way can someone fake a kiss like that. She blindsided me with that one. Here, I thought I had the upper hand, but she out-maneuvered me.

I'm just not sure she's willing to explore a real future with me. Lily's like a wild horse who belongs to no one. She'd more likely buck against all the "rules" as a hockey wife than go with the flow.

That thought freezes me in my mental tracks. Where did that come from? I haven't even dated her, and I'm already imagining what she'd be like as my actual wife?

I rip my gaze from where she's sitting with Mia and Sophie behind the net. "Then I'll die a happy yet sightless man."

Ethan snickers. "Just remember why we're here. We have a date with destiny and two teams to annihilate."

I shake my head. "You sound like Wade."

Elias leans across Ethan. "Did you see that last shot he blocked? Didn't know our T-man could bend like that. He pissed Jennings off good."

Sitting on my left, Luke joins our convo. "That guy's a goon. Don't let him get to you, right, Pay?"

"How can I forget?" I tap my side. "But I do plan to return the favor."

Luke bumps me with his shoulder. "Keep it friendly, man. We need you on the ice, not in the sin bin."

"Noted, Cap, but I'm not letting him do that to me again."

He raises his brows at me. "*We* won't let him do that again, right boys?" He makes eye contact with Ethan and Elias, our E-team, as we call them, for emphasis.

"Right, Cap," they say in unison.

Before I can get back out there, the horn blows, indicating the end of the period. As we make our way down the tunnel behind the other team, Jennings comes to a stop near the y-split, leading to the guest team locker room.

His smug expression makes him look like a pug, and his crossed arms complete his thug-like appearance. "Didn't expect to see you playing tonight, Maxwell. I hear those ribs kept you out of play for a while."

I pat my side. "Good as new. Guess you didn't hit me as hard as you thought."

Arms down, he fists his hands at his sides. "I can remedy that."

Luke steps in front of me and nudges me toward the locker room. "Playtime's over." He points at Jennings and growls, "Mess with my guy, and you mess with me. Got it?"

The briefest flash of doubt passes through his eyes, but then he presses his lips together. "See you on the ice."

Once we're in the locker room, I pull my shirt off and sit on the bench. "Great. Now he's really going to come after me."

"Don't sweat it, Pay. He'll get his."

Maybe, but now my guard is seriously up, which is probably what he was trying to do—get into my head. Even thoughts of Lily can't obliterate my trepidation about that goon, but I'm determined to play my best game.

At the start of the second period, we score a goal during the first minute, which sets the Ghost Pirates on the warpath. But Wade blocks every shot. Thankfully, Jennings hasn't tried to make good on his threat so far. Maybe he took Luke's counter to heart.

Then we hit third period, and things get...intense. With five minutes left, the Pirates shoot a goal, tying the score and taking the tension to a whole new level. On the drop, we win possession of the puck but then get an icing call. The Pirates win the next puck drop, but my line sticks to theirs like the tape on my twig.

Ethan gets the puck, then shoots it my way for a slap shot. Luke's positioned in front of the crease, ready to help bring the biscuit home while fighting off one of the Pirates' defensemen. I get into position to take a shot on goal when Jennings does his best to eliminate me with another body check. We both tumble to the ice, a tangle of legs, arms, and sticks. And the harder I try to detach from him, the more he hangs on to me. He's like a monkey who's decided I'm his favorite tree.

Just as I'm about to break free, he grabs my arm and pulls me down again, so I push him away. "Sod off!"

We both get back up on our blades, but he's in my face. "What's the matter, pretty boy? Can't handle a little scuffle? Maybe you should go back to your real job—a royal wannabe in Tillendale."

Everything in me locks up. I shove him against the boards. "You don't know what you're talking about."

"Bet I know more than you think," he sneers.

Suddenly, Luke's there, pushing his way between us. "Back off, Jennings, or I'll make you wish you'd never played today."

The whistle blows. I allow Luke to glide me back. Clearly having more to say, Jennings tries to follow, but Ethan won't let him move. Elias and two other Pirates get into a scuffle that brings the refs in, trying to separate the tangle of arms and fists.

Luke and I head toward the other side of the rink.

Coach meets us at the bench door. "You okay, Pay?"

"I'm all good. That bloke's a total nutter." If that plank

knows the truth about my family's new title, who else might know? And what if he decides he wants everyone to know as well? I may have more of a pickle on my hands than a grudge-holding doucher.

"I'll handle it. You just finish the game."

"You got it, Coach."

Except I wind up in the penalty box for two minutes. At least Jennings was penalized, too. We both hit the ice again with less than a minute left in the game and when the puck comes my way, I don't waste the chance—I wind up and let a clapper fly.

We win the game by one point. But I'm not happy. This felt more like a small win in the war I see declared in Jennings' face as he passes me on the way off the ice. This battle is far from over.

Brilliant. As if my life wasn't complicated enough.

---

The look on Lily's face when I walk out nearly makes me crack. But I do my best to appear more composed than I'm feeling at the moment. As far as my mates are concerned, Jennings is just nursing a grudge.

But I'd be a right idiot to think he'd keep my secret. It's only a matter of time before the truth comes out. Somehow, I have to get ahead of this thing. Maybe Lily will have some ideas on how to do that.

She beams a smile at me, which I assume is for the benefit of Sophie and Mia, who are standing there as well, the ever-dutiful WAGs, looking for Luke and Ethan to come out. I've seen them there so many times, half grateful I didn't have to be responsible for anyone else besides myself, and half wondering if one day there'd be someone there waiting for me.

Seeing Lily makes me wish everything about our fake relationship was real. That she could be there, waiting for me and looking so enticing in my jersey because she cared about me as her boyfriend. Or dare I say, her husband? Just not her principal.

She surprises me by wrapping her arms around me, lifting herself on tiptoe to whisper into my ear. "What happened out there?"

I pretend to nuzzle her neck so I can discreetly reply. "We need to talk."

A slight shiver runs over her, giving me some satisfaction that I can affect her like she has me. But it doesn't last long. The threat Jennings poses dominates my thoughts at the moment.

When she leans back, studying me with questions swirling in her eyes, I give a curt shake of my head, hoping she'll get the hint that this conversation needs to happen away from listening ears. Neither one of us misses the concerned glances Sophie and Mia keep darting our way.

Sophie braves the first question. "What's going on with that guy Jennings? Coach Markelson knows about it, right?"

Luke tries to nudge her toward the exit. "Let us deal with it, Soph."

Fists on her hips, she plants herself in place. "What did the therapist tell you and your dad last week about sharing burdens?"

Luke hangs his head. "Not sharing our problems shows a lack of trust."

"Right. You guys are a team on the ice, but we're all in this together off the ice." She turns toward me. "What can we do to help?"

Lily lifts her eyes to mine, revealing something akin to confusion or surprise. I'm not sure what she's thinking at the moment. And until I can tell her about this latest development, I'm just winging it with the rest of this crew.

I shrug. "Coach said he'd deal with it. But if I think of anything, I'll definitely let you know."

The others continue to chat as we make our way out to the bus waiting to take the team back to the hotel. Tomorrow, we're off to Atlanta for our game against the Gladiators.

I can tell Lily is slowing her pace to create some distance between us and the others. When they walk outside, she tugs me back. Now, only the glass doors separate us from the others. They won't be able to hear us, but they'll see everything if they bother to look.

"Tell me." Her words may be curt, but I don't miss the concern dripping from them.

"Jennings knows who I am."

Her eyes widen as she studies me. "You mean…?"

I nod. "He even clocked the name of my hometown. Fancy that."

She takes a deep breath and then lets it out. "I'll get Del on it."

Either I'm more tired than I realized, or this situation has pushed my frustration threshold to the limit. "What can she possibly do about it? Jennings is like a feral animal."

"Then we'll take him out."

I shoot my brows up. "You can't honestly mean…you're joking, right?"

She tucks her lips in as if she's trying not to smile. "Yes, you dork. We don't do things like that. But I will get Del to look into it in case there's more going on than meets the eye. And in my experience, there usually is."

The weight of this keeps growing. I run my hands down my face. "What if he tells the rest of my team? Or worse, leaks it to the press?"

She presses her hand against my chest, sending a wave of solace through me. "We'll figure it out as it comes, big guy. In the meantime, let Del and me do some digging and damage control if needed."

I cover her hand with mine and nod. On the ice, I know the fellas have my back, as I have theirs. That's held true off the ice as time has built friendships between us. But this feels deeper with Lily. Like I have a true partner running alongside me on the adventure that my life has become. She fills an empty place in me I didn't realize existed until now.

What am I going to do when she returns to England?

# Chapter Seventeen

## LILY

"Are you sure Payton's okay?" Sophie implores me with those giant eyes of hers from where she's sitting cross-legged in the middle of her bed. Mia's sprawled on the other one, yawning while trying to stay awake.

I'd have gladly gone to my room, but Sophie insisted I stop in for a quick chat. I know they're both worried about Payton and about me because they assume, as his wife, I must be worried out of my mind.

They wouldn't be too far off...I may not be married to Payton, but I am concerned. My job requires me to think ahead, plan accordingly, and move cautiously in all situations. But this fake marriage is hindering what I can do in the open.

At least Del can operate behind the scenes and investigate the situation. I sent her a cryptic message before we left the arena so she could look into how Jennings found out the truth about Payton, and if that could potentially include intel about his sister hiring a bodyguard for him.

"This thing with Jennings has him shaken up, I think. Does that happen often? Do players get these vendettas?"

Mia and Sophie exchange glances.

"Not to this degree." Mia pushes up on one arm, blinking at me with compassionate eyes. "I really hate that Payton's going through this. I just don't get what Jennings' issue is. It's weird."

Sophie nods thoughtfully. "It is. My Uncle Marty has some ties from his reporter days. I'll text him tomorrow and tell him about the situation. He might find something out."

Alarm bells go off in my head. If this uncle of hers digs too deep, he could wind up discovering Payton's secret, too. "Do you really think that's necessary?"

She shrugs. "Can't hurt."

Oh yes, it can. "Payton said Coach Markelson would handle it. Let's let that play out first."

Sophie's expression shifts to a slight frown. "What are you worried about, Lil?"

That's the photojournalist in her asking. I can tell by her tone and the way she holds her head, tilted a smidge to the side.

I need to be more careful. "I just don't want to upset Payton more than he already is. Or give this Jennings guy any more power in the situation. I ran into guys like him in the military all the time. They feed off power trips and like to be in control."

Mia squeaks. "You were in the military?" She glances to the side and says more to herself than me, "That would explain a lot."

Sophie grins with delight. "I knew there was more to your story! What was that like for you, being a woman and all?"

Deflection always works. Hopefully, she won't talk to her uncle. No need to add more fire to this growing blaze.

"Probably about what you can imagine. Mostly good. Somewhat challenging. I learned a lot there, but by the end of my tour, I knew it wasn't what I wanted." I pull my ponytail over my shoulder, running my hand over the smooth shafts. My fingers hit the fabric of my shirt, reminding me I'm still wearing Payton's jersey, and I didn't miss the way his eyes devoured me when he noticed.

"And what do you want, Lil?" Sophie asks this with a hint of mischief and a lot of curiosity.

Her question hits a deep and unexpected place in me. What do I want, really? I thought a permanent position on a security detail would check all my boxes, but now I'm not so sure anymore. The more I'm around Payton—and his friends—the less certain I am about my future. All this touchy-feely stuff is muddling with my head.

"Yeah, Lil, what do you want?" Mia is all sarcastic innuendo. "A tall drink of a British hockey player?"

I maintain my part with a coy smile. "Maybe."

But what I'd really like to say is *yes, yes, and oh yes*!

What is wrong with me?! Catching feelings for my principal violates one of our key rules. But the more time I spend with Payton, the harder it's getting. The sooner this assignment ends, the better.

Mia's phone chimes with a text. She reaches over to the nightstand and grabs it, appearing happy at first, then pensive. "Just Ethan saying good night." She raises concerned eyes to me. "He said Payton went for a walk. He's not doing great."

Without even thinking, I jump up from my chair. "I need to find him."

Sophie stands up. "Want us to go with you?"

I hold my hand up. "No, I should go alone."

Mia falls back on the bed. "Thank goodness. I don't think I can stay awake any longer."

Sophie rolls her eyes at her best friend, then shoots a compassion-filled gaze my way that tugs on my heart. "I'm here if you need me."

I know she means it, too. That longing hits me again but brings an epiphany with it this time. What if my feelings for Payton have more to do with wanting friends who really care—a community that has nothing to do with my job?

That makes much more sense than a desire to engage romantically with my client. I can work with that...and fix it. Del always says the best way to defuse worry is to identify the problem and make a plan. And the wave of relief I'm feeling confirms I'm on the right track. Next time I see Del, I'm going to thank her for those words of wisdom, even at the risk of watching her gloat.

"Thanks." I actually initiate the hug with Sophie this time. And Mia, well, I just pat her foot since she's already snoring.

The girls and I—wow, does that sound weird in my head —wound up on the same floor as the team but on different ends because the hotel was almost full. And Payton made sure I got a room with a single king-sized bed so I wouldn't have to play his wife round the clock.

First, I head to my room, texting Del for any updates while I walk down the hall. When I texted her earlier, she said she'd put a tail on Jennings. I know it's been less than two hours, but I'm still anxious to know if she's found anything out.

Lily: Anything yet?

Del: Anxious?

> Lily: More like impatient. Payton's not doing well with this.

Del: Interesting that you used the principal's name…

I stop in my tracks. She's right. Normally, it's either 'principal' or 'client.' We don't normally use names in our messages. I need to cool down and think.

> Lily: The principal is agitated and on the move.

Del: I'm still on the outside. No movement here, so he must be inside.

I give her message a thumbs-up and pocket my phone. When I turn down the hall to my room, I stop.

Payton's sitting on the floor, leaning against my door, head slumped to the side as if he's fallen asleep. I soften my steps until I reach him, then crouch down in front of him.

His right cheek is red and puffy and has a small scrape on it, probably from his scuffle with Jennings. A crease sits between his brows as though he's worried even while sleeping. Before I think about what I'm doing, I smooth my thumb over the indent.

His head jerks up. Sleepy eyes blink at me, then crinkle with a slow smile that makes every cell in my body vibrate as my heart misses a beat.

"What are you doing here, Payton? You should be asleep in your bed."

He rubs a hand down his face. "I couldn't sleep. Figured getting an update from you might help."

I rise with him as he gets to his feet. "Nothing yet. Del has a tail on Jennings."

"Sounds so mysterious." His door doze made his voice all husky and rumbly.

Along with a shrug, I pop my brows up in a casual manner for his benefit, although every cell in my body is vibrating. I learned early on that clients often take their cues from us when gauging the seriousness of a situation. "Just routine."

"In your world, maybe." One side of his mouth slants up in a sleepy yet sexy smile.

But he nailed it. Our worlds are so very different. And I don't see any way for them to possibly merge. Another reason to note what's growing between us as nothing more than simple attraction and my need for friends who aren't Del.

He waits as I unlock the door, then shuts it behind us. "Would you mind terribly if I stayed here tonight?" He points to the king-sized bed. "It's not like we haven't done this before."

I drag my gaze from the bed back to him while warring with myself. Part of me wants him to stay—that part needs to go someplace far, far away. "Won't you get in trouble?"

"I honestly don't care at the moment. But I'll set an alarm to return to my room before the rest of the blokes wake up."

We lock eyes as the air between us thickens with unspoken desire. I grab on to a hefty sense of reality—this isn't real. And it never can be.

Holding my phone up, I tilt my head toward the bed. "Go ahead and lie down. I need to discuss some things with Del."

That's not really true, although I do plan to send her a

vague message telling her Payton is okay and settled for the night. I just won't mention where he's sleeping. And I'm guessing he'll fall asleep before his head hits the pillow, thus avoiding any potential awkwardness.

He crawls under the covers, looking more like a sleepy child than a full-grown, deliciously muscled hockey player. I corral my thoughts back to a safe place and duck into the bathroom so as not to disturb him with the glow of my phone.

> Lily: The principal is secure and settled for the night.

> Del: Catch you on the flip side.

---

The sound of an alarm pops my eyes open. As a soldier, I learned not to react to sounds while sleeping because it could mean you don't stay awake, if you get my meaning.

Then I notice a weight around my waist, pinning me against something solid. I glance down. Payton's arm is draped over me, and the wall behind me is his chest. He's warm and curled against me. During the night, he must have spooned me in his sleep, and I didn't even wake up.

This man may be the end of my career if this keeps up.

Despite the persistent chiming of his alarm, he's not moving. The time on the bedside clock says it's five in the morning.

"Payton?" I whisper his name so as not to startle him awake. When he doesn't respond, I gently shake his arm.

"Huh?" His head pops up.

"Your alarm went off."

"Oh, right." He reaches behind him and taps his phone, but then, instead of getting up, he pulls me against him and snuggles in.

"Payton."

"Yeah." His voice vibrates against my shoulder.

"What are you doing?"

"Waking up."

I shift to my back as I try to pull away, but he tightens his arm around my midsection. Heat swirls there as he lifts his head and connects his sleepy gaze to mine.

It's just physical attraction. That's what I keep telling myself, but what about this warm rush of affection that's making my heart push against my chest like an oversized grapefruit? I want to smooth away the residual worry lines I see on his forehead and tell him everything will be okay. That I'll make sure of it.

"You're still wearing my jersey." His voice is rough with sleep, yet his eyes appear clear as they devour me.

By the time I left the bathroom last night, he was asleep. I didn't want to wake him by rummaging in my suitcase for my pajamas, so I slept in his jersey.

His gaze lowers to my mouth. As much as I want to give in to this, to feel his lips on mine, to let whatever's been building between us have its way, I know that's the worst thing that could happen right now. The last thing Payton needs is more controversy in his life.

I need a plan. And quick!

But it's oh so tempting. Too tempting...

The whole morning breath thing brings me back to reality. Using a move I learned in training, I flip him onto his back and jump out of the bed.

He stares up at the ceiling. "What just happened?"

"Nothing at all. And that's how it should be." I smooth

down my hair, then switch on a light, making us both squint.

Payton groans and covers his eyes. "I'm not sure I agree."

"Too bad, big guy. I don't make the rules." But I damn well have to uphold them.

I'm half asleep and probably sound like a woman about to lose her cool. But can you blame me? In bed with a hot hockey player who seems as attracted to me as I am to him? This is so not what I thought this assignment would be. I have to keep my eye on the prize like Payton keeps his on the puck.

A permanent position. That's my shot at a more normal life that includes friends like Sophie and Mia.

"You have to get back to your room, remember?"

Eyes still scrunched, he pinches the bridge of his nose. "Right."

While he sits on the edge of the bed putting his shoes on, I slip mine on. He heads for the door like a sleepy toddler. I stay close in case he needs steadying.

"Lily, I'm fully capable of walking back to my room on my own." He roughs out.

"I'm not so sure about that. Besides, I have to stay close, remember?"

Looking more vulnerable than I've ever seen him, he stops and stares at me. "I'm coming to prefer it that way."

Is he implying what I think he is? My heart pounds so loud in my ears that I almost have to raise my voice above a whisper so I can hear myself. "You're half asleep, Payton. You don't know what you're saying."

"I don't believe I've ever been more awake." His words are few, but he says the rest with his eyes, which are now imploring me to respond.

But I can't. I don't know what to say to him. That he may think he's cognizant of the situation, but he's out of his mind? That there's no way this could work between us, no matter how much I—we—might want it? Or, that the idea of falling in love with him terrifies me more than any of the threatening situations I've encountered thus far?

Because loving Payton Maxwell *would* be the most dangerous thing I've ever done.

His lips press together as he nods in resignation. "Understood."

I follow him silently past the elevators to the other end of the floor, where the rest of the team is staying. Just before he goes into his room, he pauses and gives me a curt wave.

And just like that, my heart squeezes like a proverbial schoolgirl with her very first crush.

If Payton only knew…he really and truly was.

# Chapter Eighteen

## PAYTON

"How's married life treating you, little brother?" Emalia stares at me from the small screen of my phone. I glance toward my bedroom door. On the other side, Lily is cleaning up the kitchen, which she insisted on doing because I made dinner. We ate in silence, just as we've done every evening after we got back from the away games.

If my sister only knew… "Frustrating as hell."

Since our return, Lily's been distant. She spends most of her time in her room now, writing those blasted reports she's required to do daily. But I think she's just avoiding me.

A laugh bubbles up as she throws her gaze upward. "Having trouble taking orders from your wifey?"

It's not the restrictions that are troubling me, but I won't explain that to my sister. "Keeping up this ruse is exhausting."

She makes a *tsking* sound. "You're the one who didn't want to tell your friends the truth."

"I know." But I *didn't* know, to be honest. Didn't know

how challenging this would be. Didn't know how difficult deceiving my friends would become. And I didn't know I could fall this hard for someone who's determined to keep me in the 'principal only' zone.

"By the way, why did I have to find out you were injured from the reports? You should have called me."

"Reports?" So that part's true...

Emalia pulls back in surprise. "Of course, darling. I want to know what's happening so I can keep an eye on my reckless brother."

"I'm not reckless," I say, sounding harsher than I intended.

She eyes me. "Those cracked ribs tell a different story."

"Don't blame me for that. I was simply playing hockey."

"That's my point."

I sigh. Even when we were kids and I told my sister I wanted to be a professional hockey player, she laughed and said I needed to consider a more 'worthy' path.

"I'm fine now, Em. Nothing to worry about."

Her somewhat peeved expression softens, and the vulnerable girl I remember from the past peeks out. "I do worry about you, Payton. You're my brother. Mum does, too, by the way. You should call her before she finds out what happened from some other source."

The knot in my stomach intensifies. I squeeze my eyes shut as I work up the courage to tell her about my encounter with Jennings.

"What is it, Payton? You're making that face." She frowns at me.

"What face?"

"The one you always make when you have something difficult to tell me."

I take a deep breath. "The bloke who slammed me during the game knows who I really am."

Emalia leans closer to the camera. "You mean...?"

I nod. "He suggested I go back to my real job as a royal wannabe in Tillendale."

She appears thoughtful. "Though indelicate, he has a point."

"Emalia!" I draw her name out like I used to when we fought as children.

With a twist of her shoulders, she poses for dramatic effect. "Sorry, not sorry?"

"This could be terrible. What if he leaks it to the press?" I growl.

Worry flits through the same blue eyes we inherited from our mother. "There's a good chance he will, Payton. Perhaps you should drop the facade and tell everyone the truth. That's one way to get ahead of it and lessen the potential damage. Or, better still, you could just use it as an excuse to come home."

She's right about preempting this, but I've no idea how. Yet.

"I'll mull it over."

"The part about telling the truth or coming home?"

I shoot her a scathing look. "Don't even go there."

"Fine. I'll leave it be." She raises her hands in surrender, then hesitates. "By the way, what do you think of Lily?"

Every nerve in my body goes into full alert. What did Lily share in those reports? I school my expression to stay neutral. "She's professional, diligent, and thorough."

And stronger than she looks. I won't mention that, though. But she's also stunning, sexy as hell, and challenging in the best of ways. Should I add that she has a grip on my heart that may prove fatal to my future love life if I can't have her?

She studies me, then her eyes widen. "You fancy her!"

I snort. "I don't know what you're talking about."

Emalia points at me. "There. I see it in your face. Has something happened between you two?"

"No! Of course not." At least that's the truth, even though I wish it weren't.

"Admit it. You find her attractive." My sister's like a forward digging for a rebound in the crease. Relentless.

"I'd be a buffoon not to, but as I said earlier, she's the epitome of professionalism."

"Good. I'm glad to hear she's immune to your charms."

I'm not. Quite the opposite. Somehow, I have to figure out a way to up my game. Or use my charms, as my sister calls them, to better advantage.

Judging by my sister's mysterious smile, something about this pleases her. "Why are you so interested in her?"

"I like her. We seemed to click when I interviewed her. I'm considering offering her a permanent position on my security detail."

A permanent position?

In England?

Thousands of miles away from me?

Is that why Lily seems so determined to reject my every flirtation unless we're pretending? I'm almost certain she's as attracted to me as I am to her, but she's as elusive as a panther, and as strong, considering the way she flipped me over on the bed like a WWE wrestler. Although, I will defend myself by saying I was half asleep.

"Does she know this?"

"I mentioned I'd be looking for a replacement for John.

He's retiring next month, so the timing is perfect for both of us."

A little too perfect and quite the quandary for me. I run a hand over my mouth and mumble, "Indeed, it is."

"What was that?" Her brows pinch together.

With a shake of my head, I wave it off. "Nothing, sis. Just agreeing with you."

Do I try to convince Lily that the spark between us is worth pursuing or let it fizzle so she can pursue this potential position on my sister's security detail? Knowing my sister, she'll make it clear Lily is off limits, which will make going home for visits, at the very least, awkward.

"Payton, are you all right? You look haggard. Are you getting enough rest?"

I blink back to reality. "I'm fine, Mother."

"That's not funny."

Squelching my grin fails. What's funny is how much her glare resembles our mum, but I definitely won't tell her that either. Honestly, I should know better than to poke that bear, but somehow I can't resist. Teasing my sister has always been one of my favorite things to do.

"Sorry, not sorry?"

"Ugh, you're such a brother."

"I love you too, sis."

---

After I finish my conversation with Emalia, I head to the kitchen where Lily's washing the pots by hand. I love that she remembered they don't go in the dishwasher. Her attention to detail is one of the many things I find so fascinating about her.

I grab a towel and dry the one sitting on the drainboard.

She continues to soap up the matching lid. "I can take care of that."

"I don't mind." As I reach for the next pot, her hand brushes mine. Barely a touch, but my body reacts like she just leveled me into the boards.

Heat. Awareness. A sharp, almost painful jolt of something I shouldn't feel but do, anyway. She pulls away, pretending as if it didn't happen. As if I didn't feel it. Like *she* didn't feel it.

And maybe I should do the same. Be sensible and ignore the way my pulse is still hammering. Act like the professional I'm supposed to be. There are rules, after all, and she follows them as if they're stitched into her bloody DNA.

For the first time, I don't give a damn.

Not in the reckless way. Not in a complete 'let's throw caution to the wind' way. This isn't just attraction, isn't just something I can ignore and move on from. She's under my skin, in my head, and has taken permanent residence in my heart. I couldn't shake her even if I tried.

So maybe she's right about the rules. Maybe I should be the one to let this go.

But screw it. I don't want to.

"How was your chat with your sister?" As she places the pot on the drainboard, she tries to steer clear of touching me, which is almost as satisfying as watching her try to avoid what I know she's already feeling.

But her question gives me pause. Is she asking out of genuine concern, or is this her subtle way of finding out if my sister mentioned her?

"Fine. I told her what happened. She thinks I should either come clean or go home."

Lily turns off the water and faces me. "What do you want to do, Payton?"

Right now, I want to kiss her and explore her lips with mine. To feel her settle against me as if I were her safe place because she's fast becoming mine. I want to know what it's like to hold her and wake up to her smile every morning, to wash dishes with her in the evening.

I want this to be real because I'm in love with her.

The realization knocks the breath out of me almost as much as my run-in with Jennings. I clear my throat as I attempt to breathe normally. "I'm hoping for a third option."

She considers me a moment, then takes the dish towel from me to dry her hands. "Sounds like you have some thinking to do."

"I suppose I do."

"Then I'll let you get to it." She leaves the kitchen, heading toward her room.

"More reports to write?"

She stops short of her door and turns around. "That was my plan. Did you need me for something?"

*Need you…want you…love you…*

Great. I even sound like a sop in my thoughts. I slip my hands into the pockets of my trackies and casually close the distance between us. "Actually, I was thinking I'd like to go out to dinner tomorrow evening since there's no game. Can you and your sidekick make that happen?"

"I'll talk to *Del* about it." Her emphasis is clear, but I don't miss the way the corners of her mouth tip up ever so slightly.

"Good. Then it's a date."

"More like an arrangement."

I hold my hands out. "Whatever you want to call it."

Her brows dip with her frown. "Good night, Payton."

"Good night, Lily." I stand there, watching her until the last moment our gazes connect before she shuts her door.

She thinks this is impossible. That we can't be anything more than this, but she's wrong.

And I'm determined to prove it to her.

# Chapter Nineteen

## LILY

I can't believe Del agreed to this. When I told her what Payton requested last night, I expected her to say absolutely not. Putting the principal unnecessarily out into the open is usually a hard 'no.' But since the latest suspect turned out to be an obsessed royal watcher who thought she could get a face-to-face with Dame Maxwell if she implied knowledge about their cousin's demise, Del said there was no imminent threat.

Although I agree, going out like this with Payton feels more like a date than a job. I still insisted on driving, but as soon as we walked into the Turtle Tide, he shifted his demeanor and became attentive and charming.

When he placed his hand on my lower back to guide me to our table, I thought I would melt on the spot like an ice sculpture on the beach. He even pulled out my chair for me, which was sweet, until I told him I needed to sit on the other side so I could keep eyes on the main door.

And now we're sitting at a table for two that includes a votive candle nestled in sand inside a cute glass holder resembling a seashell. Mellow yacht music plays in the background, which perfectly complements the ocean view out the windows to my left.

Payton runs his forefinger and thumb around his mouth again like he did at the airport the first time we met and at the unexpected team spaghetti dinner. I've never seen him do this any other time.

He's staring at me now. "Need any recommendations?"

"What?" I blink back to reality.

"From the menu." He points to the simple two-sided laminate still sitting untouched in front of me.

"Oh, I'm sure I can find something I like." I lift the menu, skimming it as I periodically check the entrance.

Payton follows my line of sight, then faces me. "Are you expecting someone?"

I smile for the first time since we left his apartment. "No, just part of my training."

Understanding dawns on his face. "Ah, ever watchful for danger."

"That's my job," I sing-song. A little reminder can't hurt. I don't know what's going through Payton's mind, though I have my suspicions, but he needs to understand that's all this is for me. All it can ever be.

A job.

Which could lead to an even better one if I keep my focus on why I'm here—to protect my principal against any clear or potential threat.

I finish skimming the menu. "I think I'll try the burger."

Payton pulls his brows together. "The Turtle Tide is known for its seafood, which they bring in daily from that very ocean you see out the window."

After holding my hands up, I drop them to my thighs in a light slap. "What can I say? I'm going for land food."

He lets out a chuckle that sends an unexpected shot of pleasure through me. "Surely we can do better than that."

"Why? I'm perfectly happy with a burger."

"We Brits are known for our fish and chips, but I hate to admit this chef might just outdo us."

"I didn't like them there, so I'm probably not going to like them here either."

"So, you don't care for seafood?"

"Not really." I scrunch up my face, debating on telling him how I got a serious case of food poisoning from a spoiled shrimp once, but decide to forgo the gory details. That kind of conversation doesn't fit well in a restaurant.

He sighs. "What about a grilled mahi-mahi sandwich? That's close to a burger."

The man will not let this go. "Fine. I'll try it. But if I don't like it—"

"I promise I'll order you a burger." He concedes with a gallant dip of his chin.

"With cheese," I counter, just to bring the point home.

"Fine." He slaps his menu onto the side of the table.

I do the same. "Fine."

Our server appears, takes our selections and the menus, then darts off to get our drinks. Payton fiddles with unwrapping his silverware and placing his napkin on his lap. I imagine his parents went to great lengths to teach him proper etiquette, especially considering their ties to royalty, but the whole hockey thing still throws me.

His refined and sophisticated side peeks out when he's not playing hockey. And on the ice, he's like this sexy power-house who owns it. I've found most of my assignments mundane, sometimes boring, but I find Payton's dichotomy fascinating.

Leaning forward, I fold my arms on the table. "Do you see yourself doing something else down the road?"

"Does it bother you that I'm a hockey player?" Mischief dances in his blue eyes.

"No, not at all. But there's a time limit to it, right? At some point, you'll retire."

"True, but hopefully, that won't be for a long time. Barring injuries, of course. Although I will say having my bodyguard help me shower will remain a highlight in my career."

The heat in his gaze matches the warmth rising from my neck to my cheeks. I take a sip of the ice water our server left on the table. "Can we forget that ever happened?"

"I'd rather you didn't."

"Payton!"

"What?" His attempt at innocence is comical.

I swing my gaze back and forth to make sure no one's within earshot, then lower my voice just shy of a whisper. "Stop it. I'm not your wife. I'm your bodyguard."

"Yes, I know. You remind me constantly." He grinds out.

We stare at each other as if in an impasse while the heat between us rises hot enough to cook our own food. If this keeps up, I may have to ask for a fake divorce just to keep my shot at that sweet position with his sister's security team.

I lean forward. "Why did you insist on this facade in the first place?"

His expression turns sheepish as he sighs. "I was half joking."

"What do you mean?"

"When Emalia wants me to do something I don't want to, I will suggest the most preposterous thing to make her back off."

"And this works?"

"Usually."

"But not this time."

He lets out a self-deprecating laugh. "No, but I have to admit, it's working out better than I expected."

The man really knows how to turn on the charm.

Our server returns and places our food in front of us. Payton doesn't touch his. Just stares at me, waiting to see if I'll like his recommendation, which I'm almost positive I won't.

I rarely roll my eyes. In my line of work, that's a tell. But this time, I'm willing to make a bold statement about how frustrating this man is. I even make a grunting sound so he'll know just how annoyed I am before taking a bite.

Oh. My. Word. Tangy flavors cascade over my tongue in waves as I chew. Then, the full impact of the grilled, meaty fish hits me like a burger would. I suppress a moan of pleasure in time, but clearly not my expression because he shoots me the smuggest grin I've ever seen.

"See? I was right, wasn't I?"

I wipe my mouth with my napkin. "Fine. Yes, you were right."

He slants his gaze upward, appearing thoughtful. "I think if I were to tally a score, I would be in the lead."

Maybe my last observation was wrong. Blast! That makes him right again.

"Don't get cocky." I take another bite of my sandwich, doing my best to ignore him.

"You're taking my fun away." Even when he pretends to pout, he's disarming.

And a master at redirection. I'm only now realizing he changed the subject by bringing up our shower together.

*Observation #7: Payton uses redirection when he's uncomfortable with the conversation.*

I banish the memory before my face turns red again. "Hockey is clearly fun for you, so what's your *fun* plan after hockey?"

He drops his gaze. "I hadn't thought about it, to be honest. Right now, I'm just focused on the game and being the best forward I can. For me and my team."

The way he says *my team* makes me ache all over as if I'm missing out on something. I draw circles in my ketchup with a french fry. "The camaraderie you guys have is really amazing."

His gaze turns penetrating as he studies me. "It is. I imagine you and Del have a similar dynamic."

I bark out a laugh. "Del is...well, let's just say Del is all about Del."

"But you spend a fair bit of time together, don't you?"

"Some, yes. And we're roommates. But we're not home much, and we're rarely on the same assignment."

His expression turns more serious. "What about Sophie? You two seemed to have hit it off quite well. She lights up whenever she sees you."

No, he can't go there. I can't let him create ties and connections. That will make returning home more difficult.

"Just part of my job, big guy. You created this scenario, and I'm doing my best to make it work. Speaking of which, how are we going to handle your next out-of-town game? I don't think we can pull off another girls' weekend so soon."

"Good point." He drags a hushpuppy through his tartar sauce, then pops it into his mouth, thinking as he chews.

"There's always sleuth mode." I toss my now soggy fry to the side.

"And that would be?"

"Del and I stay close, but not visible. But there's a problem."

"What's that?"

"I can't be in two places at once. Sophie wants to do another planning session for the fundraiser while the team is away. I'll have to make an excuse to get out of it."

A shadow of a smile skirts his face. "Does that mean you'll be in the same hotel?"

"Yes. Close but not seen."

"Of course." His disappointment is obvious.

Why does that send a migration of butterflies through my midsection? "As far as Sophie and Mia know, I've worked in security in the past. I'll tell them I have an interview for a remote position that sends me on location sometimes, which I can leverage as needed."

"Sounds believable."

"Good. Then we have a plan."

He nods but says nothing, appearing distracted. We finish our meal in silence until we're about to leave.

Ever the gentleman, Payton rises before I do and holds his hand out for mine. Do people really do that today? Obviously, he does. Must be part of that etiquette training he undoubtedly had to endure. But he wears it so well.

I comply to placate him, then regret it right away. Or rather, I should, but how can I when he tightens his hold, sending waves of delicious shivers over my body? But it's more than that. I feel safe with Payton. Protected. Which is so foreign to me. I'm the one who's supposed to keep him secure. Not the other way around.

Our eyes connect for the briefest moment until his gaze drops to my lips, and before I can stop it, mine drop to his. One side of his mouth lifts, revealing his sexy dimple that begs me to touch it. But I resist. I have to…but it's right there, calling to me.

He continues to hold my hand as we walk through the restaurant to leave. But instead of heading to the car, he leads me down a path toward the beach.

I tug my hand from his more out of self-preservation than an attempt to keep things professional. His touch makes me think of things I know I can't have. Not with him, anyway.

"Where are you going?"

Without stopping, he points toward the ocean where the sun is starting its descent. "Perfect timing for a sunset."

"That's not part of the plan."

He stops and faces me, his expression imploring. "Mango Key Beach is known for its soft white sands and blazing sunsets. You can't go back to England without having seen one."

I scan the perimeter around us and toward the restaurant. A scattered few people walk along the shore, but not too many to navigate or avoid. And he's right. The sky is ablaze with iridescent pinks, purples, and blues in a breathtaking display.

"Fine, but not for long."

"Not a problem. Sunsets last only a few minutes."

I tug my phone out of my back jeans pocket. "Just let me update Del so she knows why we're not heading toward the car."

Lily: Principal wants to watch the sunset.

Del: We're back to using principal again?
Hmm, was it something I said? Or he
said…?

174

She follows this with a kissing emoji that makes me want to toss my phone into the sand. The woman is downright incorrigible lately. With a snort, I pocket my phone, ignoring her comment. Sometimes, I wonder if she's trying to encourage something happening between Payton and me, but that would be ridiculous. She would never do that. At least, I don't think she would. She *is* a bit of a wild child.

"Problem?"

I catch up to where he's standing, shaking my head. "Nope." I pop my 'p' for emphasis. "We better get to it, though. The light's fading."

He takes my hand again.

"Why are you doing that?"

"Believability, remember? Someone we know might be here or recognize me. Our fans are very generous with their attention." He chuckles.

I should argue that's a great reason NOT to take a walk out in the open like this. But I want to see the sunset and the feel of Payton's skin against mine is making it difficult to think and make good decisions.

*Observation #8: Payton Maxwell is trouble.*

# Chapter Twenty

I think the memory of Lily watching the sunset will live in my head for the rest of my life. As she took in the shifting colors and reflections on the water, I memorized every facet of her. The delicate slope of her forehead and how her nose tips up at the end. That adorable indent above her chin, just below her full bottom lip that I can imagine kissing and nipping until she sighs.

Never has a woman intrigued me the way she does. It took great effort not to pull her against me and make my imaginings a reality. Didn't help that she continued to let me hold her hand as we walked the beach. I suppose I can only blame myself for that.

At one point, when the sunset reached its peak, blazing the sky like a bonfire, she squeezed my hand. But I'm not sure she realized what she did because of how enraptured she appeared.

Now we're back in the safety of my apartment, and I'm trying to think of a way to prolong our evening together.

I'd like to believe tonight helped set a precedent for the

possibility of us, but she's so difficult to read. I've never met anyone so controlled and downright stubborn. Most likely part of her job, but the way she challenges me…this crazy dynamic between us is driving me crazy.

Somehow, I have to convince Lily that this attraction we share is just a precursor to something bigger. Something better than either of us has known before, I suspect. If she'd only give it a chance.

Give me a chance.

"Can I interest you in a game, perhaps?" I'm loathe to let our evening end just yet. Her reports can surely wait another hour or two. It's not even that late yet.

"I'm not really a game person."

"We can watch something on the telly?"

She shakes her head. "Not a TV person either."

"Don't care for it?"

"Don't have the time, usually."

Well, all work and no play haven't made Lily a dull girl, but I can't imagine a life without fun and adventure. However, I do recognize the irony since my job is *playing* a game.

"What do you do for fun?"

Her gaze shifts to some faraway place in her mind. "You'd laugh at me."

I'd fully expected her to say nothing or that it was none of my business, but this…this feels like a door she's allowed to open just enough for me to catch a glimpse of the Lily inside.

"What if I promise not to laugh?"

Her supple lips lift on one side. "You have to do better than that."

"Right. Then how about a secret for a secret? You tell

me what you do for fun, and I will tell you something I've never told anyone before."

She side-eyes me. "Not even your friends?"

"Nope." I pop my 'p' like she does.

A smile slides onto her face and grows. "You swear you won't back out on me?"

With a hand on my chest, I muster as much emotion into my voice as possible. I want Lily to trust me. "I promise I will never back out on you."

A myriad of emotions swirl over her expression so quickly, I'm lost in identifying any of them.

She gives her chin a subtle lift. "I watch videos of cats and otters on TikTok."

Rolling my lips inward, I do my best not to laugh, no matter how adorable I find this. "And puppies, too, I suppose."

Her expression turns dead serious. "No. They make me suspicious."

"Suspicious? How can a cute little puppy make you suspicious?"

"They're too happy. Now tell me yours."

I run my fingers around my mouth. This will either endear her to me forever or shatter my chances with her. "When I was a teenage boy, I nicked one of my sister's romance novels."

Forget the smile. She's all out laughing now. "Why?!"

Why did I choose this secret to tell her? I hold my hands out in surrender. "I was a teenage boy who wanted to understand what all the fuss was about. I never expected to actually enjoy them."

Her eyes widen. "You still read them?!"

I spin around and head toward the kitchen. "I'm in the mood for ice cream. Care to join me?"

If it were any other woman, I'd be concerned at how she's studying me with one side of her bottom lip tucked between her teeth like I'm a piece of chocolate she's craving. Or that hamburger she wanted.

Did I just discover a way in to Lily's heart? Is my bodyguard actually a bit of a romantic?

In that case, I'll go with sweets. "I have cappuccino explosion *and* heavenly hash."

I take both containers out of the freezer and hold them up.

She runs her tongue over her bottom lip, which kills me to watch. "Both?"

"Ah, I see. You're an all-or-nothing kind of woman." The very best kind, in my book.

"If you say so." She sits on one of the barstools.

I bring two bowls from the cabinet and set them on the counter by the ice cream cartons. After dropping a scoop of each flavor into both, I slide one over to Lily and hand her a spoon.

"Thank you."

"You're most welcome, luv."

A slight blush rides up her cheeks as she focuses on her first bite.

We Brits call everyone 'luv,' but I know Americans find it odd sometimes, considering its counterpart here in the States. But I've already made peace with the fact that I'm in love with this woman, so I will let her think it's a British quirk, but I will mean it in its truest sense until I can express it in truth to her. I hope that if she hears it enough, she'll start to believe how very lovely and *worthy of love* she is.

I settle onto the stool next to hers with my bowl in hand. And then an idea strikes me. "Practice ends early tomorrow.

Can we get permission from your handler to go to the aquarium?"

She laughs and chokes at the same time. "My handler? I'm not a spy."

"Sorry. Your Del, then. School's back in session, so I'd imagine crowds will be light. Think she'll approve?"

A soft giggle rewards me. "I'll run it by her. Why do you want to go?"

"It's one of Sarabella's main attractions."

"I thought the *soft white sands and blazing sunsets* were." She mimics my accent quite well.

"Those too. But there's something at the aquarium that I think you'll rather enjoy."

"What?"

"I don't want to ruin the surprise." I smile at her, admire her.

After she finishes her ice cream, she stands up and places her bowl in the basin. "I have reports to do."

I follow behind her toward her bedroom.

She stops just shy of her door and turns around. "What are you doing, Payton?"

"Walking you to your door." I slip my hands into my trouser pockets.

"Why? We're already inside."

"If those romance books taught me anything, it was that you always walk the damsel in distress to her door to make sure she's safe."

Lily's eyes appear almost misty as if my words hit an emotional place in her. "I'm not a damsel in distress, though."

Perhaps, but I know what I just witnessed. Something tender and vulnerable peeked out just long enough for me to catch a glimpse, and I'm determined to see more.

She lets me touch her cheek. "I wouldn't be so sure about that."

# Chapter Twenty-One

## LILY

I AM NOT a damsel in distress.

Payton lives in some mysterious romantic fantasy he's devised from his dalliances with romance books. After tossing and turning most of the night, that's the only explanation I could come up with for his behavior. And he's mistaken me for his love interest in this make-believe world.

I admit, part of me wants to live and dwell in this mysterious place, too. A big part of me.

Okay, ALL of me.

But I can't entertain thoughts like this. Too much is riding on the line for me. Yet once again, Del gave the all clear. And when I questioned it, because this is way out of protocol, she reiterated there was no imminent threat or danger.

That's what she thinks. I'm the one in danger, and the threat is Payton.

I skim my conversation with Del again, convinced something is off. I've never seen her act so unprofessional. But since she's cleared our excursion to the aquarium, who am I to argue? That's subtle speak for, I don't *want* to argue, although I should.

She even had the nerve to suggest I wear that sundress she insisted I bring. I shot that one down, reminding her this isn't a vacation. It's an ASSIGNMENT. I used all caps, too.

I am so going to rip one on Del when I get home later.

Again, acting as if this were a date, Payton purchased both our tickets, ignoring me when I tried to argue.

He hands me mine. "Shall we give it a go?"

I plaster a smile on my face. He seems so intent on showing me the nuances of Sarabella that I don't have the heart to tell him that living sea life interests me about as much as the cooked variety. Although, he proved me wrong with that grilled mahi-mahi sandwich. My mouth waters just thinking about it.

"Ready if you are."

As we walk toward the first display—a school of fish swimming round and round in a circular aquarium— Payton puts his arm around me, resting his hand on my hip. Even through my jeans, the warmth of his palm radiates through the fabric and sears my skin, making me want to press closer to him. Instead, I move out of his reach, using the ruse of wanting to see the jellyfish to our right.

We do this dance at almost every aquatic feature in the place. And the more he does it, the less I want to run away. It's so tempting to just lean in...give in to these feelings swirling my insides into goo. Much like that iridescent jelly-fish I saw earlier.

So jelly. So pretty. Yet painful when stung.

That's what I'm afraid of. Whenever I allowed myself to get attached to someone or someplace, I wound up hurt. Things never seemed to work out for me, so I kept a certain amount of separation as a protective measure. So far, it's served me well, but Payton is the unexpected threat I never saw coming.

"Let's take a break before we finish the rest." He points toward a concession area. "Fancy some ice cream?"

In what world can a guy eat as much ice cream as he does and still look so ripped? "Sure, why not."

Payton gets a chocolate milkshake, which tempts me at first. Until I see they have soft serve, which is my favorite and often hard to find.

As we sit down at a small parlor table, he leans over and takes a large bite of my ice cream. His blue eyes dance with mischief, and there's a smear of chocolate on the corner of his mouth that I'm tempted to wipe away with my thumb.

Or my mouth... "Thief! Who bites ice cream?" I point to the teeth marks.

He laughs, then holds his shake toward me. "All's fair in love and war."

I don't like the implication of his raised brow. What exactly is he implying?

To get even, I nab the shake from him and take a long drink, all the while watching the fascinating shift in his expression as he watches me before handing it back. "Fair enough for you?"

"More than fair." Mischief sparkles in his blue eyes that mirror the ocean themes surrounding us. Then he wraps his lips around the straw, deliberately reminding me that mine were there just moments ago.

My insides combust.

I need a dousing of cold water more than the fish we're observing. How much more of his flirtations can I take before he wears me down? And Sophie thought he was shy? I'm mentally shaking my head at that one.

"Maybe we should leave now."

He sobers quickly. "If I promise to behave, will you let me take you to one more exhibit? I think you'll love it the most."

I don't see how another exhibit could rival the one he's been displaying, but I'm curious about what he thinks I'll *love*. Is it me, or is he using that word a lot?

"Fine. But no more of this." I wag my finger at his face.

"Of what? I'm simply drinking my shake."

"Sure you are, big guy." I finish my cone on the way to the trash can and dump the wrapper and napkin.

Payton drops his cup in the receptacle, then grabs my hand and drags me along at a quick pace. I'm tall, but he's taller and has a wider gate. Still, I manage to keep up.

"And here we are." He sweeps his hand toward a display resembling a miniature playland made of rock-like structures. Built-in slides lead to the water pooling below. I sweep my eyes over the twenty-foot expanse and stop when I notice a ball of fur rolling around the upper level.

No, two balls of fur.

Otters.

My gaze leaps to his, and then I realize my mouth is hanging open. He laughs, but not at me. More like he's delighted that I'm surprised—that *he* surprised me.

I step closer to the glass, mesmerized. I've only ever seen these adorable creatures in videos. Three more join the others in their frolic. One slides down and swims over to a small platform near the glass to my left. He sticks his paws out two holes I didn't notice before.

Payton brings his face close to my ear, flooding my senses with his woodsy scent. "He wants you to hold his paws."

Riddled with disbelief, I look at him for confirmation. "We're allowed to touch them?"

"They love it. See?" He bends over and rubs the otter's paws between his thumbs and forefingers. The little guy lifts his head, squealing with delight.

I nudge Payton over. "Let me!"

His chuckle fades into the background as I crouch down to eye level with this adorable furry animal and rub his paws. He mews his cute plaintive noises again, making me grin so big my cheeks hurt.

The otter darts away, only to be replaced by another sticking her paws through the openings. I say 'she' only because of the way she's batting her eyes at me. She lets out a high-pitched squeal, then pushes her nose against the glass and licks it.

"I think she likes you." Payton's still smiling at me as if this were the best day of his life.

It just may well be mine.

The thought makes my eyes burn with unshed tears. Payton did this for me. He took my simple pastime of watching otters and turned it into something special and meaningful to me. No one's ever done anything like that for me before.

Otter-girl wiggles away to join the others in the pool, splashing and playing with a ball while I keep my face toward the glass, giving me time to compose myself.

Payton crouches down next to me. "You all right?"

"Yeah, sure." I pretend to be fascinated by the otters tumbling and holding onto each other in the water, which I am. But I just need a few more seconds to get myself together. I'm supposed to be on the job here, not bawling over furry critters and kind gestures.

The most thoughtful and generous I've ever experienced...

*Observation #9: Payton undoes me with his charm and thoughtfulness.*

"Lily." He takes my shoulders and turns me to face him, then tips my chin up with his forefinger, which forces me to look at him. "You don't have to hide yourself from me."

I swallow. The concern in his expression hardly compares to what I see in his eyes. Something more than attraction. Something deeper. Something I've never seen before. "This...I...thank you."

He slides his hand from my chin up my jawline to cup my face. "My pleasure, luv."

Is this what being his girlfriend would be like? Not that I've had any experience in that department. A few dates here and there, but I couldn't really cultivate anything serious because my job takes me out of the city or country for weeks at a time. When I'm on the job, I'm all in. There's no room for distractions or things like maintaining a relationship.

Besides, I've never met anyone before that made me want to pursue something serious or even long for it. Until Payton...

A toddler squeals next to us as the otters swim close to the glass, startling me back to the fact that he's still touching my cheek and staring at me with sparkling blue eyes that threaten to drown me with his charm.

"Guess I should let others have some otter time." I stand up, feeling more like a shy schoolgirl around Payton than his bodyguard. No one's ever unsettled me to the degree that he does.

He remains close, studying me with quick glances he thinks I won't notice, but I do.

What I find most disconcerting is how he sees me. I'm so used to staying in the background, making myself as unnoticeable as possible, because that's what I learned to do to survive in the system. And I've used that skill well as a bodyguard.

But Payton doesn't let me stay hidden. It's like he wants to make sure I see the world and that it sees me out front and center.

And I haven't a clue what to do with that.

# Chapter Twenty-Two

## PAYTON

I think I'm getting through to Lily—that moment at the otter display...such a little thing. Yet I never expected she'd wind up so moved by a few furry animals frolicking in the water—moved to tears she didn't want me to see.

But I did see. I witnessed a side of her today that makes me ache to embrace her, to hold her close and whisper reassuring words in her ear about how I've completely fallen for her and want her in my life. But she's like a skittish wild animal, ready to flee if I approach too fast. Or flip me like a pancake, like she did in her hotel room.

I've never felt this way for anyone before, so trust me when I say I'm fully out of my element, and I'm sensing she's out of hers, too. However, I'm still determined to break through Lily's tough exterior and see the woman inside. I suspect her years in the foster system taught her to keep the truest part of herself hidden, which breaks my heart and solidifies my conviction to reach hers all at once.

I glance toward her bedroom door from the kitchen, where I'm prepping dinner. When we returned from the aquarium, she retreated to her room, using those blasted reports as an excuse again. Either she's still avoiding me, or I'm going to have to berate my sister for being such a taskmaster.

Finally, and with perfect timing, Lily emerges from her room. I have dinner prepared—a simple fare we can eat in front of the telly because I have one more surprise planned for her today.

She strolls over to the kitchen. "We could have just ordered pizza."

I sprinkle a handful of cilantro on the chicken and rice bowls I threw together. "This is also easy, yet healthier."

"How could I forget? Mr. Hockey Player must keep himself in excellent shape." She eyes me appreciatively. Am I picking up a flirtatious tone to her words?

I ease my smile up on one side. "Flattery will get you everywhere, luv."

"I wasn't trying to flatter you." She backpedals in the most delightful way.

"You implied it, then."

"I did not." She takes the bowl I offer her and sits at the counter.

Enjoying her flustered expression, I head toward the living room. "I thought we'd eat in here tonight and watch something on the telly."

"Did you forget that I'm not really into watching television?"

"Not at all. This is more like a series of clips than a program."

She joins me on the couch. "Okay, I'll give it a shot."

I turn on the telly, which I left paused on a compilation of cat videos and press play.

At first, Lily says nothing. She's not eating either. Just

stares at the first video of a kitten hissing at a cucumber with its back arched and fur standing on end.

But then she swivels her head and studies me. "What are you doing, Payton?"

I swallow the bite of chicken I was chewing. "I must say, these came out rather well. The Mexican cheese makes all the difference."

"Payton."

"Yes, luv?"

She puts her bowl on the coffee table, takes a controlled breath, and dons the expression she wears when she means business. "This isn't real. Any day now, your sister will let us know they've closed your cousin's case and determined his death was an accident. At which point, I will go back to England. You can tell your friends we didn't work out, or I changed my mind and wanted to go home, or that you realized you made a mistake and sent me off. Whichever story works."

"Can a case ever be truly settled without a body?" I can tell I'm pushing her to the limit by the way she tenses her mouth as if she's holding something back.

She lets out a long breath as she looks away. "That's a reality you just may have to accept."

"Agreed, but that doesn't help me feel any safer." I'm risking my manhood here, sounding so pathetic, but the only way I know how to appeal to her is through her role as my bodyguard. "And considering the threat Jennings could pose, now that he knows who I am, I find myself in need of protection. Possibly indefinitely."

She visibly bristles. "You can't do that."

"Do what, luv?"

"Will you stop calling me that?!"

"What? Luv? We Brits do it all the time."

"Yes, it's annoying."

"Oh, then pardon me. What would you prefer I call you instead?"

"Nothing. I mean, my name is fine." She wags her hands at me. "Don't do that!"

"Do what, lu—Lily?" I cock my smile at her just so and am rewarded with a blush.

She grabs her dinner again and drops back against the cushions with a harrumph. "Start the video."

Without a word, I press the button on the remote. The next one plays—a calico cat named Chloe who holds her owner's head with her paws like a hug and rubs her nose on his while purring like a car engine.

I chuckle. "I think she's besotted."

Call me a romantic for hoping Lily is, too. With me. Not the bloke in the video.

She shoots me a cutting glance, but I don't miss the smile playing on her lips. "Shut up and eat."

The cat videos last longer than our dinner, which pleases me to no end because Lily stays for the entire run instead of retreating to her room again. At times, she even seems to relax and lets herself laugh at the feline antics. When she tugged her ponytail loose, it was all I could do not to reach out and sift my hand through her hair to feel the silk-like strands falling around her shoulders.

Afterward, she kept true to her word about cleaning up since I cooked and started rinsing and loading the dishwasher.

I, of course, join her to help. Not out of any altruistic motivation because mine is far from selfless. The more time I have with Lily, the better my chances of winning her heart. Even if it's simply the act of washing up together.

"I can take care of this." She loads the bowl I just rinsed.

"I don't mind helping."

"I don't need your help," she says in a clipped tone.

I hand her the other bowl. "Right. Then what if I *want* to help?"

She darts guarded eyes at me. "It's your kitchen. You can do what you *want*."

Our conversation continues without words but with meaningful glances as we work in tandem like a couple operating in a familiar rhythm. My chest tightens again with a longing for something more with her, that this could be our normal routine and thoughts of what might come after cause that ache to run even deeper. I think my love and desire for Lily intensify daily.

Per her usual, she heads toward her bedroom after we finish washing up, but I follow her. And like before, she pauses at her door and turns around, striking me speechless with her beauty.

She puts her hands on her hips. "Are we doing this again?"

"Doing what? Making sure you get to your door safely?"

"Yes." Voice soft, her hazel eyes dance with questions and that same vulnerability I glimpsed at the aquarium makes an appearance. Is she about to let me in just a little more?

Of course, I mean the metaphorical kind. I wouldn't dream or expect her to invite me into her bedroom. But this feels like she's on the verge of letting me catch a glimpse of the real Lily, who protects her heart as fiercely as she safeguards her clients.

My insides erupt like our fans when we make a goal.

Score one for team Payton? "Consider it part of my royal duty."

The light in her eyes dims with the return of her earlier wariness. "I can take care of myself, Payton."

She's trying to hide again. Was it something I said, or is she afraid of the feelings I'm working so hard to stir in her?

"Never doubted you could." I take a step closer. "You don't like asking for help, do you?"

"I don't like *needing* help. There's a difference."

"Everyone *needs* help once in a while." And another step.

She lowers her arms. "I'm not everybody."

"I won't argue with you there." My last step leaves less than a foot of space between us.

A strand of her hair slips forward, tickling the edge of her eye.

I reach toward her face. "May I?"

Her eyes dart back and forth as she studies me. Just when I think she's about to turn tail and run, she nods.

Keeping my movements slow yet obvious, I brush the hair from her face. She stiffens at first, then relaxes as I rub my thumb across her cheek.

She backs up to the door, but I follow her, careful to keep my touch gentle as I cup her face.

My next move is a very calculated risk, but I'm willing to take it. I lean toward her, bringing my face close to hers. "You are the most captivating woman I have ever met, Lily Evans."

I'm close enough to kiss her. And I want to—so much— but I can't rush this. Otherwise, the hidden Lily I'm discovering might bolt like a wild animal, fleeing into the shadows. I press my lips against her forehead, relishing the softness and warmth of her smooth skin and the musky scent of her hair.

When I step back, she blinks at me. "Good night, Lily."

"Good night, Payton." She sounds tentative...unsure, which kills me, but I'm not giving up on my plan. I just need a little more time to convince her this thing between us is worth fighting for. Tomorrow morning, we head to North Florida for an away game, which means I won't see much of her for a couple of days.

So I wait until she closes her door, memorizing her allure before retreating to my room, cognizant that thoughts of Lily—her silky warmth and sultry scent—will keep me up all night.

---

We're barely holding our own against the Icemen tonight, and I know it's because of me. At the end of the second period, I missed a pass because I lost focus. The opposing team took advantage of my blunder and scored. Now we're tied, and I'm feeling scattered as I rip the tattered tape off my stick.

All I can think about is Lily. Even though she and her gal-pal Del are watching from the shadows, probably disguised, I kept searching the fans for her familiar face. I reach behind me and grab my phone from the cubby assigned to me in the guest locker room, intending to send her a text, but there's already one there.

From her.

> Lily: Quit letting the other team fluster you.
> You lose focus when that happens.

For the first time all evening, I grin. She noticed I wasn't focused. I heart her message and send a thumbs-up emoji, but what I'd rather reply is that I'd focus better if I could see her here, wearing my jersey.

But that would be a lie. She'd wind up a bigger distraction than just my thoughts of her. Even as I inhale the sweat-laden stink of the locker room, I remember the scent of her hair and the feel of her cheek against my hand.

I'm realizing I not only want Lily but *need her*, too. The thought of her going back to England and not seeing her guts me. Am I a horrible person to hope the investigation into my cousin's presumed death continues indefinitely?

Luke sits on the bench next to me and hands me the tape to redo my stick. "Here."

"Thanks."

"You seem off tonight, Pay. Everything okay?" He rests his arms on his knees, head turned toward me, waiting for an answer.

I clench my jaw. "Just a little distracted."

Elias stands nearby. "Just a little? That's an understatement, man. You're playing like a rookie."

The other guys' expressions confirm it. Not in a judgy way but out of concern, and I feel like an absolute git to have let them down. "Sorry, mates. I'll do better next period."

They nod their understanding and reassurance. After darting a concerned look at Luke, Ethan squeezes my shoulder. "We're here for you, bro."

Something passed between them I'm clearly not privy to. I shoot Luke a questioning glance.

He leans his head in closer. "Everything okay at home, Pay?"

"Right as rain. Why do you ask?" I finish taping my stick.

Appearing uncomfortable, he roughs a hand over his

mouth. "Just checking. Sophie seems to think you and Lily might be having some trouble."

I recall the conversation Lily relayed to me about her unexpected encounter with Sophie and Luke walking out of her bedroom the night of the spaghetti dinner. "Adjusting to married life, but we're sorting it out."

Sounds believable to me. Hopefully, Luke will think so too and tell Sophie there's nothing to worry about.

"Okay, I'll take your word for it. But you know we've got your back, right?"

Would they still if they knew the truth? That I not only lied about who Lily is, but also about who I am?

The temptation to tell them the truth builds again. But if I do that, Lily won't need to pretend she's my wife anymore, and knowing her, she'd put even more distance between us. The longer I can keep this charade going, the greater my chances of winning her heart.

"I appreciate that more than you know."

Luke bounces a fist on my knee, then gets to his feet. "Good. Now get your head back in the game."

Which I do. And we win by two points. All seems well in my world. For the moment, at least. But lies have a way of turning into a ticking time bomb, and this one is getting louder by the minute.

# Chapter Twenty-Three

## LILY

Today's our final meeting for the fundraiser. I arrived early at the Turtle Tide and ordered our usual drinks, with a double order of hushpuppies, to get things started. And as I sit here, waiting for Sophie and Mia, I imagine what it would be like...feel like if this were my norm.

Living in this quaint beach town, joining my new friends for lunch, working a more normal job, going to Payton's games...

What if I didn't go back to England?

Would Payton even want that?

I give myself a mental shake. Those are thoughts I shouldn't entertain.

Thankfully, Sophie bought my story about the job interview and pushed our last meeting to the day after Payton's away game. Though I keep saying to myself—and Payton—I'll be glad when this fundraiser is over, it's not true. I've come to enjoy these meetings with Sophie and Mia, which means I'm getting attached.

To them...to Payton. Becoming emotionally invested is

one of the biggest dangers of my job. So far, I've avoided it very well, but this situation has blurred all my boundaries, and now it's affecting my emotions.

Not to mention, I'm itching to pick Payton up from practice in a couple of hours. I look forward to the evenings when he's at the apartment, making dinner for us. And how he insists on walking me to my bedroom door, how careful yet attentive he is.

When I picked him up last night, he was so exhausted he dozed off in the car. But that didn't stop him from holding my hand the entire ride home. And I let him. Just more proof that my resistance is weakening.

Despite my insistence that he go to bed, he still walked me to my bedroom door again. For a moment, I thought he'd kiss me this time, and I probably would have let him do that, too. I know I shouldn't be acting so unprofessional, but he's making it difficult to resist.

He looked so adorably sleepy and in need of a hug, which is what I did without even thinking about it first. I wrapped my arms around him and pressed my face against the warmth of his chest. And I'm pretty sure he smelled my hair, then sighed.

If I shut my eyes, I can still feel the strength of his arms around me and the hardness of his torso against me. This man is going to be my destruction if I'm not careful. But oh, how I want to give in and let it happen. To let him deconstruct me piece by piece. I want to let go instead of constantly holding everything close like I always do.

But I'm simply playing a role, and I've made peace with that. Or I thought I had.

"Lily?" Sophie's voice startles me back to the present.

I blink at her and Mia's concerned expressions, berating myself for again letting these two walk up on me without noticing. I'm facing the entrance, and I still didn't pay attention to who's coming and going.

Am I losing my edge? I push a smile onto my face. "Hi, there."

Sophie slides into the booth next to me while Mia sits on the opposite side. Both are staring at me now as if I'm sick or dying.

"Are you okay?" Sophie takes my hand in hers.

"I'm fine. Just lost in my thoughts." And don't ask me what those thoughts were, or this meeting will run twice as long.

Leaning forward, Mia crosses her arms on the table. "Is there anything you want to tell us?"

I bounce my gaze between them. What am I missing here? "Nothing I can think of. Are we on track with the planning? Did I forget something?"

Sophie and Mia exchange knowing glances.

"You know you can talk to us about anything, right?" Sophie squeezes my hand.

I squirm against the booth seat, making it creak. "Um, sure. Why do I have a feeling this has nothing to do with the fundraiser?"

Again, they trade covert looks.

"Are you and Payton okay?" Mia blurts.

Sophie widens her eyes at her friend as if to say back off before facing me. "We're not here to judge. We just want to help. Both of you."

What do they know? Did they somehow find out the truth? I push a smile onto my face. Until I know the facts, I'll continue to play my part. "We're fine."

Letting go of my hand, Sophie sighs, then tugs her phone out of her brown bag. "I really didn't want to do this."

She moves deft fingers over her screen and then flips it around, showing me an image of a couple standing in a hallway by a hotel room door. I recognize Payton right away. Takes me a moment longer to realize the blonde is Del in one of her wigs. It's all very incriminating, which explains why Sophie and Mia are acting so oddly.

My first reaction is to brush it off because I trust Del. She wouldn't risk breaking cover unless it was important. But seeing her with Payton like that, combined with her not mentioning it to me AT ALL brings up something I never expected to feel.

Jealousy.

Heat rises up my neck, and the one hushpuppy I ate threatens to make a reappearance. There must be a simple explanation, but at the moment, I can't think of a reason why Del would have kept this from me. For her to initiate contact like that with the principal isn't our normal MO.

"Luke took it the night before the last away game." She puts the phone face down on the table and takes my hand again. "He wanted to talk to Payton about it on the bus ride home, but I told him to wait until I talked to you first."

I'm scrambling for what to say, how to react, or what to do. And then it hits me, I don't have to act in this situation. What I'm feeling is very real and accurate.

Even the burning behind my eyes. I clear my throat. "I didn't know about this."

As much as it pains me to admit it, it also feels good to tell the truth to these two women who mean more and more to me on a daily basis.

Sophie throws her arms around me. "I'm so sorry! This is just awful. I never took Payton to be *that* guy." She leans back to stare at me with watery eyes. "Maybe it's not what it looks like. Do you want Luke to talk to him first and find out what's going on?" She grabs her phone. "I can text him right now, and he'll do it. Trust me, you don't mess with Luke when he's dead serious. He'll get the truth out of Payton."

Mia nods in agreement with Sophie's borderline frantic diatribe. Both look fiercer than half the soldiers I did duty with. And it's all for me, for my benefit. They want to defend *me*.

The realization makes my head feel like it's floating in some surreal alternate reality. I can't ever recall a time when someone wanted to stand up for me. In the past, I was the one looking out for the younger kids in the group homes or in foster situations that were less than ideal, to put it mildly. And because of my height, sometimes, the ones I wound up protecting were older than me.

As much as I love that they want to fight this battle for me, that would just open the bigger can of worms that's hiding Payton's true identity and mine. And I can't stand the thought of how Sophie and Mia would react when they found out this whole thing has been a sham. I need to get to the bottom of whatever is going on in that picture so I can do damage control.

I press my hand down on her phone. "Thank you, but I think Payton and I should have this discussion first."

Now, even Mia looks teary-eyed. "You're so strong. I'd be a puddle on the floor if it were me."

A wan smile is all I can manage. "I probably would be if it weren't for you two." And I mean this too because I know I'll mourn the loss of their friendships when I return to England almost as much as not being with Payton anymore.

But first, I need to find out what's behind that picture. Like Mia said, I can't imagine Payton doing something like flirting with me while he's making moves on Del. She's smarter than that, and so am I.

At least, I used to believe I was. But now, my emotions are so wrapped up in all this that I'm not sure what to think.

———

After copious amounts of iced tea, hush puppies, and hugs from Sophie and Mia, I leave the restaurant, intending to send a text to Del from the car, saying we need to talk. But I know exactly where she is, and this needs to be a face-to-face conversation.

Del's rental sits by a curb near the arena, so she can keep eyes on the area from a discreet distance. I park a few cars down on the street and walk up to her rental.

She jumps when I tap on the passenger side window, then hits the button to open it. "Bloody hell, you startled me. Are you trying to break our cover?"

I reach in and unlock the door, then get in. "We need to talk."

"What's happened? You alright?" She shifts in her seat to face me.

In one swift movement, I open my phone and show her the picture I had Sophie send to me.

Del's expression turns guarded as if she's hiding something. "Dash it. I thought I did better staying in the shadows."

"What's going on, Del?"

She titters. "It's not what you think, luv. I promise."

"Then what was it?" I demand.

She hesitates, pressing her lips together. "I guess you might as well know the truth. It was Payton's idea."

Oh, no. Something *is* going on between them. How

could I be so stupid to believe Payton's interest in me was more than convenience? I should have known not to take him seriously or read so much into his words and actions. But he was so tender and caring. The otters...the cat videos...his gentle touch as he kissed my forehead.

But Del doesn't know about any of this because I haven't told her. "What did he do?"

"You know that scene in *Love, Actually*, where the guy uses signs to tell the girl he can't have that he's in love with her?"

"Yeah, you made me sit through that movie twice. How could I forget?"

"That's what he did. The sap stood below one of our cameras with a series of paper signs, asking me to help him *woo* you. He actually used that word, too, you know? *Woooo*. Who says that anymore?"

She picks up her phone, and suddenly, I'm having a déjà vu moment as she shows me a video clip from the security footage with Payton as the star of the show. He's grinning at the camera with this goofy, self-deprecating expression as he flips sheets of paper covered in black lettering, one behind another.

*Del, I need your help.*

*I'm utterly smitten with Lily.*

*I want to woo her heart.*

*Will you help me?*

*Text me. You have my number.*

Those tears return, burning the back of my eyes. "Wait? When did he do this?"

"Over a week ago."

All the outings he requested...Del readily agreeing...all the pieces fall into place.

"And you went along with it?!" I practically screech.

Her expression begs forgiveness. "How could I resist, Lil?" She gestures to the frozen image of Payton, standing there with that adorable lopsided grin and pleading eyes. "Look at him."

I am looking at him, and I'm melting inside. But I can't explore those feelings. Not yet, anyway. "Well, you should have! We're supposed to be protecting him."

"Yeah, about that…" Avoiding my gaze, she picks at a spot on the steering wheel.

"Del?" I insert a tinge of threat in my tone so she knows I mean business.

"That's what the picture at the hotel was about. I was updating Payton about his sister, who notified us the threat was over. They found his cousin on some little island. The poor sap was sunburned and near starving, but he's alive. And it *was* an accident."

"Why didn't you tell me?"

"He begged me not to. Said he needed a little more time." Her expression almost reflects the longing I've been feeling for Payton. "Lil, how often do you get a chance at true love?"

Have I misjudged Del as just a party girl when, deep down, she's a romantic at heart, yearning for something more than our fly-by-night lifestyle? Still, she's the one who taught me the ropes on not getting attached, how to stay emotionally distant, and how to guard ourselves while we protect our clients. This goes against everything she's said in the past.

"That was a huge risk, Del. What if I didn't love him?" I sound frantic, even to myself.

She smiles the biggest grin I've ever seen on her face. "And there's my confirmation."

I hold shaking fingers to my mouth. What did I just admit to her…and to myself?

Am I in love with Payton? Is that what this is—this rush of desire and longing every time I see him? The borderline emptiness I feel when he's at an away game, and I have to watch from a distance? I'm not even sure I want that position on his sister's security detail because then I'd be back in England, and Payton would be here.

If I'm going to be completely honest, I'm not sure which terrifies me more. That what I thought I wanted doesn't hold as much appeal anymore, or that I'm actually imagining…considering what my life would look like if I chose a different path.

One that included Payton.

"Guess the jig is up now that you know." She checks her watch. "Almost time to pick him up and start planning our exit, I suppose."

She stares at me, her expression pleading with me to consider another option.

"What exactly did you tell Dame Maxwell regarding our return?"

A devilish gleam I know all too well shows up in Del's eyes. "That we'd need at least another week, possibly two, to disengage from the situation in such a way as to preserve Payton's desire to stay incognito."

I do something I've never done before—I hug her. "As you Brits say, that's brilliant."

She laughs. "Just playing my part as Cupid. What are you going to tell him?"

"Nothing yet. I don't want him to know I know."

"What are you scheming at?" She smiles as she studies me.

"I'm…not sure. May have to wing this one."

Her expression turns mildly shocked. "No plan?"

"Nope."

She grins. "I like this new version of you."

"What are you talking about?"

Her epic eye roll reminds me of Mia. "The Lily who left England a few weeks ago never would have hugged me, let alone played things by ear."

She's right. I have changed. Here, I thought I was the one challenging Payton, but he's challenged me to become more open and willing to consider a future that includes more than just a stable job.

I may not have a plan, but I do have some ideas. First, I need to know Payton's really falling for me. That it's not just because I've been the unavoidable elephant in his apartment. Part of the appeal for him has to have been the chase, but will he still feel the same about me once he knows he's caught me?

"So what are you doing to do first, doll?"

"Let him think he's won me over."

"Which he has."

I give her the side-eye.

"What? You just admitted it, didn't you? If it's true, then it's not an act."

"Right, but he won't know that."

Del's eyes light up. "Oh, this is getting juicy. Then what?"

Tugging my bottom lip between my teeth, I debate whether to be real about this with her. But I feel like I've gotten closer to Del in the last ten minutes than I have over the last several years. I had no idea she would do such a thing for me as breaking protocol for the sake of love.

I just hope she's right. "Then we'll see if he still thinks he's in love with me."

Realization lights up her eyes. "You want to make sure he's really in it for you?"

I nod.

She rests a hand on mine, her expression earnest. "He'd be a fool not to want you more than anything, luv. More than that blasted puck of his."

"Or maybe just as much?" Only trying to be realistic here.

"No, don't you dare settle. Not now, not ever. And if he needs help sorting his priorities, give me a go at him."

I've no doubt she'd tell Payton a thing or two. Or three.

But I'm hoping to match his wooing attempts with a few of my own.

# Chapter Twenty-Four

Lily is driving me mad. Ever since she picked me up from practice today, the woman seems intent on tempting me in every possible way. I haven't the foggiest idea what changed between this morning and now, and I'm not complaining.

Instead of retreating to her room to 'write reports,' she's helping me make dinner. She might think I don't notice how she's intentionally brushing her arm against mine as she preps a salad, but I'm fully aware of her every touch.

Like now, she leans over me to run her fingers under the faucet, giving me full opportunity to inhale her musky floral scent—that's new. She's also wearing her hair down, which only adds to her allure. I want nothing more than to wipe the counter clean, lift her up onto it, and kiss her senseless.

"Sorry. I didn't mean to splash you."

Maybe she should splash me some more so I can cool down. But no, she brushes several water drops off my bicep, not with a towel but with an intentional caress of her hand, igniting fireworks in my head. She's so incredibly distracting that I have to drag my focus back to what I'm doing or risk cutting myself.

"No worries." I finish chopping the mushrooms for the cottage pie I'm preparing. Figured she might enjoy a little taste of home. Del may have mentioned it was one of Lily's favorites when I asked for ideas.

"When are you going to tell me what you're making?" Her facial expression is unusually open and curious.

"It's a surprise, luv." I cringe. "Sorry. I know you don't like it when I call you that."

She turns toward me, pressing a hand against my chest. The T-shirt I'm wearing does nothing to diminish the heat radiating from her palm. "What if I said I do like it?"

Is she...flirting with me? I search her face for some hint of what's going on in that pretty little head of hers. "I'd ask what changed your mind. Luv."

"I don't know. Just did." With a coy smile, she slides her hand down the front of my chest before walking away.

Takes everything in me not to grab her wrist, yank her back, and make my earlier fantasy a reality. "Lily?"

"Yes, Payton?" Now she's setting the table.

I want to ask her if she's okay, but that seems counter-productive. "How did your meeting with Sophie and Mia go?"

She pauses in thought. "It was very informational."

Did she just giggle?

I almost dump the mushrooms on the floor, but make a last-minute save and add them to the skillet to sauté. "Everything's on track for the fundraiser?"

Returning to the kitchen, she stands near me by the stove. "The kids are going to love it."

Normally, she grumbles about her meetings, citing how

she's supposed to be guarding me, not planning an event. "Sounds like you enjoyed yourself."

"I really did." She says this almost absentmindedly as she brushes her fingers through the side of my hair. "You need a haircut, by the way."

"Not until the season ends," I mumble, lost to her touch. Like I said, she's driving me bonkers.

Her hand stills. "Why?"

"Tradition. Superstition. Whatever you want to call it. We don't cut our hair or shave until the end of the season."

In a light caress that sends an ache through me, she runs her fingers from my hair down my cheek. "You're still shaving."

"I wait a little longer to stop than the other lads."

She trails her fingers down my neck toward my collarbone. I grab her hand and give her a pointed look, ready to demand she tell me what she's up to, but the open desire and affection in her eyes take my breath away. Instead, I lift her hand to my mouth and kiss the center of her palm.

A soft gasp escapes her lips, which she licks as she visibly tries to compose herself. "Is there anything else I can help with?"

I don a heated stare and make my voice gruff. "Give me a few minutes, and I'll let you know."

A deep blush blooms up from her neck and covers her cheeks. Something flashes in her eyes. Something edgy and challenging. Something I recognize…

And I nearly gasp myself with the realization.

She's playing a game with me.

I don't know what undoes me more. That she's trying to unravel me at every turn, or the bigger question of *why* is she purposely driving me wild?

When she excuses herself to use the loo, I grab my phone to text Del.

> Payton: Lily's acting a bit off. Did something happen today?

Three dots appear and go away several times. I'm about to toss my phone into the skillet when her reply finally comes through.

> Del: She'd have my head if she finds out I told you.

> Payton: Just spill the beans, woman!

> Del: Don't get your knickers in a twist.

> Payton: Stop faffing about.

> Del: She knows everything.

> Payton: Everything?

> Del: EVERYTHING

I smack my phone down.

Lily knows everything?

Head swimming, I lean on my hands against the counter as I make sense of the situation. This means she knows how I feel about her, knows about my silly antics to woo her heart, likely knows I used the word 'woo' if Del showed her my signs, and she knows my cousin was rescued and crisis averted.

To say I was relieved when Del told me he was alive and well, or soon would be after his recovery, was an utter relief. That and knowing my sister could resume her practice lifted the guilty weight I'd carried ever since returning from England.

I did think at one point that I'd have to persuade her I needed my bodyguard a little longer, but Del took care of that brilliantly. Splendid woman, that. Someone needs to give her a medal. Or knighthood, if I could convince the Queen. Or better yet, Lily and I could name our firstborn after her as a way of saying thank you, providing I can convince Lily to give me a chance.

I grab my phone again.

> Payton: Under no circumstances are you to tell her I know. Got it?

> Del: You're asking me to keep something from my partner.

> Payton: Might I remind you that you agreed to help me in the first place, and therefore, you're complicit already?

> Del: Honestly, the things one does for love.

> Payton: Cheers.

> Del: Go on then, hotshot.

The moment I hear the loo door, I grab the spoon and crack on with cooking. "Dinner won't be long."

She saunters toward me, wearing a white sundress I've never seen her in before. "Now, will you tell me what you're making?"

I do a double-take. Did she change clothes? "An English comfort food. Cottage pie."

An open smile flashes on her face, giving me a quick

picture of what she's like when she's relaxed and in the moment. "That's one of my favorites."

The sparkle in her eyes captivates me all over again, and I almost say I know but catch myself. "Mine, too."

After a long appraisal of her in that dress, I transfer the sautéed meat and mushrooms into a baking dish. The little minx upped her game, which means I will have to do the same.

She leans over, inhales the aromas, and sighs. "Wow, that smells amazing already." She blurts out a laugh when her stomach growls. "Guess I'm really famished."

Something tells me she's hungry for more than my cottage pie.

---

I never imagined a dinner could be so stimulating and yet knackering, but this competition with Lily is taking everything I have to keep up with her. She's absolutely stunning, countering my every move with one of her own as if we're playing a game of chess. And she's bloody good at it.

When we finished our meal, she stood up to clear the table, and I swear she bent over intentionally, giving me a glimpse of creamy, smooth skin above her lacy bra. As the gentleman I am, I lifted my eyes immediately, but it wasn't easy.

Now it's my move, my turn to get even. I'm handing her dishes to load into the dishwasher, one of which is a rather large spoon and the sudden source of my inspiration. I angle the bowl of it under the faucet, resulting in a steam of water saturating the front of my shirt.

"Bloody hell, I've made a mess." I turn the water off

and take my shirt off, giving her a little taste of her own medicine.

At first, her gaze skims over me in the most satisfying way. "Here, let me help." She takes the T-shirt from me and starts drying me off, the challenging gleam back in her eyes.

My brain implodes, making me unable to think— only act.

I grab her hips and lift her onto the counter on the other side of the sink and crash my lips against hers. Her hands weave into my hair as she parts her lips, giving me permission to explore deeper. Our kiss is frantic, no doubt due to how we've been teasing each other all evening. I'm so lost in her touch and the way she feels I let out a groan, which seems to spur her on.

Until she breaks the kiss and leans away. "Payton, what are we doing?"

Despite being shirtless—and breathless, I might add— the normally comfortable temperature of my apartment feels more like a sauna, and the last thing I want to do at this minute is have a discussion. However, I can't help but wonder if she's still playing a game, or is that genuine concern flitting across her face? I want to kiss her again, but not at the risk of scaring her off.

"I don't know, luv. But say the word, and we'll stop."

Her soft hands cup my face as her desire-filled eyes explore mine. I'm fascinated by the flecks of gold and green speckling her hazel irises, and I don't wish to stop looking into their depths. But there's no missing the indecision sitting there...the doubt.

I don't think I've ever felt this deeply about anyone, and I don't intend to take what's developing between us lightly. That's not how I roll.

First, covering her hands with mine, I turn my face to kiss the inside of each of her wrists, then step back. "Why don't we call it a night?"

Her eyes widen subtly, making me realize how that sounded.

"That's not what I meant." I think about tugging her against me for a simple embrace to reassure her, but then remember I'm shirtless and have little strength to resist this beauty.

"As much as I'd love that," I give her a pointed look so she'll have no doubt how utterly desirable she is, "I don't believe we should rush into anything."

"Payton, I know—"

I rest a finger against her kissable lips, aching to taste them again. But I'm not ready to let our little ruse go. Not yet. Not until I figure out exactly where this game ends and reality begins for her.

"Let's call it a night, luv. The fundraiser is tomorrow, and I dare say we'll have lots to discuss as well." Grasping her hips, I lift her off the counter while she holds onto my shoulders.

Following her toward her bedroom makes my longing for her increase. And I don't just mean physically. I want a future with this feisty woman who's unlike anyone I've ever met. As a royal and a hockey player, I've encountered my fair share of women, but I've never been one to chat them up because, to be frank, I found most of them boring.

But Lily's different. I reckon I could spend a lifetime peeling back the layers and still never get to the bottom of what makes her so bloody special. She's my ultimate adventure.

At her door, she spins around, her dress swirling about

her shapely legs, and lifts herself up to kiss me on the cheek. "Good night, Payton."

Her heady scent and warmth set my pulse racing again, and as she steps back, our gazes linger, giving me hope that this little game of hers could be very real.

Because this has been anything but a game for me since day one.

# Chapter Twenty-Five

## PAYTON

The arena is packed with fans and children milling about. Thanks to Sophie's connections in Sarabella, this fundraiser looks to be our best to date. Along with the usual concessions, the concourse is filled with game booths promising prizes and treats—all covered by our team owner. Sophie even acquired donations from various businesses in town for a silent auction arranged in the main lobby.

The blokes and I set up a miniature hockey rink on one side of the ice, run by Coach Markelson and his wife. At the other end, several of us are giving skating lessons. I dare say, the woman Wade's teaching appears more interested in his romantic talents than his skating abilities. Must be his cowboy charm. And Elias and Mathéo have their hands full with a set of five-year-old twins.

The WAGs did a smashing job, making the place feel like a carnival without having to leave the cool indoors. When I told Emalia about it, she was so impressed she insisted on helping and sent a very generous—and anonymous—donation. I thought about telling her about my feelings for Lily but feel that would put Lily's potential position with my sister at risk if things don't work out between us. As much as I want Lily to stay, if she decides to return to England, I have to prepare myself to let her go.

Speaking of whom, any moment now, Lily will appear with her rental skates so I can teach her how to skate. More opportunity to be in close proximity to her, though I confess, the anticipation has me wound tighter than a spring. I don't know how much longer I have before she finds out the truth. Or figures it out that I know she knows how I feel about her.

So, I've decided that's my strategy today. To behave as if I'm in love with Lily and act accordingly. In other words, the truth. This isn't a game for me anymore. I don't believe it ever was.

I catch sight of Lily just as she glides out onto the ice toward me. Bloody hell, if the woman didn't surprise me again by pretending she didn't know how to lace her skates. Or even ice skate. She makes a circle around me and even snows my skates when she comes to a stop in front of me.

"You've clearly skated before, you little minx." I grin at her, enjoying yet another facet of this intriguing woman.

Her mysterious expression compliments the rosiness of her cheeks from being on the ice. "One of my assignments required it."

I watch for the hint of a joke and see none. "You're not kidding, are you?"

She shakes her head. "Let's just say that, on occasion, Olympic athletes need bodyguards, too."

I spin around so I'm skating next to her and take her hand. Warm sparks shoot up my arm as she twines our fingers together. I tighten my hold, then lift her hand to my mouth for a kiss. "If I signed one of your NDAs, would you be able to tell me who?"

"Nope." She gives me a cheeky grin, reigniting the embers simmering in my chest, waiting for another chance to kiss her lush lips. Especially as our embrace last evening has run on replay in my head ever since.

I tug her closer to me so I can whisper in her ear. "Then, by royal order?"

"He wasn't British."

A 'he'? Hmm, and an athlete. I do hope she doesn't have a type. "Bugger. Call me disappointed, then."

She stops us on the ice, then lifts herself up on the toe picks of her skates and hovers her lips near mine. "Everyone's watching us, so we'd better give them a show."

Her words stop me from leaning in and tasting those soft lips again. The team mingles all around us as they play their various roles, and she's acting her part as my wife brilliantly. But that's just it. She's playing a role—her silly little game. But I don't want to pretend. I want the real thing with this woman in the worst way.

She's right there, waiting for me to follow through, so I give her a tender kiss—one I hope conveys some of what I'm feeling for her. "How's that?"

Confusion dances in her eyes again, as if she's unsure of her next move. "Payton, I—"

Before she can continue, Luke skates over to us. "Soph says to keep it G-rated, since there are children around."

I offer a sheepish grin. "Of course. I wouldn't dream of doing anything inappropriate."

Luke grunts, and then his face takes on that look I've only ever seen on the ice when he's about to drop gloves and start swinging.

Lily inserts herself between us. "Tell Sophie she has *nothing* to worry about."

His expression softens as he checks with her. "Nothing?"

"Absolutely." She smiles, then nods as if she's trying to reassure him.

Luke visibly relaxes. "Glad to hear that. She will be, too." He pats me on the shoulder. "We're good, man."

Then he skates off, leaving me utterly confused. "What was that about?"

"Nothing that concerns you. Just girl stuff." That wild gleam returns to her eyes. I think I like this version of Lily best of all. She's bold, challenging, and quite the temptress.

I take her hand and pull her back onto the ice. "Have any other tidbits you care to share about your mysterious life?"

She hums as she thinks. "I once stole a car."

"No doubt out of necessity, right?"

"Oh, totally. It was that, or my principal would've gotten shot."

I'm so flabbergasted, I skate to the boards and wrap my arms around her. Just the thought of her in danger throws my pulse into a fit. "Please tell me you don't do these kinds of things all the time."

She tilts her head up to look at me. "Not often, but it's part of the job, Payton. It's what I do."

I brush my nose against hers, pleased she doesn't stop me since no one's paying attention to us at this point. Somehow, we've wound up behind the Zamboni parked on the side for rides later. It's the perfect cover, and I'm tempted to kiss her properly, but instead, I press my lips against her temple, inhaling her sweet scent. "What if you could choose to do something else? What would you do?"

She lifts one shoulder. "I don't know. Never thought about it."

I lean back so I can see her face. "What about the future? Do you ever think about settling down? Maybe getting married, having kids? You can't very well be a mum and put yourself in danger like that?"

Her stricken expression slams me in the chest like an errant puck. I wish I could undo those last words, but it's too late. She's pulling away from me, and I'm the git who messed up our moment.

"We'd better go back to the group so we can keep up appearances." Her tone is guarded and professional again.

Everything in me slumps. "Right."

She skates away, leaving me to wonder if I've been a fool to think things could work between us. Maybe our worlds and what we want are too different after all.

# Chapter Twenty-Six

## LILY

I should have known better. How could I possibly think Payton and I could actually work out? As much as his third degree—and that's what it felt like—hurt me, I'm thankful for it because it helped me see the truth. I could never fit into his world.

Be a wife? That I could probably figure out. But a mother? I hardly remember my own, and I certainly didn't have any good role models growing up.

That stupid burn hits the back of my eyes as I fight a giant knot in the laces on my skate. I should just go home and forget about Payton. Forget about how his kiss made me dream about the possibility of a future with him. Forget about the way he's brought my heart to life in a way I never thought possible. Forget that I'm in love with him.

"Need some help?" Sophie's voice stills my hands.

When I look up, she studies my face with that concerned expression she gets when she knows someone is struggling. It's like her superpower, an empathy radar. And it's two bars strong, right between her eyebrows.

I drop my eyes, unwilling to share the pain I'm feeling. "I'm sure I can figure it out."

Which I will. I always do. Maybe that's my superpower, that I figure things out on the fly, right at the moment, whatever's needed. Anytime I wound up in a position that didn't work, I simply pivoted. Changed direction. Found a new opportunity.

But long term?

Nope. Haven't a clue. I've never stayed in one place long enough. Even as a bodyguard, I never know where my next assignment might take me or for how long. So when you know you won't be a permanent fixture, you don't make plans. You don't put down roots, either. And you certainly don't get involved with anyone. Not romantically, anyway.

In one impressive movement, Sophie lifts my foot onto her lap as she settles on the bench and starts working at the knot I somehow made twice its original size. "Everything okay with you and Payton?"

The expected response lingers right on the tip of my tongue—what I'm supposed to say as Payton's fake wife.

*We're fine. Just a little disagreement. No big deal.*

But I can't bring myself to utter those words because all these feelings I have for him have muddled my brain. Plus, I'm finding it nearly impossible to lie to this woman who's rapidly becoming a good friend—something I don't have many of.

However, there's an upside to this moment—an opportunity. Might as well use it to set up my exit. I brush back a tendril of hair falling in my face. "I'm not sure things are working out, to be honest. We may have rushed into this too fast."

Blinking, she nods thoughtfully. "You know, hockey players can be a real pain in the butt sometimes."

I don't know where she's going with this, or even why, but I can't help but agree. "Yes, they can."

"They're either at practice or a game. They wind up on the road half the time. Then there's the constant beating their bodies take, not to mention the injuries they endure." She gestures at some nonexistent entity in front of her when she's not fiddling with the knot in my laces.

I can't help but wonder if she's talking to me or herself. Maybe both?

"They're driven. Sometimes reckless even. All for a chance at a trophy they hope to win at least once before they're forced to retire because their bodies can't keep up anymore." Her magic fingers finally work the knot loose.

"Thanks." I lower my leg from her lap and tug the skate off.

"But they're like a big, messy family at the holidays. Lots of tension, but lots of love."

"And your point?" I untie my other laces without her help and place it with the other skate. I've known Sophie long enough to know she always has one. She's like a little pink bottle filled with a potion of wisdom and kindness.

"You and Payton are really great together."

A snort accompanies my head shake. "I'm not so sure about that."

She slides closer to me. "I do. I see it. And yeah, maybe you guys rushed things, but that just means it's a bit messier in the beginning. Doesn't mean the love isn't there, and that's worth fighting for."

I hear what she's saying, and if Payton and I had met under different circumstances, I might take her words to heart. But our relationship was never intended to be anything more than professional—a farce for his sake. Falling for each other wasn't part of the plan.

Resting my arms on my knees, I stare at the rink where Payton's teaching a young girl how to hold a miniature hockey stick. My heart clenches at the sight. He deserves to have that life—a wife, a kid or two. Or three, judging by how much he seems to enjoy the two other kids who skated over, asking for help, as well. A few feet away, Luke helps a little boy—without grunting, I might add—keep his balance while swinging his stick at a puck.

"You and Luke seem to have figured things out."

Her turn to snort. "Wasn't easy, let me tell you. He tried to push me away several times."

"Seriously?" I frown at her, thinking I might have been done after the first one, and definitely would have walked after the second.

That's the difference between Sophie and me. She sees the potential goodness in everyone she meets. Me? I assess everyone I encounter based on what kind of threat they might pose—a skill I learned growing up and one I fine-tuned for my profession. Size a person up before they get close enough to do any harm.

"Yeah, but I knew it wasn't about me." Her voice softens, revealing that giant heart she seems to carry around with ease.

"Still, that had to hurt, right?"

"It did, but like I said, love is worth fighting for. Even when it's messy."

Her words bring a spark of hope back to that place in my heart where Payton lives, but feeding it fuel feels so risky. "What about when it seems impossible?"

She squeezes my hand. "That's when you fight harder."

I scan the ice again for Payton, mentally taking in any potential threats near him even though I know he's not in danger anymore. He never really was.

Our gazes connect. He waves at me, but his smile doesn't reach his eyes. Instead, they seem sad—like I feel. Maybe he's having second thoughts about us. About me.

That could be a good thing, though. Doesn't change the fact that I know what he told Del, but you can't feel rejected when the person hasn't even told you how they feel about you, right?

# Chapter Twenty-Seven

PAYTON

It's been two days since the fundraiser, and Lily and I have fallen back to our usual pattern of her driving me to practice, me preparing dinner, and her retreating to her room to do her reports, which I know now is her way of avoiding me.

No more flirting or kisses, and if anything, our conversations are minimal at best. Yet, she's continued the ruse of acting as my bodyguard even though she knows there's no longer a threat, which baffles me.

I thought about confessing that I know everything and suggesting we stop the pretense, but I suppose I'm still hopeful that we can make things work between us. Could that be why she hadn't said anything yet? Is she hoping the same, or is she simply planning her exit strategy?

The latter leaves me gutted.

Normally, I crash for a good two hours before a game, but my mind has done nothing but replay our conversation, which means I didn't get any rest. And now I'm just a grumpy hockey player, looking for a way to vent some steam when I hit the ice in twenty minutes.

Fancy a fight, anyone? That's bloody well me at the moment. We're playing against the Pirates again tonight, and a part of me hopes Jennings will be his usual obnoxious self, so I have a reason to drop gloves.

"Payton." Coach Markelson waves me over.

I haven't put on my skates yet, so I pad over in my socks, following him to his office. And he shuts the door. That scenario rarely plays out well.

"What's up, Coach?"

He gestures to the seat in front of his desk. "We need to talk about Houston Jennings."

The back of my neck heats as I sit. "What about him?"

Coach raises his brows at me as if to ask if I'm that dense.

"Right." I take a deep breath, composing my words carefully. "The bloke clearly holds a grudge."

Coach nods. "Agreed, but I'm more concerned about you. How are you planning to handle him tonight?"

"Handle him?" I'd like to return in equal fervor his smash against the boards, but I'm sensing that's not what Coach has in mind.

"You know he's going to try to instigate something with you again, and the last thing we need tonight is for one of our best forwards to be in the box. Get my drift?"

In other words, no fisticuffs. "I do."

He nods. "And just so we're clear, I'm not saying let the guy get away with anything. Just maybe let your teammates help you."

I run my hands down the front of my shorts. "Got it, Coach."

"Good."

As I head back to my locker, Luke follows me with his gaze until I sit down.

"Everything okay?"

I put on a skate and work the laces. "He doesn't want me getting into anything with Jennings tonight."

He lets out his signature grunt, which says he agrees, though grudgingly. "Sounds wise."

"Right, but knowing Jennings, he'll be the one to start something."

"Then you let one of us deal with him."

Resigned to the situation, I exhale my frustration. "Coach implied the same."

"Ethan and I are paired tonight since Elias is sick. We'll keep watch." He lifts his chin toward Ethan. "Right, E?"

Tugging his jersey down, Ethan waddles over on his skates. "Whatever you need, Cap."

Luke tilts his head at me. "We're gonna make sure Jennings can't get near Pay tonight."

Ethan bumps fists with Luke. "You know it."

That's when I notice the rest of the blokes watching us, nodding. They're all ready to jump into action on my behalf —something I'd readily do for them as well. And for the first time, I don't feel utterly alone in all this.

I'm such an idiot. If I had told them the truth about my family from the get-go, they probably would have understood and not made a big deal out of some perchance title I'll likely never hold. I should have trusted them with this part of my life as I trust them on the ice.

I swallow down the regret-filled lump in my throat. "Cheers. Means a lot."

At the very least, I have my mates at the end of the day, although I'd very much like to have Lily waiting for me, too. Even better if she's wearing my jersey. I still haven't figured out what to do next—how to fix this situation my thoughtless words landed us in. The only suggestion Del had in her bag of tricks was to give Lily a minute to think.

But I can't dwell on that right now. I can't let my team down by playing distracted again. And I'll need all my wits about me to stay alert to Jennings' antics, which becomes all too clear as we hit the ice and skate the circle to warm up. Every time Jennings and I pass each other, he sneers at me.

Surprisingly, he and I rarely cross paths during the first period. And when we do, he seems hyper-focused on the game. After the second period, we're tied, and so far, I've only gotten a few sharp glances from the git. Maybe his coach had a chat with him as well, and there's nothing to worry about.

In the third period, I score a goal, putting us in the lead. Unfortunately, it's Jennings' ugly mug I have to look at for the faceoff.

Keeping Coach's warning front and center, I keep my head down, align my skates, and brace my stick on the ice. The lineman positions himself, his hand holding the puck hovering over the ice.

"I was hoping I'd get a face-to-face with His Majesty." Jennings' chirp snaps my head up. His mouthguard makes his grin almost comical.

"Just shut it, man," I growl back.

Ethan watches from the outer edge. "He's a goon, Pay. Roll it off."

I give a quick nod just as the lineman drops the puck, which I win, taking a direct shot on goal, but their goalie catches it, stopping play.

Without saying a word, Jennings skates by me but slows as he passes Luke, who shakes his head and shoves him away. Jennings must think this is all fun and games, judging by the way he's laughing.

Luke glides my way as we juggle places for the next faceoff. "Jennings seems to think you're someone important, Pay. Any idea what he's talking about?"

"Haven't the foggiest." But this moment makes the decision for me. After the game, I'll talk to Lily since she's part of this and make a plan to tell the blokes everything. Just making this choice lifts some of the heaviness I've been carrying around. The sooner I get this cleared up, the better.

I score another goal just seconds before the end of the third period and get a jolt of satisfaction when Jennings leaves the ice in a huff because we beat the Pirates again.

Telling my mates the truth isn't the only thing I want to talk to Lily about. I want to tell her I'm crazy about her—to her face. If she feels anything for me at all, we'll find a way to make our relationship work even if she wants to continue being a bodyguard.

Now that I've had time to think, I realize I should have never said the things I did to her. If I can trust her with my life, I should trust her to make her own decisions. The last thing she needs is a bloke like me telling her what to do.

I leave the locker room filled with anticipation and a rough script of what I want to say to her. She's the first thing I see when I walk out, standing there wearing a tentative smile. And my jersey. I wrap my arms around her and lower my head so only she can hear.

"I'm a right bloody idiot, aren't I?"

She tilts her head back, leveling me with those hazel eyes that capture my soul every time I look into them. "I'm not sure how to answer that. Give me some context."

"What I said at the fundraiser. I was wrong to tell you what you can or can't do. I'm properly sorry."

Her hand slides up my chest and cups my face, and then she lifts her face, pressing her lips against mine. Her touch is warm and tender, filled with so much emotion. This feels real. No acting. Not a game.

Takes everything in me not to take the kiss to the next level, but now is not the time or place. And we need to talk.

I grab her hand. "Let's go home and have a proper chat."

She lifts a brow at me.

"I meant an actual conversation." I hold our clasped hands against my chest. "There are things I need to say to you."

After a moment, she nods.

With Luke in tow, Sophie approaches us, smiling. "Anybody up for some hushpuppies?"

"As lovely as that sounds, Lily and I are heading home."

She grins at Lily. "All good?"

"We'll see." Lily glances at me and smiles as if she's promising to explain later.

Luke braces my shoulder. "Great job not letting that goon get to you, Pay."

I grin in appreciation of his praise. "Cheers, man."

He replies with a grunt while Sophie watches him with clear adoration on her face. What I wouldn't give to have Lily look at me that way. If she truly wants to continue in her profession and take the position my sister has implied she'll offer Lily upon her return, could I relinquish hockey to be with her? I still have to fulfill my contract with the Sun Kings, but perhaps we could maintain something long distance until then. I can't very well ask her to make a sacrifice if I'm not willing to do the same for her.

All these thoughts swirl through my head as we walk out of the arena and into an onslaught of shouts and flashbulbs illuminating the surrounding night. A wall of reporters and cameras surge forward, their shouted questions vying for attention.

*"How long have you been hiding your royal ties?"*
*"What does your family think about your double life?"*
*"Are you abdicating hockey to take up your title?"*
And just like that, my secret is out.

# Chapter Twenty-Eight

## LILY

Instinct and training kick in as I assess the situation and determine our best exit route.

"Oh, bloody brilliant," Payton mutters next to me as he shields his eyes against the flashes.

One journalist shoves his way from behind the rest, then lunges toward us, his phone up and recording everything. "Payton, is this your girlfriend? She's wearing your jersey. Does your family approve of her?"

I jump in front of Payton, blocking the guy from getting any closer. "Step. Back."

The journalist blinks at me, surprised. No doubt he didn't expect me to be the one to stand in his way. "I—"

"I said, back off." I match my expression to the threatening tone of my voice.

He recoils, then looks as if he's about to launch forward again, just like the rest, vying for Payton's attention. To our left, the exit route to the parking lot is blocked by news vans, and all the commotion has drawn a crowd of fans to our right. That leaves only one choice—retreat into the arena.

I spin around and herd Payton toward the door we just exited. "We need to go back inside."

He frowns at me as if he's unsure.

"Now!"

He nods and turns around.

Faces full of shock, Sophie and Luke stare at us as if we told them the end of the world had arrived, and I have a feeling in Payton's mind it has. But there's no time to explain anything to them yet. I continue to push Payton until we're well inside.

"What the hell?" Luke growls as he follows us inside.

Payton drags a hand down his face. "It's a long story."

I glance toward the door. "Where's Sophie?"

Luke tips his head in that direction. "She's trying to find out what that's all about."

Payton and I lock eyes, commiserating this unexpected turn of events without words.

Several of the other players walk out of the locker room, smiling and oblivious to the commotion until they see us standing there and then hear the muffled sounds from outside. Natural curiosity propels them toward the exit to find out what's going on.

Except for Wade, who glances between Luke and Payton. "Did the party move to the hallway?"

"That's one way of looking at it," Luke grunts.

Clearly flustered, Sophie rushes back in and points at Ethan and Mathéo. "You two guard the door and don't let anyone in." Then she points at Luke. "Go get Coach Markelson."

All three jump into action, and my respect for this woman just doubled. Now I get why she and Luke are such a good match. His grumpy side needs someone who understands and yet sets boundaries for him.

While Payton talks to Wade, I join Sophie near the door. "Were you able to find anything out?"

"Officially, they're here on an anonymous tip. Unofficially, sounds like it was Houston Jennings." She draws her brows together. "Is it true? Is Payton royalty?"

I glance back at him, unsure of what to say. This is his story to tell, not mine, but I want to help him, too. "Am I talking to Sophie, the reporter, or Sophie, the friend?"

"*Your* friend. I always put the people I care about before the job. And for the record, I'm a photojournalist."

Her stubbornness makes me smile, but her declaration sends all these warm and fuzzy feelings through me. For the first time in my life, I have genuine friends—something else I'll have to give up when I return to England.

Although Del proved to be a good friend during this odd assignment. She offered to stay and help wrap things up, but I could tell she was itching to get home, so I told her to go on ahead of me. Now, I wish she were here to navigate this situation with us.

Pressing my lips together, I nod. "Sorry. I had to ask. It's part of my job."

"What job?" She blinks her round eyes at me.

I sigh. "I'm not Payton's wife. I'm his…bodyguard."

Her mouth drops open just so as she stares at me. "Wow, didn't see that coming." She shifts her focus back to Payton. "So, Payton *is* royalty."

"More like royalty adjacent." I can tell a myriad of questions are passing through her mind as she processes this.

"So all this time…?" She rolls her lips inward as she thinks. "All that stuff I said…you two seemed so real."

Without thinking about it, my eyes find Payton and drink him in. He ran his hand through his hair at least once, leaving it a bit tousled, like the way he looks when he wakes up in the morning. He didn't bother putting his tie back on, so his shirt is unbuttoned at the top. And every time he flexes his arm, I see the definition of his biceps.

But it's his quiet strength that draws me the most. And makes me feel...safe. Maybe what's happening between us is stronger than I realized.

"Oh." A mix of mild astonishment and realization flashes across her face as she studies me.

Feeling exposed, I glance away, looking for anything else to focus on. "Yeah."

No more words. Just the press of her hand against my upper arm to say she understands. And this bundle of feelings and emotions I've been holding close feels a little lighter and manageable.

Sophie glances toward the throng outside. "We need to hold a press conference or something. Otherwise, they'll just keep hounding him."

As I nod in agreement, Coach Markelson enters the scene, trailed by Luke. Coach pulls Payton aside for a brief chat, then strides out the door to deal with the reporters. Next thing I know, the assistant coach, Derek, is herding us back into the locker room area to Coach's office.

A few minutes later, Coach joins us along with the rest of the team. "I've asked the press to give us a few minutes to get organized." He zeros in on Payton. "I think it's time you fill us in, Pay."

I stay at Payton's side as he explains his true identity and the entire situation, from his cousin's disappearance to his sister's insistence on hiring a bodyguard, which brings a room full of hockey players' eyes on me.

And crickets.

I glance at Payton, unsure what to say because the spotlight is never supposed to fall on the bodyguard.

He meets my questioning gaze. "I'm the one who insisted Lily pose as my wife, and she has been beyond supportive."

One of the rookies in the back makes a snickering comment, but Luke's grunt shuts him down.

I didn't think a burly man like Luke could appear more awkward than he does right now. With his hands in his pants pockets and shoulders near his ears, he takes on an almost sad expression. "Pay-man, why didn't you just tell us who you are? We could have helped you deal with all this."

Sophie stands next to him, giving me a look that says the same—I could have entrusted her with the truth. The rest of the guys are either nodding or making comments in agreement, all out of concern for Payton.

He holds a hand up, bringing a hush to the group. "In hindsight, I wish I had. But I thought keeping my lineage a secret was the easiest way to be a regular bloke who plays hockey."

Ethan chirps, "Is that what you call that botched play tonight?"

Chuckles rumble through the room—more snickers and chiding, but all in good fun, as if they're over it already. But more likely, they want him to know they're okay with who he is.

Wade lets out a whistle. "Let's let the past be the past, boys. Right now, we need to ask our man here what he needs to deal with this mess."

The burn behind my eyes hits me in full force. To watch these guys rally around Payton is one of the most heartening things I've ever witnessed. These people are community-bound by so much more than a stick, a puck, and a frozen floor.

Sophie steps up and rests her hand on Payton's arm. "They're not going away, so answering their questions will help keep this from ballooning into something bigger. If you're up for it."

Coach chimes in. "She's right. They're waiting to hear from you, Payton."

Payton scans the room and then gives a reluctant nod.

Keeping a quick pace, Coach leads us back down the hallway. Multiple footsteps coming from behind stop both Payton and me, causing us to turn around just short of the exit.

Every single member of the team, plus Derek, Sophie, and Mia are staring at us.

Luke lets out a snort. "You didn't think we'd let you do this by yourself, did you?"

A couple of rogue tears slip down my face before I can stop them. I look up at Payton. "I'll be right there, making sure they don't get too close."

Not that he really needs a five-foot-ten female body-guard when he has an entire team of muscled hockey players who tower over me.

Payton's eyes warm as one side of his mouth lifts in a slow smile. He brushes a thumb over my teary cheek. "Sorry to put you through this, luv."

I give him a watery smile. "Part of the job. But just so we're clear, this will not be like that movie *The Bodyguard.*"

He lets out a soft laugh. "Understood."

A voice from the back snickers. "Yeah, bodyguard my a—"

"Stop!" Luke growls.

Coach's voice breaks the silence. "Ready?"

Payton and I nod, and along with everyone behind us, we step outside in a united front to meet the press.

# Chapter Twenty-Nine

PAYTON

*Not my wife. She's my bodyguard.*

The words keep playing in my head. That and watching Lily take off my jersey as I said it in front of a dozen or more reporters. I suspect she did that out of professionalism. Or perhaps to demonstrate the truth as we answered a multitude of questions about my cousin Sebastian's supposed accident, my sister's insistence that I have a bodyguard, and my knuckle-headed decision to create this entire charade to protect my identity.

Not my best moment, that, but the press seemed to find much of it amusing by the end. Now, everyone will know the truth. Or at least, the hockey world and this quaint beach town called Sarabella that I consider home.

Although, I'm unsure how I'll feel about staying here if Lily's on the other side of the pond. That's what I wanted to talk to her about tonight before the press invaded our little bubble. But after all that went down, I don't think I'm ready for this conversation.

I must look more exhausted than I feel because Lily insisted on driving us home from the arena. Or she's still playing that game of hers. Time to bloody well clear up that rubbish.

My phone buzzes against my leg—text alerts.

Lily throws a glance my way as she stops at a traffic light. "Hope that's not more reporters."

I slip from my pocket and touch the message on the screen. "No, just the lads checking in."

Luke: You doing okay, Pay?

> Payton: If drowning in embarrassment is good, then I'm fine and dandy.

Elias: What did I miss?

Ethan: Check your news feed, man. I'm sure the story broke already. Those guys work fast.

Wade: The sooner it breaks, the sooner it will ride out with the tide.

Elias: Whoa! Pay, are you actually connected to the British Monarchy?

> Payton: Loosely. Just glad my cousin is alive and recovering well.

Elias: And Lily's your BODYGUARD!!! That's sick!

Luke: I think your fever is talking, Elias. Settle down, bro.

Elias: Figures the one time I get sick, I miss the really good stuff.

Ethan: Contrary to what you believe, Elias, the world does not revolve around you.

Elias: Hey! Sick person here. Have some compassion.

Mathéo: You know this is going to bring the fans in like crazy.

Wade: Let's not get ahead of ourselves, Barbie-man. This is like a slam into the pipes. Let the snow settle and give our guy Pay a chance to catch his breath.

Luke: Wade's right.

Ethan: What about Lily, Payton?

Payton: What about her?

Mathéo: Does this mean she's going back to England now?

Payton: I don't know.

Luke: Do you want her to?

At first, I hesitate to reply, debating how much to tell them, but then I remember how they all stood by me tonight, and I realize I don't have to carry my burdens alone anymore.

Payton: No. It guts me to think about it.

Wade: Sounds like you're in love with her, Pay.

Payton: I am. Head over skates. I think I have been since the first time I met her.

Wade: Now that's a story I can't wait to hear.

Luke: Don't tell Sophie, or she'll want to write about you two.

Payton: Wouldn't dream of it. I've had enough publicity to last a lifetime.

Ethan: Don't let her get away, man.

Payton: Not sure how to get her to stay.

Wade: Take it from me. Tell her how you feel. Or else you'll regret it.

Luke: Sounds like another story to tell there, Cowboy.

Wade: Maybe one day.

Ethan: Elias, where'd you go, man?

Mathéo: He's probably getting cozy with his toilet again.

Luke: Way to bring the convo to an end, Barbie-man. Literally...

Wade: And now we're talking potty. Get it? Not party, but potty...

Luke: Seriously, Cowboy, what's with the dad jokes?

Payton: Right, you lot. I'm off. Thanks again for having my back.

Elias: Ugh. Being sick sucks. What did I miss?

Ethan: Read the texts, man! Anytime, Payton.

Luke: Always here for you, bro.

Mathéo: Got that right.

Elias: Can somebody bring me some chicken soup?

I chuckle and pocket my phone again. The other blokes can handle that one.

The parking spots in front of my apartment are full, so Lily parks on the opposite side. Thunder rumbles in the distance, and the wind seems to pick up, blowing the palms back and forth beyond what a gentle breeze would do.

And Lily isn't moving. She's just staring out the windscreen.

I turn in my seat. "What's going on in that gorgeous head of yours, luv?"

She sends a weak smile my way, but tears sit in her eyes. "Your world."

"What about it?"

"It's...so beautiful."

"That's because you're in it." Cheeky, I know, but true. I want her to understand that my life will be forever incomplete without her in it.

She shakes her head. "No. It's because of you, Payton. You've built this wonderful life with people you love. And they care about you. So much. Seeing that tonight was amazing."

The way she pauses sends a sick feeling into my gut. There's a giant 'but' about to follow, and I'm dreading it. "What are you trying to say?"

"I know everything, Payton." She stares at me as if she's expecting some kind of retaliation. "Del told me about what you did with the signs and all the rest. I've known since the day you and I kissed."

"I know."

Her lips part with her surprise, which tempts me to crush her against me and kiss away her worries, her fears... and her doubts.

"What do you mean, you know?"

I chuckle softly. "You were acting off while we were making dinner, so I texted Del to ask what was going on. She fessed up that she told you everything."

"And you didn't say anything?!"

"I didn't want to ruin your little game of seduction." I give her a cheeky grin.

Shaking her head, she holds her hand up. "I wasn't trying to seduce you."

I bug my eyes out at her. "You changed into that sexy white dress."

She bites her lip. "I just wanted to be comfortable."

"Bloody hell, you drove me bonkers!"

She says nothing to that, and I'm too busy drinking in this gorgeous woman who quite literally inserted herself between me and the world when I think about it. All those reporters vying to take their best shot at me, how she shoved the first git away, and not to mention how she stood by me the entire time. Just like she promised.

All my life I've fought for what I wanted—what I wanted to do and be, how I wanted to live my life. And I've done it alone. So has Lily. But tonight, she contended for me. Sounds absurd to think about it, considering my dalliances with romance stories. I should be the one fighting for her.

And I do want to fight for her. Even if I have to follow her around the world. Because with her, I'm not alone anymore. Kind of a duh moment, I know. But it's true.

Another rumble of thunder pierces the night as fat raindrops pelt the car. I touch Lily's face, running my fingers along her hairline, then tuck a loose strand behind her ear and cup her cheek. "Lily, I started falling for you the day you followed me onto that airplane and began planning our ruse. None of this has been fake for me."

Her eyes dart back and forth as though she's searching for what to say. But instead of words, she lunges forward and kisses me hungrily, clinging to me almost as if she's saying goodbye. I wrap my arms around her and press her closer, refusing to believe that's the case, all the while trying to convince her I meant what I said with each nibble of her lips and stroke of my tongue against her softness.

I love her with every cell in my being. Her leaving would be like depriving me of my ability to breathe. Somehow, I have to make her see we belong together, whether that means she stays here with me. Or I go back to England with her.

Gently, I pull away from her. "What do I need to do to convince you this is real?"

Tears well in her eyes, and for a moment, I think she's going to tell me she feels the same and maybe even that she loves me.

But then she pushes me away, jumps out of the car, and runs into the pouring rain.

# Chapter Thirty

## LILY

"Lily, wait!" Payton's steps slap against the wet asphalt behind me.

What do I say to him? I want to tell him how I feel, but something's holding me back. Maybe it's because the plan was always to return to England and resume my life as part of Dame Maxwell's security team—a job I don't think I want anymore.

Or maybe I'm just afraid this is all too good to be true. That Payton will inevitably realize I'm not what he wants, and that will confirm what I've suspected all along—I don't belong anywhere. That 'home' is something others get to enjoy.

But not me.

I make it to the door of his apartment and stop, realizing I left the keys in the car. "Crap."

"Lily, please look at me."

With slow steps, I turn around to face him, even though I'd much rather be inside, hiding in my room. I could make a dash for the car, grab the keys, and run away again. But somehow, I think Payton and all his glorious muscles and quick moves would stop me before I could get through the front door.

Water drips from his hair, running rivulets down his face as he stands in the pouring rain, staring at me with that smile…the one that has officially tilted my world onto a new axis.

"Don't go back to England." He takes a step closer, bringing his soggy self almost close enough to touch.

I fist my hands at my sides to keep myself from reaching out to him. Because as much as I want the fantasy to be real, it all feels too risky. And staying was never part of the plan. "Why?"

He holds his arms out at his sides. "Isn't it obvious?"

I brush a wet strand of hair out of my eyes, wanting nothing more than to throw caution to the wind and jump into those arms. To take a literal leap and not worry about all the details like what I would do, and who I would be here.

But I can't do that, can I? "I don't know how to do this."

In lightning speed, he closes the distance between us, holding me with one hand on my lower back and, with his other, tips my chin up with his finger, forcing me to look at him. His eyes drill into me, demanding to know the truth. "Don't know or just afraid?"

Such an odd mix, to laugh and cry at the same time. Perhaps some relief as well, to let go of all pretenses and just be honest. "Both?"

My thought as his lips touch mine is how easily I could knock him off his feet to the ground right now. That's my normal MO in almost any threatening situation. And this is definitely one of them. My heart's never been in danger like this. Defending myself makes sense. Instead, I cling to him as if my life depends upon it. And maybe it does. A new life, a new place, a new beginning that includes love this time.

Could I do that? Could this be the final pivot I've been so hungry for?

Rain streams between our lips as we kiss, droplets clinging to our skin. Payton lingers for a breath, his lips brushing mine as he whispers, "I love you, Lily."

Those adorable dimples on each side of his mouth make an appearance with his tentative smile. My fingers slide over the damp rough stubble there, exploring, claiming. "I think I love you, too."

He pulls his head back. "You think?"

Heavy drops of rain and tears drop from my lashes as I blink. "I've never been in love before, so I'm not entirely sure how it feels."

"Can you see yourself building a life here?"

I glance around us as if the answer might hang from one of the nearby palm trees, swaying in the wind. "What would I do?"

"Anything you want." He says this as if he's pleading. As if his very existence depends upon my reply. "If that won't work, then I'll figure out a way to be with you in England."

"You would do that for me?" I've never felt that important to anyone before.

*Wanted.*

His eyes map my face as if he has to memorize every detail. "In a heartbeat."

Payton crushes me against him in a kiss that obliterates all the thoughts, concerns, and worries I've had since I arrived here. Rain pours over us as our embrace shifts from frantic to a slower exploration of each other.

He backs me up against the door and out of the downpour while his lips continue to tease mine with languid brushes and nips. A loud clap of thunder makes us both jump.

"We'd better get inside." He says this with a growl as if he's angry at the weather.

"I left the keys in the car."

He digs into his pocket and pulls them out.

I gasp. "You could have let us in any time."

"True, but kissing you in the rain is unforgettable." He lands a light kiss on my wet nose before unlocking the door.

We barrel in and shake off the moisture slicking our skin and clothes like two wet dogs. Payton dashes to the linen closet by my bathroom and grabs two towels, handing me one when he returns.

As I towel myself dry, I dart glances at him, unsure what to say or do next. There are no more secrets between us, just the truth. No more games or ruses. I've never been in love before and haven't a clue what to do, say, or even think, let alone expect.

The cool air in the apartment raises goose bumps on my skin, so I wrap the towel around me, warding off the chill and my doubts.

Payton notices. "Get changed and then meet me back out here, yeah?"

Nodding, I turn and head toward my door. Payton doesn't walk me to mine this time but watches from his doorway, waiting for me to go into my room. Promises fill his eyes, making me want to dash back into his arms to claim them...believe them.

Once in my bedroom, I strip off my wet clothes in record speed, opting for a soft pair of stretchy lounger pants and a T-shirt I knot at my waist. My hair's still damp, so I wrap it into a loose bun on the top of my head. When I walk out of my bedroom, Payton's already sitting on the couch, waiting for me.

"Much better." He pats the spot next to him as I approach.

He's swapped his soggy game-day suit for joggers and a T-shirt. His damp tousled hair makes him look roguish. He wraps his arm around me as I snuggle into him, his spicy scent teasing my senses.

For the first time, I feel awkward with Payton. I don't know what to say or do.

He lifts my chin as he leans in to kiss me. Soft at first, but then something ignites between us as if now that we've declared our feelings for each other, there's nothing holding us back.

Longing and desire propel us closer. As I push up to straddle his lap, he grabs my hips and helps me settle there, all without breaking our kiss. His hands roam over my back as I push my fingers into his damp hair. His kiss turns greedy, devouring and exploring, nipping and tugging.

A lingering chill causes me to press into him, into his warmth and the safety of his arms offer. His groan rumbles against my lips, demolishing any resistance I have left.

I want this. I want a life with Payton. And I want to build it here.

These thoughts push me back from him enough to rest my forehead against his, allowing us both to catch our breath. "I thought you wanted to talk."

"We will. I'm just warming you up first." Payton presses light kisses down my neck to my collarbone while his hands press against the bare skin of my lower back, sending delicious shivers through me.

My eyes flutter shut, lost in the touch of his lips and the

feel of his hands on my skin. Something tugs at the bun in my hair, loosening and setting it free.

Then everything stops.

I open my eyes and find him staring at me. Desire and wonder fill the blue depths of his eyes. "What's wrong?"

"Nothing. Nothing at all." He pushes my hair back with both hands, then tenderly cups my face.

"Then why are you staring at me like that?" I search his face for some sign of threat or danger. Is he having doubts?

He continues to devour me with his gaze. "Because you are the loveliest creature I've ever seen."

I smile, then nuzzle my nose against his. "You're not so bad yourself, big guy."

His laugh tickles against my mouth. "I still need a nickname for you."

"You'll think of something." I nip at his lips, coaxing him to kiss me again.

His hands move to my forearms, pushing me back gently. "I meant what I said, Lily. If being with you means returning to England, I'll do it in a heartbeat."

First one side, then the other, I run my fingers over the groove-like dimples bracketing his mouth. I don't think I'll ever tire of doing that. "I could never ask you to leave your life here."

"You're not. I'm offering."

*Observation #10: Payton really loves me!*

I rest my hand against his chest, over his heart, feeling the rapid rhythm that matches mine. Everything I've done has been an attempt to find a place where I belong. A home that's mine and my choosing. But what if home isn't a place but a person?

And then it hits me. Payton is the home I've longed for.

My eyes burn with the tears of that realization. Like so

many times before, I recognize this moment for what it is— a time to pivot from where I was to where I want to be. And it's my choice.

"What if I said I'd rather be here? With you?" I almost can't believe I said it out loud. The idea still scares me to some degree, but when I'm in his arms like this, nothing feels threatening. Quite the opposite, actually. I've only ever relied on myself for that sense of safety, but Payton does it for me in spades.

He breaks into a smile. "Really?"

I nod. "Really."

"You're sure?"

"Yes." I laugh, feeling lighter than I think I ever have in my life.

"Darling, you just made me the happiest man on the planet."

His endearment settles into me, making me feel special, cherished, and chosen. "Darling...I like that."

"Then we'll give it a go." He drags his lips over mine in a lazy kiss.

I know he means the nickname, but it feels like more. Like a declaration that our relationship is now official—real and out in the open for everyone to see. No more pretending or games. Although, I enjoyed our little competition very much. And it brought us together.

After one more mind-blowing kiss, I slide off his lap and stand up. "It's late. We should probably go to bed."

He's still holding my hand as if he can't bear to let me go. Disappointment drapes his face, though he makes an effort to hide it. "Right. I'll walk you to your door."

I stop in the middle of the living room, halfway between our rooms. "Payton?"

"Yes, darling?" His eyes sparkle with his words, letting

me know he intends to make good use of his endearment for me.

A fresh wave of love and gratitude for this man overwhelms me. "I think I'd rather you walked me to your door."

Payton almost gawks at first, then pulls me close and kisses my forehead like he did all the other times he walked me to my door. So patient and caring...I still can't believe he's real.

That's he's mine.

As he searches my face, I see desire flare in his eyes, but there's love there, too. So much love. "Are you certain?"

Biting my lower lip, I nod.

"I'd love nothing more." He raises my hand to his lips, watching me as his kiss sends my pulse back into chaos.

Maybe our little game isn't over after all... "Are *you* sure about that?"

He tugs me toward his door. "Yes, very. Why do you ask?"

"I was thinking about wearing your jersey. You know, like a nightshirt."

This stops him in his tracks, and the smoldering look he gives me melts me to the floor. "You are a little minx, aren't you?"

I tease his lips with mine. "If you say so, big guy."

# Chapter Thirty-One

## PAYTON

*Three weeks later*

The week Lily and I spent together before she returned to England was the happiest in my life. I didn't want to leave her for practice each day, but I suffered through, knowing she'd be there when I got home.

Of course, she came to every game we had that week, wearing my jersey, of course. I've never had to force myself to focus more during a game. And I grudgingly shared her with Sophie, too, who insisted she and Lily needed some girl time before she left.

One evening, I took her out on a proper date, which wound up interrupted twice by a couple of fans who recognized me. Thankfully, I had my bodyguard with me, and Lily did not disappoint.

Other times, I showered her with little gifts and surprises and savored each moment with her. Maybe out of fear that she'd simply vanish as if she were a figment of my imagination. Or maybe part of me feared she might change her mind once she returned to England, so I used every opportunity to convince her she belonged with me.

Letting her go was one of the hardest things I've ever had to do. But I understood. She needed to return and settle matters there. And let me tell you, the last two weeks have been pure torture. I literally ache for her return.

"Earth to Payton. Are we doing this again?" Luke gives me a friendly shove, then sits on the bench next to me in the locker room.

"Lily's supposed to fly back today." I keep staring at the opposite wall with our team logo, but all I see is her face.

Luke runs a towel over his wet hair. "Supposed to?"

I turn to face him. "What if she changes her mind?"

He grunts. "What if she doesn't?"

"Then I'll be the happiest man alive." Just like I told her that night. Probably the most memorable night of my life, actually. If Lily doesn't come back, I'll be ruined for anyone else.

Luke tilts his smile. "Then focus on that, man, and quit worrying."

Wade walks in, freshly showered from our practice. "What's got the Pay-man worked up?"

"He's worried Lily will change her mind."

Brows raised, Wade snickers. "Don't doubt a sure thing, Pay. She'll be there."

Something Wade said after the whole press debacle comes to my thoughts. "You still haven't told us your story, Cowboy."

He hums in thought. "Not much of a story to tell because I never told her how I felt."

I can't imagine loving Lily from afar, and I'm hoping it doesn't come to that. "Sorry to hear that, mate. Is she no longer available?"

Wade's gaze roams as he shrugs. "We connect here and there on social media. She's a PR genius in New York. She had a boyfriend..."

"Had?"

He scrapes a hand through his wet hair. "I think they broke up recently."

"Then you still have a chance. Didn't Coach say the owner is looking to hire a PR person? After my fiasco, I think she's on to something there. You could recommend her," I say with some excitement. It's official. I've officially joined the ranks of romantics.

"That *ship* already sailed, my friend." He chuckles. "Did a double entendre there."

Luke groans and throws his towel at him.

I lean on my knees. "I can't imagine my life without Lily."

Luke grunts. "Same here. Without Sophie, I mean. Speaking of whom, if Lily misses the wedding, she'll have to answer to my pink menace."

"That's true. But don't hold it against me if I'm hoping her return is about me."

The blokes laugh at my attempt at humor, which I appreciate. Just wish I were feeling some levity myself. I don't know why I can't shake this fear that I'll wind up one of those blokes, waiting around for the girl who never shows up.

After practice, I head straight to the airport, even though her flight won't land for several more hours. Just being here makes me feel closer to her. Kind of ironic when you think about it. Just weeks ago, I met Lily at an airport, and now I'm waiting for her in another one.

Like Wade predicted, the media attention died down

quickly, but I still wear a ball cap and sunglasses to most places these days, just in case.

Following a hasty meal in a restaurant there, I find a seat near the gate where arrivals come in. The large fish tank sponsored by the aquarium reminds me of our day there, watching the otters swim and play. The sheer joy on Lily's face while she rubbed their little paws will live forever in my mind like a marker I intend to strive toward every single day, to make her even happier than she's made me.

If she comes back.

As her arrival time draws closer, I pace around, unable to sit still any longer. The doors open, and people flood through from the other side. I examine every face, looking for hers.

The flow of arrivals dwindles, but still, no Lily and the tightness in my chest is getting stronger. Even though I spoke to her yesterday on the phone, I should have called her today. Checked in and made sure she was still certain about all of this.

I continue to stare at those opaque sliding doors, willing them to part and reveal my Lily.

Waiting...

And then, there she is. Like an angel walking through the veil from the other side, dressed in a pair of snug jeans and...my jersey?

She's wearing my jersey. The little minx took it with her.

Her face breaks into an excited grin that exceeds her otter smile, much to my pleasure, as she rushes toward me, leaping into my arms and wrapping her legs around me.

I can't imagine what we must look like, standing there in a tangle as we kiss each other hungrily to make up for the last two weeks.

But we're oblivious and don't care. Our kiss slows, then ends as she slides down.

Cupping her face, I rest my forehead against hers. "You came back."

She touches her fingers to the sides of my mouth. "Did you doubt I would?"

"Of course not."

Leaning her head away, she gives me a questioning look. "And if I ask Luke?"

"He'll tell you I did nothing but pine for you."

"And?"

I sigh. "He'll also tell you that he told me to quit worrying."

She giggles, something she's done more of lately. "I won't ask."

"Good."

After we collect her luggage, we walk hand in hand back to my car. I open the trunk and heft her suitcase inside.

"Payton, what's that?" She points to the small suitcase sitting next to hers.

"I packed a bag, just in case."

"Why?"

"To come after you, of course. In case you didn't come back." I slant a smile, totally gone for this woman.

Appearing somewhat stunned, she rests her hands on my chest. "You really meant it."

I close the trunk. "Of course I did, darling."

She brushes her lips over mine. "Take me home, Payton."

I drag my teeth across her bottom lip, making her gasp. "On one condition."

"What's that?"

"Keep the jersey on."

# Epilogue

PAYTON

*Two months later*

I may regret this. Or it could be the best day of my life.

"So, I go first?" Elias stares at the two-foot by three-foot sign with the word 'WILL' written on it in heavy black letters, all caps.

Ethan slaps him on the upper arm. "No, you tater tot. I go first." He holds his sign up with one hand and underscores Lily's name with his other like a showroom model highlighting a race car.

Scowling, Elias smacks him back. "Her name could go on the end, bro. Either way works."

Dangling his sign with the word 'MARRY' by his side, Wade waddles over in his goalie pads, looking more menacing than the entire lot. "You fellas best take a chill pill. You're stressing the Pay-man out."

Here I am, sitting on the bench, holding a sign with 'ME' scrawled on it and, in my other hand, a velvet box with the ring I had designed for Lily while she was in

England. Took every bit of strength I had not to ask her to marry me at the airport after she walked through those doors, ran to me, and wrapped herself around me like a hungry kitten.

And each day afterward. But I wanted to do one of those grand gestures like I've read in my sister's romance books. Something that would show Lily how much I love her, and how much I want to spend every day of my life with her. And that's why I hatched this plan with the help of my mates. In fact, the day Lily flew back to England, I hosted another team dinner with the ulterior motive of asking for their ideas and assistance.

When I explained how I'd used signs to enlist Delilah's help, Luke said I should do it again, this time for Lily. And he was right. I hope he still is because even my sweat is sweating at this point. It's bad enough I have to wait until the season's over to officially marry this woman.

If she says yes, that is.

Luke inserts himself between me and the other blokes. "We got this, Pay. Don't we, boys?" He shoots a threatening look at the others, who nod obediently. "And she's going to love it."

Breath shaky, I get to my feet. "I bloody well hope so."

I know Lily loves me. She's told me so many a time over the last two months. But I'm moving fast, and a part of me still thinks she'll wake up one day and decide she made a huge mistake by staying.

Anytime that fear rears its ugly head, I remember what I told her. That I'd follow her if that were the case. And I still feel that way, but it still boils down to her heart and if I've truly made her mine. Because that woman pretty much owns me.

At the sound of a text chirp, Luke reaches into his

locker for his phone. "Sophie's on her way with Lily." He looks at me with some concern. "You ready?"

I think about what I'm about to do, and a surge of wild energy buzzes through me. "More than ready."

Wade whistles. "You heard the man. It's showtime."

---

## Lily

The horn blows, and I, like all the rest of the Sun Kings fans, jump to my feet, cheering and celebrating another win. The guys are having their best season so far, according to Sophie and Mia, who are jumping up and down on either side of me. They've been teaching me about hockey so I can understand the game better.

Payton has, too, but having these two giving me play-by-play explanations has been surprisingly fun. Especially when they get their noses bent out of shape when the refs miss a penalty call, and I can relate. Even though he can handle himself, seeing a player from the opposing team get rough with Payton riles up the bodyguard in me.

By the way, I've traded in being a bodyguard for becoming a college student. I don't know what I want to pursue yet, but since I've had to study people most of my life, I figure psychology might be a good place to start.

As the guys leave the ice, I sit back down to watch the top scorers come out and give their sticks to the kids. I think this is my favorite part of the game, especially when it's Payton. Or Wade. In all his bulky gear, he acts like a giant teddy bear.

After checking her phone, Sophie grabs my arm,

tugging me back to my feet. "Let's get down to the waiting area."

"Don't you want to watch Luke skate out and give his stick away?" I protest.

"Seen it once, you've seen them all." She continues to pull on my arm, dragging me toward the aisle.

"What's with you two?" Obviously, they're up to something. Maybe it's a surprise party. I always wanted to experience one of those.

"Nothing. I'm just ready to get Ethan and go home." Mia pushes me from behind, giggling, which tells me they're definitely up to something.

Okay. I'll play along. I can still pretend to be surprised.

My conviction wanes though, when Sophie bypasses the family waiting area and heads to the players' entrance. Luke's standing there, holding the door open, still dressed in his gear and skates.

Sophie pats him on the chest. "Thanks, babe."

He grunts, but one side of his mouth tips up.

Sophie drags me inside and down a hallway while Mia tries to keep up.

"Are you guys going to tell me what's going on?"

"Not yet." Sophie throws over her shoulder.

Luke gets ahead of us and skates into the rink. I catch sight of Ethan's jersey and Wade's big goalie pads, but no Payton.

That's when I realize Sophie is leading me in that direction as well. "Are we allowed to go on the ice like this?"

"Only for special occasions," Mia calls out from behind me.

The idea that they involved the entire team sends a flush of warmth through me, warding off the cold as I gingerly step out into the rink. I only wish I knew what was going on.

Mia and Sophie flank me like soldiers, and the guys line up on the ice, facing us. But I still can't find Payton.

Hands behind his back, Ethan skates forward and stops. He brings his hands around to the front, revealing a small poster board with my name on it.

Then Elias glides up and does the same. Except his has the word 'WILL' on it.

Luke is next, and his board says 'YOU.'

Looking rather sheepish, Wade approaches, flipping his card, which says 'MARRY.'

My hand flies to my mouth as tears burn my eyes.

Payton skates out from behind the wall of hockey players, heading right for me as he flips his sign, which says 'ME,' of course. As he gets closer, he goes down on one knee and slides to me, his eyes filled with so much love— love I never expected to find or have returned, not like this.

My tears turn into a sob as Payton swaps his sign for a ring box, which he opens. Inside, a silver band with a diamond sits nestled in a lily-shaped setting.

I can't speak, so I simply nod. After Payton stands and slips the ring on my finger, I throw myself into his arms so hard that we glide backward as I kiss him with all the love exploding from my heart.

When we come to a stop, Payton sets me down but keeps his hands on my waist. Everyone is clapping and cheering, including some remaining fans in the arena.

I kiss the dimples on each side of Payton's mouth. "You work fast."

He cups my face in a lingering, sweet kiss. "Just making our marriage official."

"I love you so much. And I love that you included Sophie, Mia, and the team."

"We're like a big, messy family."

"And stinky."

He laughs as I twist around so I can thank everyone, but I start to slip.

Payton catches me. "I've got you, darling."

Every time he calls me that, I know he's saying he loves me. Besides all the times he says the actual words. Something I'm still getting used to hearing.

Tears spring back as I'm overwhelmed with so many feelings. So many BIG feelings. This man I was supposed to protect and keep from harm turned out to be the best thing that ever happened to me.

"Thank you for saving me, big guy."

"No, Lily, you saved me."

"But you were never in danger."

His thumb brushes my cheek, his voice low and sure. "That's where you're mistaken, darling. Before you, I was alone, convinced I had everything I needed already. And that's the worst kind of danger."

I bob my head because I know what he means. Probably better than anyone.

But now, none of that matters because he's mine, and I'm his.

"Let's go home, big guy." I pat his chest. "And keep your jersey on."

# More by Dineen Miller

vinci-books.com/bloomedmessy

**A flower shop. A former bully. One year to find out if love is worth the mess.**

When my aunt dies and leaves me her old flower shop, I have to run it for a year before I can move away and chase my dreams in New York. Then Kade Maverick turns up: the guy who bullied me in high school. He seems changed and is willing to help me fix up the store. But I'm going back to New York when my year is up, and he's just not a part of those plans. Right?

Turn the page for a free preview…

# Bloomed to Be Messy: Chapter One

## AMANDA

"Wait...can you read that part again?" Sitting in a lawyer's office on a Saturday afternoon is not what I call fun. And neither would my Aunt Paula. But here we are, just two weeks after her sudden departure from the living and one week after the funeral.

My aunt's lawyer, Mr. Tate, clears his throat as he shuffles papers on his desk. "You have to run the business for one year before you can sell or close it."

"From what date?" One needs to be clear on these things, right? Because, if I'm understanding things correctly, this is about to mess with my plans.

Big time.

He checks the document again. "The date of her death."

I bounce forward in my high-backed chair and slap down the top of the pages so I can see the proverbial fine print. "Well, look at that. Says from the day of her death."

"That's correct." In lawyer-y fashion, he shakes the papers back up. "Shall I continue?"

"Yes, please. Sorry." I give him a grin-like grimace and shrug.

As Mr. Tate continues to read the stipulations of the will, sunlight streams through the bay window to my right, warming the right side of my body. I turn to gaze out at the bustle of this small Florida beach town that moves with the ebb and flow of tourism.

Mango Lane runs the entirety of downtown Sarabella and is known for its quaint shops and bistros that are mostly comprised of converted houses originally built around the turn of the twentieth century. Along with a close-knit community, the business district here shares a special camaraderie that hasn't changed much in twenty years.

By the way, mangos are to Sarabella, Florida, as garlic is to Gilroy, California.

Big.

We even have a festival in the fall that boasts foods made out of mangos that you never imagined possible, like mango wine and savory mango fries made from green mangos. And the tourists make sure to arrive in time to attend this event that draws vendors, from all over the state of Florida and beyond, who sell their wares.

Being back here brings a flood of memories. Mostly good. Some not so much.

I left several years ago to pursue my own dreams, convinced my days of living under swaying palms and my mother's brow-raising reputation were over. Yet now I'm yanked back by Aunt Paula, whom I adored, but she always had a unique gift of meddling.

Yes, I'm calling it a gift. Otherwise, I'd stomp out of the lawyer's office, refusing to take over the flower business my aunt has so *graciously* willed to me—a ready-made business that has nothing to do with my dreams of being a communications and product designer in the Big Apple, something I'd imagined since being a high school senior in art club. Plus, New York had one of the best art schools in the country.

I *could* cite Mad Men as part of what cultivated my interest in the advertising world, but it only fueled it. In reality, Aunt Paula is to blame for that one because her father—whom I never had the pleasure to meet—was a real live Don Draper in his day. He even had the same first name!

Thus, I grew up listening to her stories about him and his life as an ad man in NYC that bordered on the scandalous at times. So in reality, she helped set the trajectory of my life, even though she would never have admitted it.

Not that I wanted to do something scandalous. I just wanted more. More adventure and excitement, to see more of this big wide world I lived in. And more distance from my mother's notoriety, which never seems to fade when you live in a place with people who have long memories and sometimes loose tongues.

And finally—the final decider—I wanted out of this beach town that hummed half of the year and slept the other.

Mr. Tate's throat clearing snaps me back to the present.

I give him a smile to reassure him I'm listening. Well, half listening. Most of what he's relaying now has to do with his law firm's involvement in the handling of the will, so I'll just go back to justifying my decision to get out of Dodge nine years ago and reminisce about how well things have worked out.

Well...mostly...

When I moved to New York to go to art college, I figured the Big Apple had room for one more designer. So did my former classmate and current roommate, Sasha, who's more of a fine artist. And since graduation, we've managed to scrape by (not starving, mind you) in a tiny two-bedroom walk-up. Not exactly ideal for creating art, let me tell you.

I'm still more of a production assistant at this point, and Sasha has to work on her paintings on the fire escape, which leaves a lot to be desired but makes cleanup very easy. As long as the downstairs neighbor doesn't happen to be outside at the moment. That's a story I relish telling at any and all opportunities.

But we've persevered, sustained mostly by the belief that our next break was just around the corner. Which one? We had no clue. We just kept turning those corners as they came. Early on, we lived mostly on ramen noodles, peanut butter and jelly sandwiches, and the fancy appetizers at the art shows I frequented with Sasha. Plus, the occasional event my boss needed me to help him schmooze old and new clients.

Over time, Sasha and I have upgraded our menu and splurge on an occasional night out on the town. Not exactly how I imagined my life would look at this point, but it is what it is, right?

"Ms. Wilde, do you have any other questions?" My aunt's lawyer blinks at me through his designer glasses as he neatens the stack of papers in front of him. He sits behind a broad desk with a stack of folders on one end, an overflowing inbox on the other, and a wall of books behind him that appears rather dusty on the upper shelves. Just like his head.

"Did I understand you correctly, her condo is mortgage free?"

He shuffles through a separate stack of papers on his

desk. "That's correct. Just the property taxes due at the end of the year, and the monthly HOA fee."

Mr. Tate clears his throat before giving exact figures with his official lawyer expression of authority. I had no idea how pricy living in this beach town had become, which has sprouted and expanded quite a bit in the last five years alone. Not so sleepy anymore, it seems. I do a quick calculation in my head. Less than what I pay for my half of the rent in New York but not by as much as you'd think.

He continues reading where he left off, but my mind has flitted to yet another thought.

"Any stipulations about selling *it*?" Even I can hear the edge of desperation trying to peek its way out in my voice. Maybe Aunt Paula's meddling—I mean generosity, of course—could be used to my advantage for once.

And the way Mr. Tate raises one brow tells me he knows exactly where I'm headed with this. "Once the transfer of ownership is complete, it's yours to do with as you wish. But if you don't mind a word of advice?"

"Yours or Aunt Paula's?"

"Mine."

I give him a nod.

"Sarabella has grown a lot in the years you've been away. Property is valued at an all-time high, but that has thrust rental prices through the roof as well. A one-bedroom apartment would cost you more than twice the HOA fees on your aunt's place."

Okay, closer to New York rates than I thought. "So, keep the condo?"

Now his other brow rises to create a uniform, fur-lined wrinkle in his brow. "You need a place to live, don't you?"

Boxed in again by my crafty aunt. She always did have an interesting sense of humor that tended to break the rules of decorum but in very subtle ways. To meet her was to be immediately enchanted by her Savannah-born and raised southern charm. The woman knew how to get people to do what she thought was best for them. All out of love, she would tell you. But despite that somewhat irritating trait (only because she was usually right), she was one of the strongest and noblest people I've ever met.

Mr. Tate clears his throat again.

Clearly, he's trained his guttural sounds and facial muscles from years of lawyering. (And yes, that's a word. I looked it up.)

"Any other questions?"

"No, just trying to figure out what my aunt is up to."

He gives me a knowing smile that tells me he knew Aunt Paula better than most. "Paula always had a mission."

"That's one way of saying it."

Mr. Tate either didn't hear my mumble or chooses to ignore me as he slides a set of keys across his desk. "These are to the store and her condo."

I hook the ring on my finger and count five keys. "That only accounts for two keys."

"Paula loved a good mystery, too."

I drop the keys into my bag as I stand and extend my hand. "Thank you, Mr. Tate. I'd like to say it's been a pleasure, but the verdict is still out on that." I smile and give him a short laugh so he'll know it's nothing personal. I know who's still pulling the strings in this scenario, even if she's watching from the heavens she so dearly loved.

After shaking my hand, Mr. Tate comes from behind his desk to walk me out. He's taller than I realized and towers a good ten inches above me. And I'm not short. Now I understand why he's seated in his family picture that sits on the shelf behind his desk. The camera would have been hard-pressed to fit his wife and kids without him looking like a giant.

"I'm here if you need anything. Paula was very special to my family, as well as the firm. Please don't hesitate to call if you need anything, Mandy."

"Amanda, please." What I don't say is that since my mother, born Josephine Wilde, hijacked my nickname to create her stage name, Mandy Wild, I preferred not to bring her up at all in this scenario. But knowing my aunt as I do—did—Mr. Tate is probably aware of our history to some degree.

He blinks and drops his gaze. "Of course. I forgot…" He clears his throat and his gray sideburns stand out against the blush darkening his cheeks. "Whatever you need, I'm happy to help…Amanda."

"Thank you, Mr. Tate. I'm sure I'll be in touch."

I leave the Law Offices of Tate and Tate, which makes me think of the expression 'tit for tat'—a phrase that aptly describes this scenario. My aunt's scheme could very well be her way of telling me moving to New York was a mistake, which at this point in my life, I could be persuaded to see it that way if she were still alive and having this conversation with me.

But she's not and now I'm a prisoner in her little scheme for the next year or more. The next task on my agenda is to let my roommate know that I'll be gone for a while. Maybe she can sublet my room.

And then?

Check out the flower shop I now own and am required to run successfully for an entire year.

As I walk up the steps and unlock the back door of the shop, I'm transported to the past and the fragrant memory of flowers and greenery. I spent most days after school helping Aunt Paula at the shop and always had a guaranteed job during the summer, which was a mixed bag of love and hate. As in, loved having money to spend at the movies or at the mall but hated being stuck at the shop, working while my friends hung out at the beach.

But as I open the door, the putrid stench of rotted flowers assaults me, making me gag. Seems things have been neglected much longer than anyone realized. And let me tell you, the smell of rotting greenery is like none other.

The culprit is a large garbage can of discarded flowers and clippings that clearly never made it to the dumpster before Aunt Paula's sudden departure. With my hand over my mouth and nose, I drag the can outside, walk a few steps away, and inhale the humid mid-morning air that carries a hint of the beach in its scent.

For a moment I'm tempted to lock the door and head in that direction—to the beach and deal with whatever else lurked in the flower shop of death tomorrow. But I've never been one to put off what I can get done today. Especially in light of the big picture. The sooner I get the place up and running again, the better my chances of making it through this next year so I can move on to my original plan. Maybe even with a financial cushion to give me more time to make NYC notice my creative talents.

I snicker out loud at my own thoughts. What does that tell you?

"Mandy?"

I whip around and see a face that brings a flood of childhood memories that includes building sand castles on the beach and hanging out at the movie theatre on Friday nights. All the wonderful memories of growing up in Sarabella.

"Zane!" A flood of warm affection launches me into his bear hug.

"How are you doing?" He steps back but hangs onto my hands, giving me that look that requires only the truth. "I wanted to stop by sooner, but I had to fly out for a conference in California right after the funeral."

Zane Albright is the quintessential surfer, who turned his childhood passion for the beach into a full-blown career. He worked as a lifeguard at Mango Key Beach straight out of high school. Not long after, he revamped the training program for the Sarabella County Lifeguards and now he's Director of Operations.

"A conference full of lifeguards? That sounds like way more fun than a funeral."

"Seriously, how are you?" Zane gives me his concerned, big brother look, which always made things seem better in high school. He's also the only one who completely supported my dream of moving to New York.

"I'm okay."

Overwhelmed by the concern I see in his eyes, I drop my chin, feeling the heavy weight of grief twisting around my neck like the string in my gym shorts caught in the dryer. I refuse to shed more tears over my aunt while I'm still wrangling the mess she's left me to clean up.

Maybe it's payback for all the years she wound up raising me while she waited for my mother—her little sister—to "hit it big" and come back to claim her daughter. "I still can't believe she's gone."

His voice rumbles up in a deep baritone. "I know."

I shield my eyes against the sun that's now peeking over Zane's sun-bleached head and blasting me with its brightness and heat. Sweat trickles down my back. Though nearing its end, summer is still very much present, as is the humidity.

"What are you doing here? Why aren't you at the beach?" I finish my words with a laugh.

"Mom figured you'd need some help. She called me when you left Mr. Tate's office."

Sally is the owner of The Pink Hibiscus, a super cute clothing boutique, and has been my Aunt Paula's best friend since they opened their shops around the same time. Supporting each other in their businesses translated into a close friendship in other areas of life, which meant Zane and I pretty much grew up together.

"How did she know when I left his office?" I know the answer to this question, but I still have to ask.

"She told him to call her when you left."

The small town grapevine was alive and well in Sarabella. I look over my shoulder at the can of putrid death oozing its noxious smell like an evil gas looking for a new victim. Who knows what else lies in store for me inside? Maybe giant cockroaches have invaded and set up shop. Or one of those ornery raccoons Aunt Paula always complained about raiding the dumpster behind her shop because she shared it with Peppery Pete's Wine and Cheese Shop.

Now there's a rank smell in the summer.

Zane glances at his watch. "I can spare a couple of hours before I go on duty. How about I help you figure things out?"

Gratitude nearly brings me to tears again. "Thanks. I can really use the help."

He winks at me before grabbing the garbage can and tipping it over into the dumpster. His face scrunches up as he turns his head away, revealing his pure disgust, which says a lot for a guy who's had to deal with red tide and rotting fish.

Therefore, I am vindicated that I nearly barfed my own putridity at my first encounter with what shall forever be referred to as 'The Can.' God only knows—Him and my Aunt Paula, that is—what else lies in wait for me in the place.

Somehow having Zane's help to navigate the unknown jungle inside boosts my lagging confidence that I might be able to handle what lies in store. In *that* store. I go back inside and scan the back room, which used to be a kitchen when the place was a residence. A plant cooler sits where a refrigerator used to go and a work counter and stool filled the place where a stove might have once stood.

At least that's what I imagined as a child when I helped my aunt. The cabinets needed some paint and small repairs —one seemed to be missing its door—and smears of green, yellow, and red stained the wood table. Evidence of who knows how many floral arrangements crafted over the thirty-plus years my aunt owned the shop.

The storefront itself is spacious and thankfully free of giant cockroaches and angry raccoons. Aunt Paula didn't have much set up display-wise, except for a rickety greeting card display near the counter, a bookshelf with various mugs and decorative pots displaying plant themes, and a table near the front door that touts several dead flower arrangements, an emaciated cactus, and a few orchids that still have blooms—the only things still living in the place.

Three glass-front coolers line the wall to the right, one unlit. The flowers and greenery in the buckets inside have either dried out or drooped over the sides. I can only imagine the stench waiting inside to greet me. Although the baby's breath seems to have persevered.

Does baby breath ever die or does it just dry out?

Zane comes alongside me, toting the can he just emptied. "How about I empty the coolers while you water what's still living over there?"

He must have seen the look of horror on my face as I stared at the contents. "Thanks. Not sure I can handle any more of that smell."

I open the front door to create a cross breeze, giving up the air conditioning for some hot but fresh air. Outside, I turn around to look at the sign above the door.

Bloomed to Be Wilde.

If you're thinking of the Steppenwolf song, you're on target. My aunt loved that song. So much so she modeled the name of the flower shop after the title, using the spelling of our last name, which aptly describes the women in my family, it seems. Aunt Paula said it was the family motto, which my mother seemed to have lived up to in spades.

And here I stand, the new owner of her legacy.

I glance upward and sigh. Aunt Paula had to be loving this.

# Bloomed to Be Messy: Chapter Two

## KADE

"What did you expect to find out?"

I'm sitting on the sofa in my mother's small but immaculate trailer, wishing I were back in my studio, torching metal. There's a certain satisfaction in controlled destruction. That probably sounds strange, but if you knew my past, you'd understand.

But now my future is about to get way more complicated.

By a four-year-old.

"I didn't know Shannon was struggling."

"Maybe you would if you bothered to check in more often with your family. After she lost her job, she had to move in with a friend. Things got overwhelming for her."

I run my hands through my hair and let out a long exhale. "I'm sorry. Business has picked up over the last year."

What I don't say is that my reputation in Sarabella has grown. An increase in custom home builders wanting original metal work detailing for homes has doubled my orders in the last six months alone, thanks to the popularity of a couple of DIY home shows on TV and social media.

But that won't matter to my mother. She only sees the man who left the confines of a toxic family that boasts a long line of motorcycle-riding 'bad boys.'

Cliché, I know, but we do exist.

However, I shifted gears five years ago in order to pursue a more creative and lucrative future. It's not that I don't love my family…I do, but I no longer share their perspective that life deals us what we get and we're stuck with it. Nor do I subscribe to the belief that men who are creative and artistic are somehow…unmanly.

Plus, watching a person die brings life-changing side effects. Don't ask me how I know.

Do I need therapy?

Maybe?

Probably.

Right now, all I know is I'm doing what I love and now I may have to redirect for a compact human being whose big green eyes and dimpled smile melt my every resistance.

"I'm so glad life worked out for you while the rest of us are stuck here in the muck."

Acknowledging her comment will only feed her pessimism. I learned not so long ago that you can't reason a person out of a place they didn't reason themselves into to begin with.

I also know she's still bitter. "What else did she say?"

My mother shrugs. "Just that she needed time to get back on her feet, which I was happy to give her. Elly is my granddaughter, and I want the very best for her."

We interrupt this guilt-laden dialogue to interject that this is my mother's way of reminding me of all she's done for me. She's the queen of passive-aggressive dialogue and part of the reason I had to get out of close proximity. The constant reminders of how much I've disappointed her became life-sucking.

"But then this happened," she gestures to the brace encasing her foot and ankle, "and there's no way I can keep up with a four-year-old."

I nod but say nothing because I'm trying to picture how to adjust my life to accommodate a child. Which isn't mine, by the way. Just want to be clear on that. Eliana is my niece. And the daughter of my brother Devon.

"Of course not." I rise from the couch. "Where is she now?"

"Preschool, or what we used to call daycare. My neighbor dropped her off for me. Figured it might be easier for us to figure this out without little pitchers around."

"Little pitchers?"

My mother waves me off. "An old expression. Means big ears, even though hers are small." A hoarse laugh rumbles in her chest.

"When does she get back?"

My mother looks up at me with an expression I've come to recognize as her loaded gun. "That's up to you, now isn't it? Her bag is packed on the bed, and they're expecting you by three."

Unbelievable. "You could have told me this before I drove out here."

"Why? And spoil the fun?"

"No, so I could have planned for a passenger. I rode my motorcycle." I notice her flinch as I check my watch. Maybe she cares more than she lets on. All I know is I have about an hour to get back to Sarabella, get my truck, and come back to pick up the squirt.

I push up to my feet, careful not to let my work boots bump against her coffee table.

A flash of regret moves behind her eyes so fast that I would have missed it had I not been looking for some sort of recognition. But it's gone before it can do anything to soften the hardness that's settled permanently around her mouth. "Then I guess you better figure something out quick."

And now I've clamped my jaw so tight I can only nod. I grab Eliana's bag from a makeshift cot in the corner of the tiny bedroom.

At the front door, I pause. Despite the chasm between us, she's still my mother, and I'm a duty-bound son. "Do you need anything? Help with anything around here? I can come by this weekend."

She waves me off. "No, I've got great neighbors and people who love me nearby."

Guilt trip received. I exhale, drop my chin, and count to ten. "Bye, Mom."

My mother just stares at me. She doesn't move. Doesn't say a word.

I'm guessing she's disappointed again that I didn't allow her to manipulate me, but as I said, I can't reason someone out of a place they've chosen to be in.

I close the door and stride to where my motorcycle sits. After lashing down Eliana's small bag, I hop on, pulling my helmet over my head, and then crank the motor.

The ride home will give me some time to think and plan, as will the ride back.

Because I don't have a clue about how to take care of a four-year-old.

In a split second, Eliana recognizes me and comes running. "Uncle Kade!"

Her little pink backpack bounces behind her as she runs toward me. I scoop her up with a grunt, realizing she's grown nearly half a foot since I last saw her. And in preschool, no less.

"Hey, squirt."

Her little arms hang onto my shoulders as she stares into my eyes. "You smell funny."

"Yep. I was working."

"Why are you picking me up today?"

My gut clenches because I see Devon staring back at me through green eyes that are an exact duplicate of his, even down to the freckle in the right one. I have one too, but in the opposite eye. Mom said we got our green eyes from our father, who left town around the time Devon was born. Which left me to become the man of the house.

"Because Grandma sent me to take you on an adventure."

Her little mouth forms a circle to match her rounded eyes. "Do I get to ride on your motorbike?"

She couldn't get the hang of the word "cycle" when she was younger because of a lisp she's mostly outgrown. Bike became her default and stuck.

"No, not yet. You're still a squirt."

She wiggles to let me know she wants to get down. When her feet hit the floor, she stands straight with her shoulders back and her chin up. She lifts her heels off the floor to look taller. "But look how big I am now."

I squat down and hold her hands. "Yes, you are, but this adventure is bigger than my motorbike."

She frowns, but her eyes are round with wonder. "Bigger than a motorbike?"

I can picture her father's proud smile right now at his daughter's awe of motorcycles. But my mother would kill me if I let Eliana anywhere near one. Shannon, too, for that matter.

"Way bigger. You get to come stay with me for a while. And you can see my metal shop."

"What's a metal shop?"

"A place where I make things out of metal with a blowtorch."

"What's a blowtorch?" Torch sounds more like *torsh* with her residual lisp peeking out.

"I'll have to show you. So, what do you think?"

She lowers her chin. "Did I do something wrong?"

I can almost hear the "r" in wrong this time. She really has grown a lot since I last saw her. As much as I don't want to admit it, my mother was right. I've been too busy and away too much.

I hug Eliana. "No, squirt, not at all. Why would you ask that?"

"Because Mommy said she needed a break and now Grandma does, too."

I smooth a rogue, pale brown wisp behind her ear. Even her hair has grown, judging by the Rapunzel braid she now sports. Braiding hair—another thing I'm going to have to learn.

"Grandma broke her foot, which means she can't run around and play very well right now."

"So she called you?"

"Yeah, is that okay?" I almost hold my breath because if she says 'no,' I've no idea what to do next.

The corners of her mouth lift slightly as she nods, looking at me again with Devon's eyes. "Yeah, as long as you promise I can sit on your motorbike."

I stand and tousle her bangs. "I'll think about it."

Eliana crosses her arms and pouts. "All right."

As I take her hand, the teacher walks over, holding out a slip of paper. "Mr. Maverick, can you sign this so we have it on record that you picked Eliana up?"

Nodding, I take the slip of paper and pen.

"Will Eliana be coming back?"

That's a good question. One I don't have an answer to, though. "Uh, I'm not sure, to be honest."

She gives me a sympathetic smile that makes me think she's more aware of what's been going on with Shannon than I am. "No problem. I'll just mark down on her file that she'll be away for a while."

"Thanks, I appreciate it."

She points toward an odd-looking chair near the doorway. "Don't forget her booster seat."

I scrawl my name on the blank line and hand the paper and pen back to her.

A simple slip of paper, yet somehow I feel like I've signed up for something way bigger than I can handle.

**Grab your copy...**
**vinci-books.com/bloomedmessy**

# Things I Noticed While *Totally* Not Falling for Payton

Strictly professional.
Absolutely not personal.
Okay, maybe a little personal by #10.

Observation #1: If my principal's talking, he's distracted and much easier to manage.

Observation #2: When flustered, the principal loses track of details.

Observation #3: Payton is more athletic than he looks. And very competitive.

Observation #4: Payton is ticklish.

Observation #5: Payton is mischievous, and his kisses are dangerous.

Observation #6: Payton is a bit of a thrill seeker.

Observation #7: Payton uses redirection when he's uncomfortable with the conversation.

Observation #8: Payton Maxwell is trouble.

Observation #9: Payton undoes me with his charm and thoughtfulness.

Observation #10: Payton really loves me!

# About the Author

Dineen Miller is an Amazon best-selling and award-winning author who loves to write closed door romantic comedy, where witty banter, sizzling chemistry, and unforgettable characters leave readers smiling long after the last page.

She's a dog-mom to two furry rescues that answer to wiggle butt and snuggle boy, and she's married to a punny guy, who thinks she's unique.

# Acknowledgments

A very special thanks to Donna Marco for her stellar input. I love you! You're not only my mom, but my biggest cheerleader. Thank you for all the encouragement, Mom!

Great appreciation to my editors, Alice Shepherd and Judy DeVries for your keen eyes and encouraging words. Makes me so happy to hear when you love my stories. Thank you for catching all my goofs.

To Sophie Britton and Vinci Books, thank you for taking a chance on me and my books. And for all of your hard work. I'm looking forward to what the future holds.

And finally, to all of you, lovely readers, who took a plunge with me into the first installment of the Romancing the Sun Kings series, and now book two, Payton and Lily's story—thank you. These two took on a life of their own and pushed me to write them accordingly. I hope they delighted you as much as they did me.

I can't wait to write Wade's story. In fact, he's already pestering me to get started. More soon!

May you live authentically, love fully, and laugh often.

And watch hockey!